Chasing De

By Gary Flint

ISBN: 9798750643448

Chapters

A Walk in the Park

'Quiet. A solitude not shared with a breath, even. I feel I am here, wherever here is, but nothing else. Cold: so cold my hands are turgid and gloved by frost. No movement, no reflex, just a view forward. Desolation, darkness: no glimmer of hope. Why am I here? Is there no one who can help? Wait . . . in the distance . . . someone's coming. I cannot shout. I have no voice. He is getting closer, my Samaritan.'

It was winter. Jim loved this time of year. Outside was cold, frosty; the sky was blue with the low-lying sun barely visible on the horizon. On such a morning, it felt good to be alive. Cocking back his head and filling his nostrils with air he welcomed that each inhalation of breath was obvious and unique.

Beads of moisture clung to Jim's heavy beard and although his face felt chapped, the evolutionary overcoat was performing well. He was warm, comfortable against the elements. Jim had grown the beard a few years earlier as a fashion statement rather than for any practical reason. Now, today, all the preening and oiling of his facial hair seemed justified.

As he walked through the park, his feet crushed the frozen shards of grass beneath him. There had been a dusting of snow but a cruel seasonal wind had cleared pathways along the park, partly exposing the turgid earth below. The open ground was cracked, barren of life. Only the hardy survived winter and perhaps only the foolhardy ventured out on such a morning but it did not deter Jim. It was a routine he enjoyed: a morning stroll with his dog.

He followed the same path as he did most mornings, but rarely saw the same things: nature's artistry made sure of that. Up ahead, but never too far away, was his dog, Barnstable. He was getting old and his age was now starting to curb his enthusiasm. Every few yards or so, Barnstable turned his head and gave a cursory glance to ensure his master was in tow. Jim just smiled at his need for re assurance.

As Jim walked further, he blinked awkwardly to moisten his eyes. Would he ever find contact lenses that actually did the job? He had contemplated laser eye surgery but was too cautious, and social media tales of things going wrong had calmed his interest. Jim supposed his lot in life was to walk around permanently looking as if he had just seen Bambi's mum killed in the famous Disney movie. The sun was rising and the cold chill of the wind clawed at his eyes, making him stretch them to reduce the increasing discomfort.

Meanwhile, Barnstable was head down and grazing. His nose shovelled the frosty earth, giving his beard a greyer tinge. Occasionally, a jet of moisture from his nostrils belched into the air, followed by a brief shake of the head to eject any unwanted passengers. The dog continued on his route then suddenly came to a stop. He rolled on his back, wriggled from side to side and emitted a sound of pure contentment that anyone would envy. There was nothing more gratifying than watching a dog playing; even an old dog could cast a shadow back to their youth when indulging in such a simple pleasure.

As Jim watched Barnstable squirm and throw tufts of frost into the air, he pondered if he would be able to repeat those actions when he reached the dog's age. Barnstable was seventy in human years and if Jim were to copy his actions, he would probably end up stuffed full of diazepam, be fed rice pudding for the rest of his life and wheeled in front of a TV showing daytime programmes until it was time for bed at six. Cynical, yes: accurate, who knew? It just made you think. Would he be better off as an old dog or an old man?

As Jim continued to think about it, he chuckled to himself. In both scenarios, age brought certain truths home. There would always be someone to wipe your arse and pick up your shit.

Jim carried on walking; occasionally kicking clumps of snow into the air and watching it drift back to the ground. He felt like an environmental hooligan, purposely smudging winters tapestry. Realising his actions were more suited to a teenager than someone in his early fifties, he stopped and felt rightly scolded.

After a few more steps, he looked up and saw Barnstable run towards a small, frost-covered bush. The season had long since stripped away foliage, and branches hung down like the shattered, upturned arms of an umbrella after a storm. The plants skeleton was clearly visible, with its decaying vegetation forming a carpet along the same path as its spring time shadow.

There was something unusual ahead: Barnstable stopped, transfixed; his body taught and alert.

'Hey, mate. What's up boy?' Jim shouted. No response. There was no change in his little friend's demeanour.

'Barnie, come on boy,' Jim called again, in a softer tone. Still no response: something was definitely wrong.

As Jim got closer, Barnstable started to move, inching steadily towards the thicket. His bravery kicked into gear by the presence of his master. He stopped moving again, his gaze still drawn towards the bush as Jim reached the dog's side. Jim crouched down and grabbed his collar to stop him moving closer to his target. He held Barnstable tightly and, as he moved his head for a better view, he could see a figure sat in the middle of the bush. It looked like it was upright, with its legs crossed and head facing forward. Whoever it was must be freezing. While Jim had been walking he had not seen anyone else nearby and assumed that the figure must have been there a while.

Jim offered an introduction. 'Hello! Are you OK?' There was no reply.

'Hello, I said are you OK?' he repeated, this time more loudly. As Jim listened for a reply, he twisted his neck to the side, angling his ear for a sound. He heard birdsong, dogs barking in the distance, and the grumble of a far-off car, but no voice.

He looked around. There was no one else there. He wanted to walk away; perhaps if it had been any other time than winter, he might have done so. But this was no place for anyone to be exposed to the elements for a long time.

Jim decided to move closer. As he did, Barnstable pressed tightly to his side. This spooked Jim more: if he had not already suspected it, Barnstable's behaviour was telling him something was wrong with a capital W.

Edging nearer, he was able see more. It was definitely a man and, although the man's head was slightly stooped, he could see that he was sporting a thick, unkempt beard. Jim looked to the man's hands, which were exposed. The skin was blue, shrouded by body hair that the frost had changed to icy wire.

Shit, Jim thought. He looked up again, seeking help. There was no one. He looked at Barnstable; felt him trembling. He crouched down and gave him a cuddle.

'It's OK boy,' he said, trying to sound reassuring, but both of them knew differently.

Jim returned his focus to the man and as he squatted beside him he could see under the man's hood, which had been masking his face.

'Christ Almighty!' he cried.

Barnstable, startled, gave a retaliatory bark, spooked by his master's impromptu cry. Jim pulled Barnstable to his chest in an attempt to comfort both of them. Under the hood, the man's eyes were open and glazed over; his mouth set in an awkward smile. It was a smile you would see towards the end of a wedding when everyone is tired and wishing for a break from the camera.

Jim looked more closely, his curiosity overriding his fear, and stretched out his hand to touch the man's bare skin. It was stone cold, like meat from a freezer, but was as coarse as rock, devoid of life. This wasn't a man any more: this was a body.

Jim swallowed, lifted his hand and pushed away the man's hood. He turned away sharply, gagging and slowing his quickening breath. Parts of the man's beard had been hacked off and replaced by staples which pinned into both sides of his face, holding a distorted smile in place. Curls of skin pressed against the metal anchors. Each staple had been punched precisely into both cheeks.

That was enough. Jim turned away, his stomach churning. Shaking, he reached down and pulled Barnstable closer.

‘It’s all right Barnie,’ he said, trying to reassure himself rather than his dog.

Jim walked away from the man and scrambled in his jacket pocket for his phone. Layers of cloth seemed to impede him as he pawed for the handset.

‘Come on,’ he gasped. Eventually, his fingers pulled the mobile free.

He dialled the emergency number and asked for the police. The call was relatively brief. Jim gave his name, explained the situation and what he had discovered. He could hear lots of police terminology in the background and, judging by the operator’s *Papa, Charlie*-style instructions, he assumed that the call was being dealt with. Jim was asked to stay with the body and the call ended.

He looked around and still could not see anyone. Perhaps early Christmas festivities were keeping people in their beds. Jim moved Barnstable further off and averted both their gazes away from the dead man. He had seen enough.

At that moment in time Jim felt like the only man on the planet. Well the only one living. *How did this man end up like this? You don’t do that to yourself?*

Soon, he could hear the wail of a police car siren and then saw, as the noise grew louder, a blue tinge of light echo off the keeper’s office near the park entrance. Jim watched as a squad car pulled up and two uniformed figures emerged.

Jim was about two hundred yards from the road, so he waved his arms in the air to attract the police officers’ attention. One of them waved back in acknowledgement. As they got closer he saw that one of the officers, who was puffing out plumes of condensation into the freezing air, was considerably slower than the other. *Obviously not the Flying Squad or a tactical unit* Jim thought, but at that point he no longer cared. He just wanted this responsibility off his hands. He had only gone out to walk his dog.

The quicker of the two officers, a young female PC, was soon with him. She spoke clearly and empathetically.

‘Mr Thomas, isn’t it?’

‘Yes,’ Jim replied.

‘I’m PC Roper. You said there was a dead body?’

‘Yes, over there in the thicket. Just be careful, the man’s face, it’s . . .’ Jim swallowed deeply again and stared at the ground. ‘You’ll see for yourself.’

Roper moved towards the body, carefully scanning the immediate area. Barnstable moved to follow, but Jim pulled him to his side.

Jim watched the officers. This was surreal. It was like to a play, with him sitting on the outside looking in, Jim thought. How did he get involved with this? After all, he was only walking his dog; something he did most days. Maybe if he blinked hard enough he would open his eyes and be in a different scene: anywhere but here and now.

By this time, both of the officers were standing with the body. The other officer stooped to stare at the man’s face; Roper was on her police radio. *Thank God*, Jim thought, *I can carry on. I have done my bit.*

Roper returned to Jim, leaving the other officer with the body. Jim noticed the other officer was a burly man: overweight, and straining to stand from a crouched position. Years ago, he would have been called fat: today, he would be termed obese and receive emotional support. Jim surprised himself that even in these circumstances his cynicism still rose to the fore. There was no doubt that society was certainly different now as opposed to when he was younger.

Jim often thought of his past, particularly since he had moved back home. He’d grown up locally and recalled his schooldays. He had been a chubby kid and had been called ‘fat’, ‘lard arse’, ‘Mr Piggy’. In fact, he had walked by his old school yard recently. The buildings were the same; there was even the same smell of school dinners. Jim had peered into the playground through the meshed fence that surrounded it. Perhaps all the playgrounds in the world were the same. There was no democracy in the playground when it came to being different to the herd. Fat, thin, bespectacled, coloured, rich, poor, spotty: they all got it. There was a pecking order that had been in existence since man had first appeared on the planet, and social dilemmas had played out ever since.

Jim tried to recall further details of his school days. What was the school bully's name? Every school had at least one: the one who smoked first, the one who swore first. What was his name? Surely he could remember his name. Someone who caused so much pain and grief you don't easily forget. Perhaps his psyche had hidden it away. He recalled seeing him French-kiss his girlfriend outside the classroom while everyone else was inside. The voyeurs all realised it was a show. It was done to set an example, a demonstration to the plebs that he was more mature than them. Jim did not recollect feeling jealous or envious: it hadn't even stirred anything in his teenage crotch. The bully's gal seemed to go along for the ride and security of being his mate. He remembered *her* name: Abby Merrymen, and by all accounts she had made many men merry. Jim recollected once seeing her exposed neck. It was leopard printed with love bites. Boy she was one classy lady. Now, Jim thought how suited they really were at the time.

Roper approached and woke Jim from his temporary trance. But he didn't stop pondering the bully's name. He knew it had been unusual. The kids had given him a tag line but it was to remain a mystery for the time being. Jim glanced up at Roper; his eyes were stinging and beginning to run.

'Sorry, Mr Thomas, it must be upsetting for you.' The PC foraged around in her pocket, pulled out a tissue and offered it.

Jim, was surprised at the gesture, then realised he must be looking tearful.

'No, I'm fine! It's my new contact lenses. It takes a while to get used to them.' Although he understood that his explanation was only partly the cause. 'Please, PC Roper, call me Jim,' he said. 'Mr Thomas throws me a curveball. I can't remember the last time anyone used my full name.'

Roper smiled back, her cheeks chapped a ruddy colour by the slap of winter chill.

Jim felt warmed by Roper's actions and gazed at her face. In any other situation she would be pretty, and perhaps life would have taken another path for both of them. Not here though, not now.

‘Jim, are you sure you are OK? Could you answer some questions? I’m sorry; I need to take some details down.’

‘Of course,’ Jim replied, and began telling her about the morning’s events.

They were both deep in conversation when their attention was diverted.

‘Whose is this dog, crying out loud?’ the portly officer bellowed.

Jim looked at his side and saw that Barnstable wasn’t there. The extendable lead had loosened and Barnstable, obviously bored, had gone for a wander.

Jim looked up and saw his dog hurry towards him from the direction of the tirade. ‘Sorry, he is mine. Is there a problem officer?’

The burly officer turned. Jim instantly saw three stripes on his epaulettes: a sergeant.

‘You could say that, sir. He has just taken a dump at the side of the body,’ said the Sergeant.

‘Sorry Sergeant Crane, I was taking the statement. Our attention was elsewhere,’ Roper explained.

‘A dead body, and a contaminated crime scene: the perfect start to the day,’ Sergeant Crane bellowed, staring at Jim with a gaze of disgust.

Jim stood open-mouthed at a vision from his past: his bully. He remembered the nickname: Crane the Pain. It was him. After all these years, Crane still looked at him in the same way. For one instant, Jim wanted to lower his head, to break eye contact. That had sometimes worked in the schoolyard, but not now and certainly not today. Boys had become men and life had given Jim the confidence to confront his bully, but he had also learnt the art of patience. No matter how many painful memories challenged him, Jim refrained from responding.

Roper walked over quickly to Crane and Jim watched them talking. Crane was gesturing and pointing to the dog mess. Roper grabbed his arm and pointed in Jim’s direction.

Jim recognised she was trying to diffuse the situation and wondered if Roper was trying to highlight the fact that he had just discovered a dead body: no amount of dog mess was going to cover that up.

Crane walked towards Jim, muttering under his breath.

'Sorry, Mr Thomas.'

Jim looked at Crane: it was a look that transcended the years: a vision from the playground. Everything was telling Jim to address the years of abuse he had suffered at Crane's hand. He had heard stories of bullies getting their comeuppance but now was not the time.

Looking closer at his former foe, Jim almost pitied Crane. It appeared as if life had started to inflict its own retribution for his past sins. His face was bloated; his cheeks tainted red by alcohol rather than the wintry conditions. It was obvious to Jim that Crane apologising for any upset he had caused was as uncomfortable to him as eating a salad. *Fat arsehole*, Jim thought.

Crane, disturbed by Jim's lack of response, kept talking. 'Sorry, it's just been a testing morning.'

Jim continued to stare, but his gaze started to soften as he replied, 'Difficult for all of us.'

Crane looked Jim up and down. 'PC Roper said that you live locally. How long have you lived here?'

'You probably don't remember me. We went to the same school. I looked a lot different then. I was a tubby kid, spotty. Obviously didn't have this beard back then.'

Jim wondered if Crane would remember. They had never directly communicated at school. Socially, they were from different groups. Their only interaction had been through physical or mental violence and that had been in one direction way, towards him.

Crane looked at Jim more inquisitively then his mouth arced into a smile. 'My God, I don't believe it – little Jimmy. Christ, you *have* changed. Of course I remember you – you were one of the clever kids. Not like me! I had to concentrate on physical education as I never had your brains.'

Jim was shocked. *He does remember me!* How could that be? Had Crane kept a mental log of his victims? Jim wondered if it had been jealousy that had prompted Crane the Pain's actions all those years ago.

As Jim contemplated a reason for Crane's past deeds, he looked at him with an anger built from mental rehearsals of reprisals. *You'll get yours, Crane*, he thought.

'So, what happened to you? I heard you'd moved away,' Crane asked.

'Yeah, I stopped on at school and after getting my A levels I went to university, got my degree. I then worked overseas. I spent eight years working in Japan. Eating rice every day soon gave me a better waistline.'

'What did you do in Japan?'

'Computer programming, I was working with some really clever guys in Tokyo. Made a mint with some software I created out there, so I don't need to work much now. Just blue-chip clients, when I feel like it.'

Jim loved that: one up for the clever class. He wanted to say more and tell Crane of his wealth, but prudence intervened. He glanced over to the body: money meant nothing once you were dead.

There was a brief silence.

'I guess we both made a success of our lives,' Crane said.

Jim smiled. The pressure cooker of sarcasm inside him was about to blow, but the brutality of his current situation turned down the heat.

'I guess you could say that,' he replied.

Crane turned and looked at Barnstable. 'What's the dog's name?'

'Barnstable.'

'Barnstable', Crane repeated. 'I suppose it stands for something clever or significant event, an unusual name like that. Not a common name like Toby, Spot or Jack.'

Crane appeared to turn to an imaginary playground. Almost looking for acceptance in a game of one-upmanship.

Jim could see that the dog was looking bored with the morning's activities. His walk had been cut short and he was ready for a snooze, warranted by his age.

Still staring down at Barnstable, Jim said softly, 'I couldn't tell you where his name came from. He was given it by a previous owner, before I adopted him.'

Jim watched Crane's face change from a smirk to a more awkward frown. His eyes danced around, seeking solace. It's funny, how our eyes can hold the key to our soul, Jim pondered. It certainly seemed true with Crane. It looked like his pupils were playing a game of *pong* with his eye sockets.

Crane stuttered and spoke again. 'I remember your parents. I'm sorry – I hadn't made the connection. I was there at the accident; I was one of the first on the scene. We did what we could, but it was no use. Is that what made you come home?'

It was Jim's turn to feel awkward and swallow a huge spoon of guilt. He recalled the phone call he had received in the early hours one morning. He was working abroad and the time difference partly explained the caller's lively voice. As Jim had cleared sleep from his head and listened to the conversation, the gravity of the situation became apparent. His parents had been killed in a car crash. Jim's father had been driving and had hit a tree at speed. The police said it was dangerous driving but to Jim's father it was normal driving, he had dementia. Both his parents had. But they seemed to be at the, *they can cope stage.* They just seemed forgetful and slightly confused to friends. Anyway, if they had gotten worst who would have decided that they needed help? Jim was working away, so he certainly couldn't. His interactions with his parents were scarce. He occasionally called home but it was brief and more from a sense of duty than a real desire to speak to them. When he did call, the majority of time he would talk to his mother, Gwen. It was easier. In Gwen's eyes, Jim could do no wrong. He was still her little boy but his father, Henry, was different. Henry was a belligerent man and also quite selfish. He resented the fact that Jim had left home and deep down the fact that he made such a success of his career. Henry would often explain to Jim that he could have done the same if he had not had a young child to bring up. And so the seeds of responsibility and guilt had been planted firmly within Jim. Henry just watered and nurtured them with tainted conversations aimed at his son.

Jim returned home to arrange their funeral. It was a brief affair. He had not organised anything like this before and just threw money in the right direction. Things seemed to go along smoothly. There were only a few guests present as most had already taken the same journey as his parents.

After the funeral, Jim returned to the family home. The last time he had been there was about three years ago. Nothing had changed. The kitchen still contained the same biscuit barrel he remembered from his child hood. As he had stood in the living room, he took a deep breath. He smelt his past, he smelt his home. He recalled memories of a younger Jim nestling in his mother's arms as she swayed him to sleep. He thought of past Christmases. Good times, evoking images of his father carving the turkey, joking around the table. It was a small family but it had been a rich one. In his youth, times had been happy. Age just seemed to sour things as he got older.

Here and now, he understood this was still his home and as hypocritical that might seem to some, he realised he had to stay.

Back at the park Jim and Crane looked at one another. The playground disappeared for once and was replaced with a shared empathy.

Roper reappeared. 'Sarge, it looks like CID are here.'

All three looked over to two men dressed in plain clothes walking towards them.

'Excuse me Jim, me and PC Roper had better brief them. Are you OK here for a bit longer?' Crane said in a softer tone.

'Yes, of course, whatever needs to happen.'

Crane and Roper made their way over to the two men. Out of Jim's earshot Crane started to relay parts of Jim's history, and particularly the details of his parents' deaths, to Roper.

'Can you remember the old couple that died in the car smash? They both had dementia, the man was driving and he hit the tree?'

Roper nodded.

Crane continued, 'Jim was their son.'

Roper blew through her lips. 'He's had a tough time, and now this.'

‘Perhaps if he had been at home, he could have helped his parents more. Perhaps they would still be here.’

‘That’s a tough shout Sarge.’

‘I would never leave my parents in a situation like that. No matter how much money I was earning,’ Crane said.

Roper did not answer and an uneasy atmosphere hung between them, broken by the two arriving officers.

Jim watched Crane and Roper talking to the two plain-clothes officers. Crane pointed to the body, then to Jim and more noticeably, Barnstable. One of the officers glanced at Jim then turned to Crane and they both entered into a more heated debate. Jim saw Crane hang his head.

The officer who had spoken to Crane walked towards Jim. As he approached, Jim could see he was smartly dressed. He wore a thick wool coat, his collar pulled high to keep out the winter chill. Getting closer, Jim noticed frost had started to cling to his trouser bottoms. He walked tentatively, trying his best to avoid skidding.

‘Mr Thomas, I’m Detective Inspector Rand. Are you OK?’

Jim, taken aback by the show of concern, choked as he replied, ‘Yes, sorry, no. If I am honest, I don’t know if I am or not. I am starting to feel a bit cold now.’

‘Not the morning you were expecting, I guess. It’s the same for all of us. Listen, we will move things along for you. I know PC Roper has taken some details from you but my colleague, DC Yates, needs to get a statement from you. Then you get off home. Keeping you here any longer would be doing no good. We can take it from here.’

We can take it from here: that’s all Jim had wanted to hear since he had found the hooded man. Jim looked over at the body, and Rand followed his gaze.

‘Do you think you will find the person who did this to him, the murderer?’ Jim asked.

‘Sorry Mr Thomas. What makes you think he has been murdered, Mr Thomas?’

‘You’ll see his face, the cuts, staples put in his cheeks. I can’t see how anyone could do that to themselves or even want to do that,’ said Jim.

'We'll find that out Mr Thomas. I assure you sir, that all procedures will be followed. As to a murder or not, our investigations will determine that.'

'Oh, I'm sorry DI Rand. My dog messed near the body. I hope it will not impede the case, the Sergeant seemed to think it might.'

Rand smiled and said, 'The Sergeant did explain, Mr Thomas, and no, I can't see it causing too much of a problem. In the scheme of things it is nothing. It seems ironic to joke but after all, it's probably the only thing here at the moment that is steaming.'

Jim forced a smile and nodded. He speculated if that had been the topic of the heated conversation he had witnessed between Crane and Rand earlier.

'I am going to go back to my colleagues. I'll tell my DC to come over.' Rand said, turning, walking back towards the body. The other plain-clothes officer was already there. Both looked under the hood of the dead man and grimaced. Rand looked around the immediate area, searching for clues, but a fresh dusting of snow in the early hours of that morning had tainted their chances of finding any real evidence.

Jim watched for a few moments more. Rand and Yates scribbled on notepads and whispered to one another. Crane and Roper stood back and watched the play unfold.

At the park entrance more vehicles started to appear. People wearing white paper suits and wellingtons trailed towards the body. Jim had seen plenty of crime shows on TV and assumed they must be "Scene of Crimes" staff. One of the members of the troop was heavily weighed down, holding large bags in their hands and the inevitable happened. Jim watched them skid on some loose snow and unable to correct their balance due to their load, fall to the ground. The officers stood around the body turned as they heard the noise of the bags hit the frozen earth. Crane burst out laughing. He held his stomach as his body shuddered with enjoyment.

'Honestly, this job gets better.' He blurted out as he watched the stricken person scramble to their knees. Rand, Yates and Roper all looked at Crane in disgust.

Crane returned their gazes and still giggling spoke, 'What? You have got to admit that was funny.' Neither of them joined in with Crane's joviality. They all looked back at their fallen comrade.

Jim watched as the once pristine suited accident victim brushed themselves down. Other members of the party came to their assistance, checking they were ok. Brown stains scuffed the suits knees and elbows but Jim also noticed to muddy circles on their chest. Obviously a woman he thought. The accident victim didn't look large enough to have man boobs. There was certainly nobody trying to brush dirt away from that area, prudence intervened.

The temporary excitement ended as the team arrived at the body. Crane shook his head and wiped his eyes, 'God I wish I had videoed that. I'd be an internet sensation.'

DI Rand intervened firmly, 'Sergeant Crane, remember where you are!' There was a brief silence, a general pause in motion. Then the entourage started to work again.

Jim started to feel the cold. He picked up Barnstable, who promptly rested his head over his shoulder. Large tufts of hot vapour spouted into the air from the pet's nose, like the puffs of a teenager vaping their first e-cigarette.

Jim shouted over to the two CID detectives, 'Excuse me, can I go now? We are both starting to feel really cold!'

Rand raise his head, spoke to Yates and then they both walked towards Jim. Jim noticed Crane, his headed tilted to avoid detection, whisper to Roper. Roper responded with a shake of her head. Was that another defamatory comment from Crane, Jim wondered? He was honestly beyond caring at the moment. The morning's events had been far too rich for his blood.

'I'm sorry, Mr Thomas. DC Yates will just take a quick statement from you then you can go. We may need to ask more questions, but we can do that at the station later or tomorrow. We could come to you. Whichever is easier?' Rand peered at Jim more closely. 'Mr Thomas, are you sure you're OK? I can have an officer come around later anyway, to make sure?'

Jim did not respond immediately. His normal reaction would have been to say yes, and let bravado absorb any feeling of vulnerability but the truth was that seeing the body and being exposed to such trauma was starting to play havoc with his mind.

‘I think that might help. Could it be PC Roper? She seems a good listener,’ Jim said.

Rand glanced over at Roper, ‘I’ll ask, Mr Thomas. I can’t see why not. Are you in all day? We have your address don’t we?’

‘Yes and yes.’

Rand offered Jim his hand and Jim, moving Barnstable to one side, shook it tentatively.

‘I’m sorry we had to meet like this Mr Thomas. Please go and get warm, get a drink,’ Rand said.

Jim doffed an imaginary cap and started to make his way home, taking one last glance at the body. He looked around the park as he left. A few isolated figures were in the distance, they were also walking their dogs. Jim wondered if he had been a little bit later, perhaps if he had slept an extra hour in bed, they might have found the body and he could have been the one peering at the commotion. If’s, what’s and maybe’s didn’t matter. It was what it was now. His head hung low, he thought how cold the world had become that morning, and perhaps just a little darker.

All these people. An audience, of sorts, but none offering me any warmth. Cold, so cold, but at least my Samaritan has not left me alone. Goodbye, my friend. I think we may meet again.

Fifty Eight Pounds

The Previous Day

The floor was cold. Stacks of the previous week's newspapers were not proving to be the best insulation. Michael's rear sat upon piles of old headlines. A lot might argue that was the best place for them. Better they remained there kissing someone's arse cheeks than trying to get a point across. He shivered trying to keep warm. Layering up with what clothes he possessed but they were not bought for the specific purpose of keeping him warm. They consisted from what he had found or had been donated. His appearance was not his priority. There was no colour coordination or time spent grooming. He had no ambition for any of that. When winter arrived and you had no home, the season bit hard.

All the street dwellers hated the winter. It didn't mean cosy nights around the fire and choosing Christmas presents. It only meant one thing to them, survival. If they woke up the following day it was a bonus. For some they chose not to, preferring death than further suffering. The front of a Christmas card, a typical winter's scene did not bring merriment to them.

Michael had positioned himself at the entrance of the town train station. He had discovered the optimum place of visibility to the travelling public. It was a perfect pitch, a place to tug at heart strings and tease out compassion from the people passing by. There had been a previous tenant for the patch but they had gone, left. Michael didn't know where too, he didn't care. This was prime real estate in this world of dog eat dog. It afforded no inquisition or sympathies for anyone.

The spot was close enough to attract the penny donators from the masses but not too close as to cause offence to anyone. If you crossed the demarcation zone, the imaginary line dotted by the authorities or landlords you risked retribution. That did not necessarily mean a visit from the law. Quite often, private security firms, who administered a lot of the local buildings, enacted their own idea of justice. It was Dickensian, harsh and swift. Experience had taught Michael to tread very carefully to ensure his safety and not bring unwarranted attention upon himself.

It was evening. Michael was awaiting the last few trains carrying passengers to arrive at the station. At this time of day, they mainly returned people home from work. These travellers were his bread and butter. They provided a steady revenue stream for him but at this time of year there was an added bonus. Another type of passenger might pass his way. He may get lucky. There might be a few festive shoppers on board. With their arms laden full of presents, stomachs warmed by mulled wine and heads swooned by carol singers. As they talked of Christmas card lists with one another, Michael hoped they might stop and give money as he sat, cup in hand, waving for a donation.

Occasionally, there was always the kind soul who went to the trouble to buy him a coffee and a sandwich. He thanked them gracefully and blessed them, but money was a more tangible commodity. It bought the things he needed, stuff he craved. Things like lager, not the weak stuff, Export, the nine percent gear. It gave you a buzz. It only took a few cans of the right stuff to get you going, it helped you forget. A few cans more and you were on a beach somewhere sipping a cocktail.

Michael heard the rumble of the train pull in, its brakes hissed as it came to a halt. The clanging of the running gear on the track was a dead giveaway. It wouldn't be long now. He prepped himself for the passengers. He then heard the muffled station announcer confirming the traveller's destination. Looking around he swiftly tidied up his make shift seat and pulled down his woollen hat. He took a small bottle of hand gel and cleaned his hands before putting on a pair of fingerless mittens. Experience had taught him that he could appeal to more of an audience if he didn't appear too dirty. People seemed to be more willing to give to a cleaner vagrant. As hypocritical as that seemed it worked in practice.

The footsteps of the passengers grew louder. Michael looked at them as they passed, his hand holding out his begging cup. Frequently, arms shot out from the precession, causing his cup to rattle with coins that had been donated.

'Thank you. Bless you. You are very kind,' Michael responded to the clatter of money being given. He then noticed a small group of ladies approaching. Their arms brimming full of gifts, all tastefully shop wrapped, held in expensive corporate logo bags. They looked like they had completed a trolley dash in Harrods; now more resembling a hastily decorated Christmas tree. As they approached, they had not noticed Michael. Their seasonal jollities seemed to blind their awareness of his presence. One of the women accidentally caught Michael's foot, she tripped and barely managed to keep her footing. Stumbling and juggling her presents without dropping any, she kept her balance like a tight rope walker. Turning around, she looked at her obstacle. Michael clutched his ankle, grimacing. The woman's initial anger and embarrassment turned to concern.

'I'm sorry, so sorry. Are you OK?'

Michael held the injured joint in his hands. Rubbing the bone up and down, he looked at the woman angrily, 'Can't you watch where you are going!' he barked.

'I'm so sorry. Listen I am parked nearby, let me take you to A&E.' Michael laughed sarcastically and replied, 'A&E, really, do you think they will give me the time of day.'

The woman looked more intently at Michael and understood.

'Can you stand on it? Put a bit of weight on it' she asked.

Michael stood, nervously placing his aching foot to the floor and whimpered. It didn't hurt him too much but he had a captive audience; compensation was ringing around his head. The woman's friends watched on, keeping a distance, not wanting to get directly involved. One of them beckoned

Michael's culprit over towards her. Pulling her to one side, she whispered something in her ear. Listening, the woman who had caught his foot, looked him up and down. Then the two women parted. She placed her presents on the floor and approached Michael.

'Is there something else I can help with?'

'What exactly?' replied Michael. The woman got closer but not too close as to be uncomfortable. She reached in her pocket, produced her purse and took out two twenty pound notes. 'Would this help?' Michael looked at her outstretched hand holding the money.

'I suppose I could get something to ease the pain.' He took the notes from her hand, stuffing them hastily into his coat pocket. The woman pulled back her hand swiftly, as if it had been bitten by a snake.

'So you will be alright now?' Michael continued with his act, tentatively leaning on the injured limb.

'There's a chemist up the road. I'll see if he has some painkillers.'

'Would you like me to walk you there? I don't mind, my friends can help?' Michael looked at the woman's friends whose eyes had widened at her last statement. Half of him wanted to say *yes*, see what their reaction would be. He realised deep down it wasn't a genuine offer. Anyway he didn't want to go to the chemist, it was the off licence he needed.

'No thank you. I will be fine.'

That was what she wanted to hear. The forty pound had cleared her conscience and now she could get back to her festive plans her friends.

Michael watched her leave. The troop reloaded with presents, scurried away from the station. He wanted to shout to them, say he'd changed his mind but all in all, he had had a good result. Totting up the coins in his begging cup and with the forty pound in notes, he had made fifty eight pound. Not a bad day at the office. Walking around perfectly, pain free, he put the newspapers he had been sitting on into a bag, then tossed it over his shoulder. He made his way to the off licence.

Looking back, all that remained was a slightly dryer patch than the surrounding area. The meagre insulation afforded from the paper had prevented any frost from forming. The conditions would soon put that right.

As he walked, he was aware that all the useful passengers had gone. Michael did not hang around for the later ones, the revellers. They normally meant trouble. The only donations they seemed to be liberal with were violence and bodily fluids. It was time he made his way back to his temporary home via the booze shop. It was warmer there and safer.

He made his way steadily to the high street, passing several people along the way. There was no communication between them. He did not offer season's greetings or even a simple *Hello*. Previous journeys had taught him that there would have been no response, other than one of abuse. Most people avoided him, moved to the other side of the road if he was in their way. Then they didn't have to make conversation. The problem had disappeared. If they confronted one another, what could it have led too? *You never know what these people want?* He seemed to be marked with the same sign of contempt as a suicide bomber. If people only knew how he ended up here, if people only took the time to know? Perhaps they would not be so quick to judge.

Light snow had started to fall. It clung to his coat and face. He desperately needed something to warm him up. A quick short cut and he would soon be able to buy his pick me up. *Fifty eight pounds, a positive bounty*, he thought. Without question, the booze shelf would be open for him tonight. All that money, how long would he have to work in a fast food chain to earn that?

He laughed as he imagined himself adorned in the corporate uniform of a burger chain, wearing a T shirt and baseball hat. Speaking down the microphone of a drive through, he might ask, 'Hello can I take you order. What's that Sir? You would like fifty eight pounds worth of burgers please and hold the mayo.' He joked to himself as he continued on his way.

He turned onto an avenue that led directly to the high street. He knew this way like the back of his hand. It was a quicker route. It was a bit darker, quieter than the main road but took about fifteen minutes from his journey. He wasn't scared, it was not late. The youths and drunks were not out yet so he felt assured with his decision.

As he walked, Michael looked up at the streetlights. He could stare at them directly. They still had old gas filled bulbs, the ones that took an age to get bright. Firing up red, slowly turning orange as you watched them glow. They had not been superseded by the latest LED ones that lit the high street. The ones you dare not look at unless you wanted your vision blind spotted for a few hours.

In between each lamppost was a shaded area, made darker by the falling snow. The drifting flakes seeming to absorb the last fragments of light. Michael was not fazed by the shadows. He had nothing to worry about. All was good in his world. He had fifty eight pounds in his pocket.

Looking along the alleyway he could see the brighter neon lights from the shops on the high street. They called to him with a promise of riches.

Out of the corner of his eye, he thought he saw something, a man. Turning to look closer he saw a figure withdraw into the shadow of the street light. Michael sensed he was there and the dull glow of the light still shone on his boot. That was enough for him. He was in no mood to confront anyone. Pulling his bag tighter over of his shoulder and covering the mouth of the pocket which contained his money, he ran slipping and sliding towards the high street.

The green bawdy neon light of the off licence soon greeted him. Michael cast a glance back down the alley. The man had gone. All he saw was the slowly falling snow meandering on its path to the frozen pavement.

Bing Bong. The door chimed as Michael entered the store. The shop keeper raised his eyes at the alarm, glanced over towards the open door, keen to see who had entered. It was an action he repeated umpteen times a day, normally returning his attention to what he had been doing, but not with his current customer. He'd had many previous dealings with Michael. He was more than aware he had to keep his wits about him. If Michael was drunk it would be hard work, if he was sober then peace would reign in his small world.

'You Ok Michael?' the shopkeeper asked to test the water.

'Good as can be expected Mr Singh. It's turning bitter out there.' The shopkeeper, Mr Singh, breathed a little easier. He recognised Michael's response as being sober. *That will do nicely*, he thought.

Michael didn't browse the goods he knew what he wanted, straight to the good stuff. Standing before an array of liquor, he squinted at the bottles, pointing at the labels with his finger. He mumbled to himself, 'Chinese, Polish, Indian. All cheap stuff, where is the Russian gear?'

'Can I help you Michael,' asked Mr Singh, carefully watching his movements.

'I'm after the Russian vodka. The dear stuff, I can't see it.'

'Let me get it for you.' Mr Singh eased passed Michael, stretched out his arm and grabbed an ornately shaped bottle. 'You sure this is what you want?'

'Yes Mr Singh. Sorry didn't look there. I am not normally as flush as I am today.' Michael leant toward the shopkeeper and whispered, 'I've got fifty eight pounds.'

'Good for you Michael. Let me put you a burger in the microwave or a hot pie. They are not expensive. I bet you are hungry?'

'No thanks Mr Singh. I'm saving up. Gonna' buy me a yacht and sail to the south of France. Get a rich wife, live the good life, *La Vie en Rose*.' Mr Singh smiled and followed Michael to the counter.

‘Listen Michael, it is cold out there. Let me cook you a pie, it’s on the house. You need something to eat. This stuff is no good for you?’

Michael shook his head, ‘Thanks, but no thanks.’

Taking out his money, he paid and left. As the door to the shop closed shut, Mr Singh watched Michael through the glass panes. He unscrewed the lid from the bottle of vodka and took a huge swig. Michael looked back into the shop, saluted Mr Singh and walked away.

The visit to the off licence was rapidly becoming a distant memory as Michael was already half way down his vodka. The bottles curvy shape fitted comfortably in his hand. Even the snow that slid down its sides didn’t cause his grasp to ease.

Up ahead he saw a few people gathered outside a takeaway. Getting nearer, he recognised the normal scurry of staff leaving with boxes of food primed for delivery. Michael held back slightly. He’d walked this path before and remembered being on the receiving end of some serious shit from a group of local youths. It looked quiet at the moment, all clear. *Just let ’em come,* he thought. If they decided to show their faces he was ready for them. A vodka fuelled Michael was a different proposition to the sober one they messed with last time.

The bright glare beaming threw the takeaways window lit the concrete slabs outside. Michael walked, following the cemented lines, placing one foot in front of the other. It was as though he had been asked to prove he wasn’t drunk. Stood squarely facing the takeaway window he looked at his reflection. His tatty clothes hung from his gaunt frame. They fit were they could, which was infrequent. His beard was unkempt, rough, not manicured and displayed remnants of his last meal. Definitely *not marriage material* he thought.

‘Looking good!’ Michael said giddily. He took another long slug of vodka. As he lowered the bottle, a wider audience joined his reflection in the window. Two youths now stood either side of him.

'Well, well, who do we have here?' One of the lads asked in a muffled tone. They all wore hoodies. Their hoods pulled over the heads, with scarves raised to their noses. Michael spun around to face them. He looked closer, too close for comfort. A couple of the lads backed away slightly.

'I know you. Yeah, I know you. It's the little boys that gave me shit last time. Little boys, you're just little boys, scared little boys.' All four of the lads watched him, one answered,

'What you say you tramp. You'd better shut up your mouth man or we will fuck you up. You gotta' pay to be here. This place is owned by us.'

Michael looked at each of the lads in turn, wobblingly slightly as he focused, 'Little boys. Go home. Haven't you got homework?'

He giggled, turned from them and started to walk away. The youths watched him leave. Michael, now about five metres away, turned around and waved back,

'Nighty, night, don't let the bed bugs bite.'

He then helped himself to another drink.

From inside the takeaway one of the staff had one eye on what was happening outside. Looking past a customer's shoulders, they watched the gang of youths follow Michael. There was little doubt in their mind the evening would not end well for someone.

Michael reached a bench in small clearing. The seat was covered with fresh white snow. He sat down, not giving a care if he got wet or not. The dwindling bottle of vodka was clutched close to his side. He patted its neck and smiled.

The bench was surrounded by flats and tenements. They were about five storeys high. A mixture of household lights twinkled on or off within the buildings. It resembled an amateur mosaic created against a white background.

'I'll soon be leaving all this behind. None of this were I'm going. *La Vie en Rose*.' Michael whispered to himself.

He looked upwards and let the slowly falling snow rest on his face. The cold, moist flakes sobered him slightly. Another drink countered that. The warm sensation of the libation comforted him as it slid down his throat. He didn't recognise the flavour or taste of his drink anymore, it just served a key purpose. It took him from his current situation to where he wanted to be, his special place. A place made of dreams which cradled and nurtured his aspirations. It was Michael's dreamscape, the good life, *La Vie en Rose*. In this world, he had built a beautiful vision in his mind. He lived in the south of France. He owned a huge mansion on the water front with a yacht moored alongside. He had a supermodel wife and two kids. He would kiss her on the cheek every morning, fling open the balcony windows of their bedroom and breathe in the fresh air, warmed by a Mediterranean breeze. His children would run around on the lawn below, a girl and a boy, watched carefully by their nanny. They needed a nanny, Michael and his wife had to be away from home frequently as they attended "World Film Premieres". They regularly rubbed shoulders with the stars, had dinner with them. Michael was so popular, the centre of attention. His phone contact list brimmed with the names of the rich and famous. It was a socially absorbing list of names that opened doors to the most exclusive of places. There was nowhere refused him entry, all wanted a piece of him.

It was a life he conjured over time. That's one thing Michael had plenty of. An exotic vision constructed and rehearsed countless times. Its inspiration from an image he had seen on one of the magazines he used to keep the cold and wind at bay. This picture engraved in his mind, kept him warm through winter and gave him a glimmer of optimism for any hint of a future.

It could happen. Of course it could, Michael reasoned. He came up with a plan. *I will use the change I have, from today and buy lottery tickets. Yeah, that will work. I'll go public with my winnings. Hold a big cheque before everyone, show 'em all*, he thought. He shook his head, laughed, then shouted, 'You will all be shocked then. You won't turn away from me then. Won't cross the road, you will all want to be my friend then!'

He held his head back over his shoulders and started to sing, 'Oh the good life, fool of fun seems to be the ideal,' Michael paid a drunken tribute to Tony Bennet's iconic song.

He continued his slurry rendition, 'Mm, the good life lets you hide all the sadness you feel.'

His joy was cut short by a voice from behind him.

'I don't know about that man. There ain't no happiness for you. You ain't going nowhere 'till you pay the piper.'

Michael felt an arm reach from behind and tighten around his neck. He struggled, caught off balance, dropping his bottle to the ground. It was the gang he encountered earlier. Three youths raced to the front of him and started repeatedly punching him in the stomach. Michael's thick clothing marginally muted the beating. This wasn't his first attack; living as he did it was a consequence of his very existence. Punch after punch rained in around his midriff. He coughed up stale vodka from his mouth. Reaching to break the hold around his neck, left him further exposed and the blows had more of an affect. He was trapped. His assailants hold was too strong to weaken. The youth anchoring Michaels neck spoke to the rest, 'Check his pockets. He should have some money, he's bought a bottle.'

One of the others rifled inside Michael's pockets. He came across his money and grabbed the notes, 'Got it, let's leave this piece of shit.'

Michael's was released, thrown to the floor. Discarded like a piece of rubbish. Two of the youths kicked him in his stomach, one leaned down, spat in his face and spoke, 'this is our turf ya' skunk. You come here, you owe rent. You listening?'

Michael lay on the floor. His cheek pressed against the cold ground. He watched the youths walk away, laughing and counting the money they had just stolen.

Slowly he managed to manoeuvre to a crouch position. His sides ache, he could taste blood in his mouth. He watched red spittle drop to the floor. The pure white carpet of snow inked stained, a result of his injuries. Climbing back on the bench, he reached and gathered his bottle from the ground. Unscrewing the top, he took another long, satisfying drink. The bottle emptied. Michael shook it, straining the last dregs inside. He tossed the spent bottle to the side and heard it thud as it landed. The thoughts of the south of France had gone, *La Vie en Rose* had disappeared. He needed to get home, somewhere safe, he needed time to repair. Using the back of the bench to stand, he stumbled his way off the housing estate.

Michael now stuck to the shadows. He recognised the dark kept him safe. He stopped several times as he heard noise, revelry up ahead. Senses still heavily muted by alcohol, he skidded, slipped his way closer home. 'Damn it,' he shouted as he stumbled to the floor. The pain from his attack was starting to kick in more and more. He didn't suspect anything was broken, he just felt bruised. Tomorrow he expected his skin to look like a maroon leopard skin coat, mottled and blotchy. Not that anyone would see it. There were no showers or bathing facilities where he lived.

He grabbed at the base of a lamppost to straighten himself up. The structures frozen steel burnt at his fingers. One step ahead of the other he carried on. The weather was getting worse. The wind had picked up and the white stuff was falling heavier. Clumps of snow clung to his beard and back. His footing was getting tricky, any progress severely impeded. The journey home would be a long one.

Whether it was the conditions, his drunken state or his injuries, Michael fell to the floor again. 'Arghh!' he shouted.

'Enough. That's enough. I am staying here. I'll wait it out until the morning.' He curled into the foetal position and surrendered. Clutching his ribs, he did what he could to get comfortable. If comfortable was the right word.

A few minutes later Michael heard a voice, 'Can I help you?' He looked up through falling snow. His eyes straining to see and replied, 'I'm just trying to get home. I've slipped.'

'Come on, let me help.' A strong arm reached down and lifted him up easily. Michael grimaced.

'Have you hurt yourself falling,' his aid asked.

'Yes, I think so but I am OK.'

'Have you got a long way to go?'

'The old car park, I live there.'

'That's the other end of town. In this weather and in your state, you'll never make it.'

'What state? I haven't been drinking if that's what you think,' Michael bellowed angrily.

'No sorry. I didn't mean that. I meant from your fall. You must have gone with a bang.'

Michael realised he had over reacted but he had grown tired of being questioned over his drinking in the past. He wasn't an alcoholic. He just liked a drink, it calmed him down. He slept better after a drink. He didn't need to drink. It just made things seem better.

His helper replied, 'I'm sorry. I didn't mean to offend. I have an idea. I live closer. Let me help you to my house, I'll pick up my car, drive you home from there.' Michael looked at the man. He seemed right enough, a kind soul. At that moment, there didn't seem much of an alternative. Michael gladly accepted.

The man steadied Michael and looped his arm to form a crutch under his shoulder. As they walked slowly forward, a blizzard forced them to lower their heads in an attempt to parry the harsh conditions. The worsening weather held them in their tracks.

Michael's helper spoke again, 'I have an idea. It's quicker if we take a short cut over the park. We will be home in five minutes.' Michael agreed. Both the men migrated from the dull radiance of the street towards the darkness of park. The only glimpse of light either saw was the tainted reflection of the snow covered ground. Even, the sky refused to help them, heavy with winter weather.

Michael spoke, 'You know, I was having a good day. Fifty eight pounds I had today. I think my luck has changed. It's going to be all good from here on in. Tell me, what's your name friend?' The man answered, 'You don't need to know my name.'

Michael never reached the other side of the park.

Slash, slash, but no pain. You tear at my face, my skin but I feel no pain. I have no voice. Is it the end? Cold, so cold. Goodbye La Vie en Rose.

Beginnings

The present

Jim was soon home. He paused for a moment of normality in familiar surroundings. As he stood enjoying the silence, he remembered the morning's events and genuinely felt sad for the man he had discovered. His brief trance was interrupted by the chortling of the boiling kettle; an everyday sound that reminded you that shit needed to go on. Making a drink, he took a biscuit from the family biscuit barrel and could do nothing else but think about the day. He had too many questions in his head and wasn't sure who could answer them anyway. What was this man doing in the park? Who could do that to him?

Jim looked at Barnstable, who had curled up into a ball on his dog bed. Once again, Jim envied him. He wanted the dog's world, without conscience and responsibility. Jim crouched on the floor and huddled beside Barnstable. He placed his arm on the sleeping pet. Barnstable nuzzled his head into his master and both of them slowly drifted into sleep.

Jim was awoken by Barnstable twitching, followed a few seconds later by a knock at the front door. Jim rose up, shrugging off the pain in his shoulder, which had been contorted by his unplanned slumber.

Jim could see a fluorescent top through the door's opaque window: police? He glanced at his watch and was shocked to see he had been asleep for four hours. Rubbing his eyes quickly, he opened the door. It was PC Roper, as promised.

Jim made tea and they sat together in Jim's living room.

'Nice place you have here – been here long?'

'It was my parents'. After they died, I decided to stay and do the place up. I've travelled a lot and I'd grown tired of that life.'

'I spoke to Sgt Crane. He said he remembered you from school.'

Jim thought about his response. He toyed with whether to tell the truth or not. To expose Crane for his past deeds. He looked at Roper, her face full of compassion, and decided to trust her.

'The truth is, PC Roper, that most of the kids we were at school with would remember Sgt Crane – or Crane the Pain, as we called him then. He was not a nice man. To put it bluntly, he was a bully.' Jim fell silent and waited for a response.

Roper stared at the floor, then back at Jim. 'That's not the first time I've had heard that. I've been based here about three years and a lot of people I have come across say the same.'

'Look, the past is the past and today's events have put it in perspective for me. I suppose we were all different then. If you asked Crane about his past, he would probably tell you a different story.' He stood and walked to the window.

'Can I ask, do you know who the man is yet; the one I found this morning . . . the body?'

Roper looked away and Jim sensed she was struggling to reply.

He tried again. 'I know you can't tell me much. It's just that it looked like someone who didn't have a penny in life. I feel a kind of responsibility for it.'

Roper raised her head. 'You said *it* instead of *him*.'

'I'm sorry PC Roper, but I just saw a body. I didn't know who he was. I suppose it's subconsciously how I'm dealing with it.'

Roper was weighing him up; she seemed to be peering in at his soul. 'If I tell you what we've discovered, you can't repeat it. Can I trust you?'

Jim gazed at Roper. His features softened and he replied, 'I understand, PC Roper. And I assure you that it will not go any further. I just need to try and make sense of it all . . . the brutality, the loss of life.'

Roper took a deep breath and began. 'We're not sure of his name yet but we do know that he'd been living rough in the old town car park. It's an area where vagrants, for want of a better word, live – it's dry and relatively secure. It is where they call home. We found a serviette issued by the local soup kitchen in his pocket. Their charity's logo was on it. We don't know his name yet: some of the other vagrants gave us a nickname but we need to verify it. These people, they're not the most reliable of witnesses.'

Jim could not understand the delay in identifying the dead man. He had worked in a world awash with data, where an individual's social and physical characteristics were mapped to their electronic footprint. It had been just over six hours since the body's discovery and he assumed the police would have found a name by now.

'The old town car park? I thought it was derelict. I played there as a kid. How many people live there?'

'There's a small community. They keep themselves to themselves and we only go there to deal with the usual drink or drug incidents. The car park is quite isolated now, since everything moved over to the new precinct.'

Jim held his head in his hands. Questions swirled around in his mind until the blood throbbed in his temples. 'I'm sorry PC Roper, I was going to ask why they were there at all, but why wouldn't they be? I've seen a lot of the world and witnessed poverty first-hand. Coming home, I perhaps believed that I'd left those sorts of problems behind.'

'Jim, will you be OK? I need to get back, but I can call again or you can come to the station anytime.'

'Thank you, PC Roper.'

'It's Susan, Jim. PC Roper is my Sunday name,' she smiled.

'Susan it is then.'

Roper turned back to him at the front door. 'Just one last thing: we're keeping this from the Press. They don't know anything and if they should find out they could cause problems for the investigation and scare off potential witnesses. Could you please not talk to anyone about today?'

'No problem, I'm not a big lover of the Press anyway.'

Jim watched her go. Perhaps in another time, another place, Jim and Susan might have meant more to each other.

The remainder of the evening passed as usual for Jim. He watched pre-Christmas shows on the TV. He and Barnstable sat in front of an open fire, cheered by the heat. Maybe it was the warmth, or the rhythmic sound coming from the crackling logs on the fire, but after just a short while Jim dozed. He was exhausted by the day's events. When he woke it was cold; the fire had long since died. Its red embers had been replaced by grey piles of soot which rested against a spent hollow carcass left from a burned out log. The TV was showing post-watershed entertainment, where naked titillation is the order of the day. He looked at Barnstable, who had curled closer to him as the heat from the fire had diminished.

'Come on Barnie, bed time,' Jim said to his slumber buddy.

Jim glided through his bedtime routine on automatic pilot. He fastened the fireguard to the hearth, turned off the TV, then the lamps, and locked the front door. Lastly, he went to turn off the Christmas tree lights then realised that he had not put them on. A simple action missed, which drew his attention back to the trials of the day. Jim made his way to bed, his head slightly lower, shoulders slightly heavier.

Barnstable jumped onto the bed, paced around, prodded the quilt with his paws to obtain a position of optimum comfort, and lay down. Jim watched him in the reflection of his bathroom mirror and smiled. Running water from the tap into the white ceramic basin, he cupped his hands, splashed his face, and cautiously held his fingers to his eyes to remove his contact lenses. Jim had completed this action many times but could not watch himself doing it. If he watched other people do the same, it always made him squirm. He had pondered yet rejected eye surgery countless times, and realised wearing glasses just made the condition worse. He concluded that this was his lot in life, and that there were many people worse off than him. So he had just got to get on with it.

Jim looked up and into the mirror through his tear-smeared eyes. There was a different view in the reflection. On his bed he saw an upturned, frost-encrusted boot. The tread was worn and held grass within its rubber teeth. Jim reached out to the mirror and turned it to allow a better view of the bedroom.

Sitting on the bed, the head with its stapled grin looking down, was the body. Ice hung in sharp angles from its frozen clothes. Behind the body Jim could see Barnstable was still fast asleep. The dog's lack of interest made Jim realise that this was more apparition than reality and, like Ebenezer Scrooge from

Dickens' *A Christmas Carol*, he thought, 'There is more of gravy than grave about you, sir.'

Angered by the intrusion, Jim stared at the body in the reflection and, not wishing to speak out aloud and disturb his loyal friend, began an internal dialogue with the apparition.

I realised you would be here. That's why I am not shocked to see you. But why? Do I owe you something? I just found you: is this to be my life going forward? Seeing a continual image of you?

Jim moved his head from side to side, trying to instigate a modicum of reason. He was starting to get angrier, so began the mental tirade again.

I have a question for you. Your death – were you an innocent victim? You have my sympathy but what about your part in it? and what gives you the right to torment me? I was walking my dog and now this.

Jim looked away from the mirror and rubbed his eyes to clear his vision before looking back at the bed. There was nothing there but a sleeping dog. He heard the sound of his breathing, which was heavier than usual due to his heart pumping faster: the result of a mind that was toying with reality.

Jim calmed himself and made his way to the bed. He pulled back the quilt, reached out his arm and cuddled Barnstable close again. Jim nuzzled his face into the dog's back. Barnstable let out a sympathetic whimper and fatigue quickly forced them both to sleep.

Sleep well, my Samaritan. This may be my last visit. If I had a voice, I would answer your questions. You are the only hope for truth. It must be you. I am cold, so cold.

The next morning, Jim awoke as normal but his mind soon raced back to the previous day. He struggled to make sense of any of it but was determined not to let yesterday's events impose themselves on his life. He needed to rationalise the situation and move on.

A few days passed as Jim tried to get back to some kind of normal. He still took his dog for walks but avoided taking Barnstable along the same route in the park. The local TV channels reported a body had been found but that the police had stated there were no suspicious circumstances.

Jim smirked as he listened to the news: *great detective work by England's' finest.* He wasn't too bothered. He hadn't the ambition or energy to argue the contrary, even if he recognised that what was being shared was a blatant lie.

Returning from a shopping trip, he found a card pushed through his door. The front of the card bore a police emblem and at the bottom was PC Roper's contact number: on the reverse, a brief, handwritten note:

Hello Jim,

I hope you are OK. I just wondered if we could catch up.

Susan

Jim perused the note and deliberated what to do next. If he ignored it, would he be able to just carry on and forget everything? He knew that would not work. So should he contact Susan, say, 'What the hell?' and mention the obvious omissions from the Press reports? He did not want to be involved any further, but there was no avoiding it, so he felt he had to make contact.

He picked up the phone and dialled the number on the card. Susan didn't pick up, so he left a message and waited for a return call. Recent events aside, Jim realised that he wanted to see Susan again.

At last, Susan returned the call and arranged to visit Jim later that afternoon. Jim sensed from her voice that she was genuinely concerned for his welfare. The fact was that in Susan's absence Jim had become attracted to her, so he welcomed her attention.

Jim swiftly tidied up around the house: he plumped cushions; sprayed air freshener. He laughed, thinking how far into a relationship you had to be before you stopped using air freshener. At what point did familiarity overcome making an impression? Was there a mutually agreeable juncture when breaking wind was allowed? Jim had not been with anyone long term or even short term to find out. Work had always seem to get in the way or it had been put there as an excuse.

Jim started with excitement at the sound of the doorbell. He opened the door and there was Susan: they greeted each other with smiles and exchanged looks that went beyond the formal pleasantries.

'Please come in Susan. Would you like a drink?'

'Love one, thank you – tea, white with none please. Staple diet of the Police Force.'

Jim smirked and replied, 'Please sit down, I'll bring it over.'

Susan made her way to the sofa, with Barnstable in close attendance.

'How have you been? I guess you've seen the news?' Susan asked.

Jim walked over clutching the drinks, 'If I'm honest I'm trying to get on with things. Yes, I did see the news. No suspicious circumstances – if that was the case, I hope I don't die as naturally as that.'

Susan looked at him steadily. 'I'm not going to lie: when I saw the Press release I thought of your response. I admire you for not creating merry hell. We want to keep as much detail as possible away from the public at the moment, and protect your anonymity. Whoever did this is still at large and our best chance of catching them is to keep the situation under control.'

Susan took a gulp of tea: it was far too hot to drink but she needed an interruption to the conversation.

Jim sat back on his freshly plumped cushions and breathed in the spring scent of the air freshener. 'It's OK Susan, whatever it takes. I can't comment, I'm not a detective and I don't want to be one. Things have calmed down for me after the first night.'

Susan looked at him, puzzled. 'The first *night*? Did something else happen?'

Shit, shit, shit! The word was being tossed around like a hot potato in Jim's head. 'I . . . er . . .' he stammered. *Shit! I'm going to sound deranged.*

'I was getting ready for bed and I saw the body on my bed. The dead body, the one I found but I have not seen it, *him*, since.' Jim coloured up, his face tinged cherry.

‘What you went through is bound to affect you. It just proves you are human. I would imagine it’s a kind of post-traumatic stress reaction. I am pleased you felt confident enough to tell me. I can get someone to come and see you. Talk to you. We have professionals, people trained to help with these sort of things.’ she said.

‘As I said, it was just the first night, thanks but no thanks. I’ll be OK.’ Jim rubbed his eyes, which had started to strain. ‘Contact lenses – you can’t live with them and you’re blind without them.’

Susan reached out, took Jim’s hand and offered a reassurance. ‘Jim, you’ve done so well. I admire you – we all do.’

Jim felt the warmth from Susan’s hand. “Have you found out anything else about him?’

‘Not really. We’re still questioning people. We have confirmation he came from the old car park but it’s difficult to get any accurate information. I can understand it: the people there don’t trust the police. Unfortunately, our interactions with them are normally not in their favour.’

‘Really, like what?’

‘Their main contact with us is a purely professional one. I suppose their way of life is a kind of living, and I sympathise with that, but we cannot ignore the law.’

Susan pulled her hand away and Jim immediately saw a change in her attitude. She placed her half-filled teacup on the table and stood to leave. ‘I had better get back,’ she said. Jim, the body has been released, so he can be buried. Social Services are arranging the funeral.’

‘I can imagine that it will be a cheap affair. Could I pay for a better send-off for him? I didn’t know him, but I think he deserves that.’

‘I don’t see why not. If you’re sure, I will get Social Services to speak to you.’

They moved to the door and exchanged goodbyes without making eye contact.

A week passed, during which time Jim was contacted by Social Services. Their nonchalant attitude left Jim questioning how social the service actually was. How did he know the man? Why would you offer to pay for the funeral? Jim simply argued that an act of human kindness and a demonstration of sympathy for a fellow human being should be enough. Didn't we consider those options anymore? He got his way and arranged to pay for the funeral: nothing lavish, but certainly something more befitting someone of substance; not just a name etched on a poorly made casket.

Jim arranged to attend the funeral and was advised again by the police to avoid the Press, as they would undoubtedly be in attendance and prying.

The day of the funeral arrived. Jim made his way to the church, clad in dark clothes, having decided that a suit wouldn't be appropriate, and because the cold December weather demanded warmer layers. The last time Jim had worn his only suit had been to his parents' funeral. He questioned the hypocrisy of their funeral to this one. The passing of a loved family and the burial of a murder victim did not seem to make comfortable bedfellows.

As Jim approached the church, he surveyed its familiar stone façade and felt that the gargoyles adorning it were leering down at him. The gravel driveway, cemented by melting snow, shifted beneath his feet as he walked.

Jim stood back from the mourners already at the church, who were all were huddled in small groups. The branches on the trees surrounding the church hung down, heavily laden with snow. Perched on a branch, a customary crow cawed an involuntary chorus.

Jim spotted the Press straightaway. They were the only ones laughing, standing around clutching coffee cups, waiting for the show to start. At the side of the church entrance, slightly out of the field of view from the Press, stood another group of people: a man and two women. One of the women was dressed in black, the hood of her coat raised to keep out the cold. The other two wore a miss mash of garb and looked slightly dishevelled.

Jim wondered if they knew the dead man. Curiosity got the better of him, and he made his way over to them. As he approached he could see them more clearly and smiled his introduction. 'I am sorry, I don't mean to be rude but could I ask, did you know the man who is being buried today?'

All three looked at each other and then the more smartly dressed woman replied, 'Why, are you one of the Press vipers? You don't look like one.'

'No. I found him in the park. I wondered if you knew him.'

Three pairs of eyes focused on him: three faces softened. First came a handshake, and then a hug.

The man spoke first, 'My name is Charles and our Samaritan, what is your name?'

Jim puzzled over being called a Samaritan: he was sure he had heard the word used recently, but could not remember where. 'I'm Jim,' he replied, looking at Charles' long checked coat, which had patches on the sleeves. He was wearing a cravat around his neck, more as a fashion statement than for practical purposes. Charles' neck was part stubble and chafed, as if shaved with a long-worn razor. As Charles smiled, Jim could see his stained teeth, obviously caused by nicotine: a quick glance at Charles' ochre-tarnished fingers confirmed his thought. 'Why do you see me as a Samaritan?' Jim asked.

Charles stared deeply into Jim's eyes. It was a gaze that took time; analytical and intense. 'You found a soul, Jim. You obviously became aware of that soul's predicament and you endeavoured to ensure that his last experience of this world would be one of respect and not of reliance on the State. For that sir, Rome salutes you.' Charles stepped back and bowed graciously in front of him.

Jim smiled, surprised and bemused by Charles' gesture. The moment was interrupted as two Press men approached them. Jim saw them over Charles' shoulder and assumed that they had been attracted by Charles' erratic behaviour.

Charles whispered, 'Don't avert your eyes, Jim. I gather by your gaze we have approaching guests, not so welcome as yourself. Please, allow me.'

Charles turned towards his two women companions, who had been watching and listening to their conversation. He looked directly at one of the women and said calmly, 'Lizzie, we are in need of your talents. Be a dear and pay homage to our approaching visitors. I think they may knock at our castle door but we certainly do not want to lower the drawbridge and allow them entry.'

One of the women stepped forward. She was small and slim, though her large bosom filled the gaping top of her coat. Jim noticed she was pretty for her age, which he guessed was about sixty. Her skin was clear and she had a natural complexion not covered in makeup, with auburn hair draped over her shoulders. As she approached and stood next to them she smiled a perfect white smile: too perfect. It was a smile that Jim guessed lived in a glass by the side of the bed every night.

'Am I to understand from all that bullshit bingo that you want me to piss these gentlemen off? Is that correct?' Lizzie said.

'If you would be so gracious, Lizzie.'

Turning to Jim, Lizzie looked him up and down and said, 'You're a fine looking man. Never been one for beards myself. I find they get in the way, but in your case I'll make an allowance. I won't be two ticks then we can have a proper chat.'

Lizzie headed straight for the approaching reporters. They met about twenty yards from Jim. He could see them all smiling and exchanging chit-chat. Jim arched his neck and, keeping his focus on Lizzie, asked Charles, 'Is she some kind of diplomat? She seems to be holding their attention.'

'Lizzie has a special talent with men. I fear they do not know who they are dealing with.'

Jim was intrigued and watched the rapport develop between Lizzie and the reporters.

Every so often, Lizzie would waft her hair from side to side, as if she were auditioning for a shampoo commercial. Jim noticed her slowly unbuttoning her coat, each side of the garment gently blowing in the breeze. What happened next was so bizarre that a poet would not have been able to describe it accurately. From behind, Jim realised that Lizzie was rubbing her hands around her crotch vigorously. The two reporters stared at her lower half, shocked and aghast.

After a few seconds, Lizzie threw her outstretched fingers under their noses and mouthed something at them. Both journalists backed up and skidded away from her. They shouted angrily but Lizzie was doubled up with laughter as she watched the two men retreat.

Jim stared open-mouthed at Lizzie. He giggled then shook his head, and thought of the historic moments of his age. He remembered where he had been when Princess Diana had died. He knew where he'd been when the twin towers had been destroyed and now he would recall the moment when a woman masturbated in front of some reporters in a churchyard.

Lizzie turned towards Jim and Charles. She laughed and wiped her fingers on her coat as she approached. Her dress was raised at one side at the front, revealing a pair of black knickers. The second lady of the group shouted towards her, 'Lizzie, please tidy yourself up. You're outside a house of God.'

Jim watched as Lizzie joined them, dressing herself and buttoning her coat back up. *This is crazy, am I actually here?* Jim pondered. *What the hell!*

Lizzie stood face to face with Jim and said, 'Sometimes, shock and awe is the only way.'

Jim stared, speechless.

'Oh, close your mouth, or I might put something in it,' Lizzie said, leaning forward and kissing Jim tenderly on the lips. Jim didn't, couldn't move: there was only one person in control and it certainly wasn't him. Jim took a short breath and looked at the others, and then they all burst into laughter.

The laughter subsided and the smarter dressed woman said, 'Come on you pair – give the man a chance. Go over there and have a smoke. Let me have a chat with him.'

Under instruction, Charles and Lizzie moved away. Jim could see Charles rummaging in his pocket and produce a packet of cigarettes. Soon he and Lizzie were puffing away. Jim watched the smoke billow into the air like hot vapour escaping a steam train. A lack of breeze made the fumes hang like clouds above them.

'Hello Jim, I'm Chrissy. I know those two seem quite extreme but they have good hearts.'

Jim, still shell- shocked by the whole event, replied,

'Is their behaviour normal? I mean Lizzie, what she did and Charles how he acts and talks.'

'For both of them, that was normal but not for you. But if we're going to get philosophical, what *is* normal? Your idea of normal life is something Lizzie and Charles once had but now they have a new normal.'

Jim's curiosity was now in overdrive. 'How do you know them Chrissy? You look, dress, and speak as though you are part of *my* normal.'

'I am between both worlds, Jim. I work at the food bank that serves their community in the old car park. That's how we knew Michael, the man you found. He was a very kind and quiet man.'

'His name was Michael,' Jim said then gazed at the ground, suddenly embarrassed. 'I'm sorry, I didn't know his name.'

'The police didn't tell you?' Chrissy enquired.

'No, they said they couldn't track down his details.'

'Hmm,' Chrissy murmured, 'sometimes, you need more focus.'

'What do you mean?'

'If it had been a politician or even a member of the mainstream, a Joe or Josephine Public, perhaps they would have discovered the name by now,' Chrissy said.

Charles and Lizzie returned.

Charles spoke in a tobacco-perfumed voice, 'Jim, our Samaritan, are you our saviour?'

'Charles, Lizzie, – I'm sorry for your loss but you keep calling me Samaritan and now saviour. I'm just a man who found a body. I'm not sure what else I can do.'

Jim looked at the three of them: Chrissy was staring up at the sky while Lizzie and Charles stared back at him.

'I think it's fate I'm afraid, Jim. I think you will be the man to catch another man,' Charles answered.

'Catch a man? I'm as confused as ever!' Jim replied heatedly.

Charles grabbed Lizzie's hand and continued to stare at Jim. He then spoke with a quiver in his voice, born of emotion.

‘Michael was not the first to die. He was one of six that we know of. There may be more. You see, our community has no government or accountability.’

Tears started to stream slowly down Charles’ face and through the furrows of skin created by a lifetime of hardship.

‘There are more? More people dead? You mean there is a serial killer? What about the police? How could this be allowed to happen? No one knows?’ Jim blurted out.

So many questions – too many questions – and too few answers: Jim shook his head. Inside, he was torn. He had only discovered a body, now this. *Shit! Shit! Shit!*

He thought about what Chrissy had said: was this their normal? *Shit!* Could he turn away? Ignore the last hour or so? Somehow he couldn’t: he felt some kind of obligation, he had discovered the body afterall. Jim said, ‘Listen, it is getting colder, can we go somewhere after the funeral and talk?’ All agreed.

The funeral service was swift. Jim stood with his new found friends and joined in hymns whilst lamenting Michaels passing. The church was even colder than outside. Jim noticed Charles hoping from one foot to another trying to keep warm. Odd laces tied his boots. Jim pondered how many miles they had trod. Lizzie was at Jim’s side. She purposely stood close. Close enough for Jim to feel the warmth from her body. Every so often she turned, looked Jim in the eye, coyly smiling.

There were no other mourners. Even the Police didn’t show up. Jim mulled over what Charles had just told him, more people dead. Perhaps embarrassment kept the authorities from attending the funeral. He really wanted to leave the church, ring Susan and ask what the hell was going on. But common decency intervened and stopped him in his tracks.

Jim looked up at the gabled church roof, then down to the intricate stained glass windows. One of the windows depicted a saint, beneath a halo; holding a staff. Either side of him where sheep and a small child looked up at him adoringly. Jim wondered was this is path, was he to be shepherd with Charles and Lizzie his sheep.

The service concluded. As they all left the church, Jim noticed there was only Chrissy and himself who left money in the church offering bowl. Charles and Lizzie just shook the rector's hand and thanked him for his kind words.

Outside, snow had started to fall. The press had long gone realising there would be no morsels for them to chew on. Lizzie's action, however extreme, seemed to have done the trick. Jim turned to the group, 'Can I get you all a drink? I could do with one.'

'Sorry, I have to go.' Chrissy replied, 'But thank you.'

'Lead on McDuff,' Charles answered. Lizzie just shrugged her shoulders. The group split. Chrissy left and Jim led the other two to a nearby pub.

The pub was only a few streets from the church. This was sorely welcome as the snow was getting heavier and Jim was concerned for the welfare of his new friend's in such harsh conditions.

Inside the building was warm and welcoming. There were not many other people drinking or eating. The ones already there cast a derisory glance towards Jim's party as they entered. Recognising the mood in the room, Jim manoeuvred them to a vacant table in a quiet corner. 'Right, what can I get you?' Jim asked politely.

Without hesitation, Charles replied first, 'A tot of whiskey if you wouldn't mind kind Sir. Oh, and not the cheap stuff. It plays havoc with my chest.' Lizzie was in the process of removing her coat, 'What he says, thanks. But I think my chest is alright. What do you think Jim?' Jim looked at Lizzie. She was leaning forward and her low cut top was perfectly displaying her bosom.

'I'll go and get the drinks.' Jim averted his gaze, made his way to the bar. He just smirked. He ordered the drinks and then wondered when Charles had last been able to afford a decent whisky. It didn't bother Jim anyway. He was not cash strapped and in a strange way welcomed the company. As the barmen returned with the drinks he took Jim's money, leant over and quietly spoke, 'Not everyone likes that sort in their pub but me I don't mind while they are paying and behaving.'

‘What sort?’ Jim replied.

‘Your friend’s over there.’

‘Why what’s up with them?’

‘Listen, I am just saying.’ The barmen continued, ‘So long as there is no trouble.’

Jim stood back from the bar. Looked at the barmen’s face and balanced the three drinks in his hands. He turned and made his way to Charles and Lizzie. His short journey to the table seemed an age. The words from the barmen echoed around his head.

‘Everything OK?’ Charles asked.

‘Yes fine.’ Jim said unconvincingly.

Lizzie had picked up a food menu from the table and was scanning it.

‘I’m sorry. I should have asked, are you both hungry?’ Jim questioned.

‘Well a nice steak would go down a treat. And for you Lizzie, does anything take you fancy?’

‘Does anything take my fancy? Well there is someone definitely taking my fancy but as for food I wouldn’t mind the fish.’

Jim acknowledged their order and made his back to the bar. He loved it. He rubbed the barmen’s nose in it with his request and ordered more drinks. Jim let him know, they were going nowhere in a hurry.

The food arrived. Jim’s friends ate up. Clean plates were the order of the day. He watched Charles and Lizzie wipe their mouths with serviettes. Jim thought, *were these people so different to him.*

Lizzie rose from the table, ‘Excuse me gents, I need the bathroom.’

‘I think it is to our right, over there.’ Jim automatically replied, pointing his finger to show the way.

‘I’ll find it,’ Lizzie then leant forward and whispered, ‘Perhaps you would like to follow me. We could be alone for a while.’

Jim smiled awkwardly. Lizzie left. He blushed cherry red and blew out air from his mouth, 'Jesus Charles, is she always like this?'

'Only to the chosen few Jim, you should count yourself lucky.'

Lucky, was not the word Jim would have chosen. Threatened, intimidated, they seemed more appropriate.

Charles broke Jim's train of thought. 'Jim let me ask you again while we are alone. I go back to my question at the church. Are you to be our saviour?' Slam. One word but a harsh welcome back to the real word for Jim.

'Charles I don't doubt your predicament and I want to help but what can I do? I have no experience or skill in dealing with something like this.' Charles sat rubbing his finger around the top of his empty glass.

'What about the Police. I could go to them. Tell them I know there are more killings. It may get things moving?' Jim said trying to restart the conversation.

Charles just remained rubbing his finger around the tumbler. He stopped and then spoke, 'Jim I am speaking out of selfishness and for the ones I hold dear. I have nothing left in this world only a few close friends. The question I have toiled with for so long is where we are on the killers list?'

Quiet. There was no talking, just two people thinking. Jim's head was awash with thoughts. Actions and their consequences played out in his mind. He had a simple dilemma to decide. He could walk away or help. There was only one conclusion. Jim ended the silence, 'What can I do to help?' Charles grabbed Jim's hand. Jim could feel it clench his own. Charles' wiry grip shook it acknowledging, 'We have work to do. Let me show you our world. I will introduce you to the Broken Land.'

Lizzie returned from the bathroom, 'Eye, eye, what's going on here? Holding hands are we.' Jim instantly moved his hand away.

'Moving in on my turf Charles? He's mine or he soon will be.'

Lizzie sat back down, reached over, took one of Jim's hands and held it. Jim just went along with it, what else could he do.

‘With it being so dull in this corner we could have a séance.’ She stared at Jim, gently shrugging her shoulders. Her chest moved gently. Jim noticed a pendant sat around her neck, rock in between her cleavage. Lizzie knew what she was doing. *Eyes up* Jim reminded himself.

‘Who would you contact in the afterlife?’ Lizzie asked, still looking directly at Jim. Charles may as well have been absent. Lizzie was in the zone, she was spinning her web, ready to catch Jim.

‘I’m not sure, never really thought about it.’

‘I would contact Michael, who we buried today. I’d ask him how he died.’ Charles interrupted the conversation sombrely. The mood changed in an instant. Jim remembered why he was here in the first place, why he had met his two new friends.

‘I think it’s time we were going it’s getting late. It has been a long day, my dog will be ready for his evening walk,’ Jim said. All three got up to leave and made their way outside. The evening had turned as gloomy as the weather. It was dank and the air seemed heavy with moisture. A stagnant fog hung around the streetlights and the noise from passing traffic seemed amplified. They all said their goodbyes and Lizzie pecked Jim on the cheek. Jim explained he lived in the opposite part of town to both and started to make his way home. This wasn’t true but Jim needed time to think on his own. He needed time away from both of them. As he meandered along his route he mulled over his decision, *What have I done? Who are these people? What on earth is the Broken Land?*

The Broken Land

Jim woke the day after the funeral. His head was still spinning as he tried to come to terms with the previous day's events. It was the level of task that now presented itself that caused him the most angst. Jim wanted to jilt the idea of helping to find the killer. It felt like a bad taste left by a one-night stand, but he knew this was different. He had only just met Charles and Lizzie, but deep down he did not want them added to a murderer's tally.

Jim paced around the bathroom, catching his reflection in the mirror. *Where do I start? I'm not a detective! I was just walking my dog. What about these people, and the Broken Land*? He squeezed his eyes and felt around to replace his contact lenses. The job never got any easier, but after a few seconds he caught sight of his blinking features again, reflected in the mirror. As he watched his pupils dilate, he realised he had to fulfil his commitment to his new friends, however hasty that decision appeared.

The last conversation Jim had had with Charles outside the pub involved Charles giving directions to the old car park and the Broken Land. Jim knew roughly where it was as he had played there as a child.

Jim performed that morning's routine in a trance. His attention was elsewhere. He ate his breakfast and washed himself with an added purpose. Barnstable went on his walk but with little encouragement from his master. He just got the occasional word to hurry him on his way. Even the dog sensed the tension in the lead and knew something was out of the ordinary. Time suddenly had more of a purpose for Jim.

Eventually, curiosity got the better of him, so Jim made his way to the Broken Land.

Jim left Barnstable at home. The dog watched his departing master through a breath-fogged window. The sort of window you may have drawn faces on as a child.

Charles advised Jim to leave his car a distance away from the car park, to ensure its safety. Jim complied: he was not in any mood to be dealing with repairs as a result of vandalism. When he arrived there were other cars parked there, so he felt reassured that it was relatively secure.

As he got closer to his destination, he saw the car park up ahead. The image jolted his memory. He recalled that there were two levels to the old car park. The stark concrete walls, drab and grey, were tattooed with old graffiti. Rain stained the vibrantly sprayed images, causing dirt to run down them like mascara running down the face of an elderly clown playing his last performance in the circus. The floor was carpeted with paper and litter. It all looked forgotten and one could only feel sad. If you had seen this on the TV you would compare it to a post-apocalyptic town. A place where you might have to fight for your life every day, just to survive.

As Jim entered the lower section, he saw signs of habitation and, to the right, he noticed some sort of activity taking place: a small queue of people waiting in line for something. It looked like hot food was being ladled into bowls and Jim assumed it was a food station.

Everyone seemed to look in Jim's direction. No one spoke. They all just kept a careful eye on him. He stood out like a saw thumb. Jim was not dressed particularly smart but he looked clean and none of his clothes were in a dire need of repair. Significantly different to the people who surrounded him.

Should he say that he knew Charles, he was a friend and he knew Lizzie and she was…well, Jim didn't know what Lizzie was to him. There was no doubt she had stirred something within him that had been dormant for a long time.

As he drew closer, he recognised Chrissy from the church, serving people. He stood to the back of the dwindling line and waited for an opportunity to approach her, occasionally raising his head from the line in the hope of making eye contact, but her focus was firmly on the meals. Finally, the queue had gone. People scurried out of Jim's way, hiding their food as they left. Between the small stack of bowls and the plumes of heat from the pans, Jim eventually caught Chrissy's gaze. She smiled and said, 'Hello, Jim! So after yesterday you still came to see us?'

'Yes but I am not going to lie, I did have to think long and hard about it. Somehow it seemed the natural course of action but I'm struggling to find anything natural or familiar any longer. My normal is not a place I recognise any more and yesterday, well . . .'

Chrissy watched Jim toil with his thoughts and offered an explanation. 'I've been doing this job for a while. I know Charles and Lizzie well. Their behaviours, how they act, as well as those of others that live here, do not surprise me anymore. Listen . . . please, sit down. I'll pour us a drink of something hot and tell you what I know. I guess you have questions.'

Chrissy pulled a chair from under a table. The table had rough edges and paint-splashed legs, its true condition hidden by a tatty, makeshift tablecloth. Jim copied Chrissy. His chair wobbled and creaked. He decided not to put too much confidence in leaning back on it.

Jim indeed had questions. Plenty of them, loaded ready to fire. He wanted to ask them all. Each one, desperate for an answer but potentially, missing its target. But for the time being Jim held back and decided to be patient. He needed to figure out his next course of action. *Slowly, slowly, catchy monkey*, he thought.

Chrissy poured them both a cup of coffee. Jim took his cup and placed it on the table. The table also wobbled from side to side, its legs sat awkwardly on the ground and tried to balance. *God,* he thought, *it's like being at a fun fair, if Chrissy brings candy floss and sits me in front of a contorted mirror that will top things off.*

He took a swig from the drink. It was a strong coffee: no Americano, latte or cappuccino here. Jim masked his reaction. He didn't like strong coffee and often wondered how people entertained drinking expresso. It seemed like a dark brown poison to him. He often joked to himself that you could always spot an expresso drinker. They were the ones speaking in tongues, climbing walls, with massive bags under their eyes due to lack of sleep. Anyway, back to the real world. The taste of chicory had diluted in his mouth, Jim perched forward, ready to listen to Chrissy. Chrissy sat opposite and began. 'I've been here for three years, part of a volunteer group that serves meals to the community.

Believe it or not, I like it here. It gives me a purpose and I enjoy talking to the residents. My husband passed away a while ago and after he had gone I sat in the house, wondering what to do with myself. You soon get bored of breakfast TV and the countless adverts telling you, you're getting old and you need to arrange your funeral. So I looked for something to do with my life. I met someone who worked here, so I came along to try it and stayed. There are now only four of us and we take turns to cover the meal rotas. There used to be more but people left. This place is not for everyone. You have to be pretty thick skinned to work here. It is a straight forward operation. The food is donated. We just collect it already prepared from a council-run kitchen. Most of the year it is straight forward, not much changes. Christmas is always busier and more complicated. Not by the residents but because of the hypocrites who watch the Salvation Army adverts on TV and find that they cannot digest their Christmas dinners unless they have helped to feed the less fortunate. It's quite funny, watching the residents turn them inside and out. You see Jim, this is their home: whether for a few days or a lifetime. Some stay for a long time, like Charles and Lizzie, and some just pass through. I suppose you've wondered how all this works, how the residents got to be here in the first place. I asked the same question when I first started, but my enthusiasm was soon curbed after I had worked here a while.

'Some of the people trusted me to tell me their life stories. After I had listened, as a consequence, I no longer pass judgement on any of them. I found sleep became harder for a long time when I knew of their situations and my commitment to this role only strengthened as a result of it.'

Chrissy paused and took a drink of coffee and Jim did the same, searching for a chip-free edge to sip from.

'Can I ask about Charles and Lizzie please? Is that OK?'

Chrissy cradled her cup and savoured its warmth. 'Charles and Lizzie, I love them both. I suppose they are the governors of the community or, to give it Charles' title, the Broken Land. I'll let Charles explain his reasoning for the name. I will start with Charles and leave Lizzie until last. You would need a free mind to understand Lizzie,' Chrissy giggled. Jim had a strong idea what she meant. He had only met Lizzie once and felt like he had been put in a washing machine on fast spin.

'Charles was an actor, believe it or not. He had a few roles on TV soaps: bit parts. He mainly performed plays in the theatre – Shakespeare and the like. One of our former residents remembered seeing him in something and said he was good. One key thing to understand about Charles is his intellect. He is really clever, but you have to decipher his language to understand him.'

'If Charles had all that, how did he end up here?'

'Charles said it was society that poisoned his soul and stifled his talent. It's funny how alcoholics look for mitigation rather than the truth. One drink too many became his life and it soon spiralled out of control. Slurred and forgotten lines do not bring applause, only exit doors. He's lived here for about seven years, so I was told. Charles and Lizzie live in the lower section of the car park, towards the far end. It's more secure, warm, and they get electricity from the street light nearby. It's where the lifers live. That's what they call the long-term residents.

Jim listened, absorbed.

'They will be here soon, so you can chat, get their take on things. I only see their lives from the outside. I bless myself that I am not in their situation. Community, the Broken Land, whatever it is called, I am glad I am not living in it.'

'What about Lizzie?'

Chrissy smiled. 'Lizzie is a dilemma. She is the best and worst of things. As I said earlier, with all these people it is best not to judge. Until you are in their position, have experienced a portion of their lives, my advice is to accept it and let it be. Lizzie is a nymphomaniac. Talk to her she will openly tell you. There are no veils of embarrassment; she just loves sex. She is not a prostitute. I warn you, do not go there. Just because Lizzie is here, in this situation, does not mean she has to sell herself. I have not seen her partners but Charles has mentioned she has a few, and they are Lizzie's choice. I suppose they are just fulfilling a need for both sides. You have met Lizzie: she is certainly an attractive woman and always looks after herself.'

Jim had been sitting with his mouth open up to that point and realised that Chrissy had noticed. 'I'm sorry Chrissy. It's just, erm . . . new to me,' he said.

'I've told you Jim, please remember to keep an open mind. Charles and Lizzie are just two of many here. We have to be thankful for what we have, and cherish what they can only wish for.' She looked up and over Jim's shoulder.

'Here's Charles now. I will get him some hot food ready. I'm sure he will be happy you're here.'

Charles spotted Jim and altered his normal walk. He began to sway and perform an exaggerated dance. He held his hands out in front of him, as though waltzing with an imaginary partner. Jim could not help but laugh, thinking, *now that's the way to make an entrance*. Arriving at Jim's side, Charles said, 'Good to see you again our saviour. Difficult day yesterday . . . I wasn't sure if we had scared you off. I'll get my food from this angel and then we can talk, if that's OK?' Charles smiled in Chrissy's direction exposing his brown tinged teeth. Jim wondered when they had last seen a toothbrush and reasoned that one good brushing could potentially take the lot out.

Jim grinned towards Charles. He had not felt this nervous since he had had to hand his homework in late at school. In most situations throughout life you have some idea of what is coming next, what to expect, but not here. Jim was in a state of anticipation, on the back foot. He watched Charles as nervous as a fledgling director at the premiere of their work. He knew he was as alien to this world as Charles would be to his. Jim thought of Dorothy's words from the *Wizard of Oz*: 'We're not in Kansas anymore.' He knew exactly what she meant.

Charles took his food from Chrissy and gestured to Jim to follow him to a nearby vacant table. They both sat down and Charles politely asked, 'Do you mind if I tuck in?'

‘Of course not, please, enjoy,’ Jim replied, watching attentively as Charles spooned the meal into his mouth. He noticed it wasn’t a ravenous munching from hunger but rather the calculated digestion of someone who was actually enjoying their food. Jim questioned why he thought it would have been any different. He recalled Chrissy’s comment: ‘Don’t judge.’

Charles finished his meal, wiped his mouth with his sleeve and said, ‘I bet you have a million questions.’

Jim nodded.

‘Tell me, where do you want to start?’

‘Why do you call this place the Broken Land?’

Charles began: it was a lesson in life, a lesson for society, a lesson to cause a neck-tie knot adjustment of attitude in the masses.

‘Here and now our community, like many others of its sort, sits in a place that it is easy to ignore. Its foundations are built from charity and sympathies. Our rules and way of life have evolved from necessity. All who live here strive to live until tomorrow, not beyond it. We measure our future in hours rather than days, weeks or months. This is not a sob story or a plea for help. It is simple and the truth. However difficult a conversation this maybe, we would be liars or contemptuous if we believed it to be unique. Look at both of us, our different situations. We do not exist in the same society, although we are on the same planet. There is a chasm between us and why is this? It comes to value and what use are we, the people here, to this world? The residents of the Broken Land tick the ‘no fixed abode’ column, which means we can’t vote and so we are the forgotten. Here, we’re quite lucky: we are left alone, there’s no police, and limited drug problems. The drug users, the young, are in the town centre, where funds and product are easier to obtain. That is why we are the Broken Land.’

Jim looked at Charles and swallowed deeply. Charles noticed his unease. ‘It’s OK Jim,’ he said, ‘this is how it is. I came up with an analogy that fits how our small society works in practice. The Broken Land can be represented as a bucket or a pail. We, the inhabitants, are the water within it. The sides of the bucket are our boundaries. It’s a small ecosystem of its own.

There is a gentle trickle of new people who add to our population and at the bottom of the bucket is a hole, letting some water out as people leave. As a rule, there is equilibrium, with water leaving the bucket and additional water being added – by which I mean people leaving the community and new people arriving. At the moment we have a slightly bigger hole in the bottom of the bucket in the shape of our killer. That needs addressing, and that's where you come in: our saviour.'

Jim had hoped naïvely that Charles had forgotten the conversation at the church but it was clear that that was not going to happen. As Jim pondered, he recognised Charles was still staring at him.

'Charles, I get what you mean but I am struggling to understand still how I can help. Why haven't the police done more, if there are more bodies?'

Charles, still steely-eyed and focused on Jim, replied,

'I can only assume it's the principle of the Broken Land. I still keep up to date with the news and recognise the pressures on the police force. How much time and money would the investigation cost? Does helping the likes of us win votes? Is our plight as important as your average tax-paying Joe getting his burglary investigated? Politically we are polar opposites but morally obviously not.

'Jim, I base this on fact. I know six lifers have been taken from here. They are never found here but we get to know, especially when the police come and ask the same questions each time about those who have gone missing. If I am honest I can give the police or any investigation some leeway. Some of the lifers here would not give you the most credible evidence, most would rather not. A face in the limelight without makeup might reveal a life best kept in the shadows. Or simply put, it is easier to stay out of the way.'

Jim's eyes felt grainy and he blinked excessively to create tears.

'You OK?' Charles asked.

'It's my bloody contact lenses, Charles. Not like your problems,' Jim said, rubbing his eyes.

Jim's vision returned. He noticed Charles looking over his shoulder. He could hear heavy footsteps approaching. As Jim turned, the owner of the footsteps was beside them. It was a man. He was massive. His huge frame looked like a coat thrown over a refrigerator door. Charles smiled at him and said, 'Turnip!'

The giant nodded towards Charles, cast Jim a fleeting glance, and carried on walking.

Christ, Jim thought as he watched him go, *that guy must have his own orbit. If he says it's Sunday on a Wednesday, you go to church.*

Charles said, 'Sorry, were where we?'

'Turnip's some kind of nickname, right?'

'Turnip? No, that's all he says. He's been here about two years and that is the limit of his vocabulary. Now, where were we?'

Jim was quickly learning to pick up his dropped jaw. *Turnip! All he can say is bloody turnip and that is normal for him!* Jim retuned to Charles' gaze.

Charles' face softened. 'I'm sorry Jim,' he said, 'this place can come as quite a shock. Not everyone can spend time in the Broken Land or even peer across its border. I forget how this must appear. I am fortunate: I can still remember both sides. I can flit between the two worlds, or I think I can. Looking at your face, I realise I am probably not the actor I was.'

Jim sat in a state of pure confusion. He felt worried, tormented, embarrassed, and he didn't know what to make of any of it. Used to a world of code, models and logical discipline, this was an algorithm he was struggling to process. However, he realised that he was hooked. As bizarre as the conversation had been, he wanted to know more about the Broken Land. Deep down, however, he worried what might happen if he dug further into the closet: what unexpected skeletons might he encounter?

Jim looked up at Charles again. The winter sun was starting to wane and heavy shadows surrounded them. The air had turned noticeably colder as the stark, slab walls absorbed the last few degrees gleaned from the afternoon's token sunlight.

‘What do we do next Charles? Have you any idea how to proceed? I thought about leaking the story to the Press via social media. I could easily hide the source – it might attract some attention.’

Charles rubbed his stubbly chin with his tobacco-stained fingers and replied, ‘I have given this some thought. I have deliberated on a plan. Are you familiar with Newton’s third law of motion? He said for every action there is an opposite reaction. The reaction to us going public would be cause for concern for me. If you will indulge me, I hope to explain.

‘The Broken Land, our community, is all we have. It is our host. We are parasites, and finding another host could be a treacherous journey, not easily achieved. If the Press were to run our story, where would it end? It might be easier for society to remove the Broken Land all together, thereby removing the problem. I believe we have to adopt a more cunning approach. Sometimes, a drip can be enough to start the crack in the dam wall, but we could also keep a modicum of control.’

Jim listened. It was obvious that Charles had given it a lot of thought. He felt he was not in a position to question his approach. ‘So what’s the answer?’ he asked.

Charles pulled up the collar of his coat and pressed it around his neck. ‘Information: I think we need to find out what the police have. We can then make a decision. Do you think you could obtain that?’

Jim nodded. ‘If I can get access to the station I think I can. I have worked on a lot of corporate IT systems in my career. I am sure that is where the information, or at least some of it, will be held. They won’t know I have accessed it; it’s what I do. But how can I get access?’

‘You are tormented by the whole experience. Who was the man who died, you wonder? Could you help the police further? You are curious and eager to help, like every good citizen. Do you get my drift?’ Charles answered.

‘I am not an actor Charles, but I will give it a go.’ Jim said shrugging his shoulders as he also began to feel the cold. He knew the value of information. It had given him a career and made him wealthy but he also recognised it could carry a burden. He had sat and listened to Charles intently and worried about adding to his woes. The description of the Broken Land seemed accurate enough to him and he was in no position to contradict or pose an argument. He just felt ashamed he had not been aware of their way of life before. Jim then reasoned if he had known would he have openly offered assistance. Could he have been another Chrissy?

His mental deliberations were rudely interrupted by the sound of a fracas near the food station. Charles rose from his chair, 'Excuse me a moment Jim.' Jim watched on as Charles headed over to where a heated argument was taking place between Chrissy and another man. As Charles got closer, the man stretched out his arm towards him, waving his fist. Jim rose swiftly from his chair, heading over to help Charles. Getting nearer, Jim heard the man ranting,

'Do you know who I am?' He then started to sing, mimicking Elvis Presley. 'Wise men say, only fools rush in. Viva Las Vegas. You are all wrong. I ain't dead, the King lives. Thank you for very much. Uh! Err!'

Charles just let him continue. The man then started to twist his hips and sang again, 'I went to a party at the county jail...'

Jim looked at Chrissy, then Charles, then back to the man. *What the hell is going on? When is this guy going to stop?* Charles gently lowered the man's arm. His movements started to slow and he stopped singing. Charles placed both his arms around him, hugging him gently. The man mumbled under his breath, 'Thank you very much. Thank you very much.' Jim stood back as Charles cradled the man's head on his chest. He heard him whisper in his ear,

'It's OK. I am here. You are safe. I am here.'

The man calmed and clung to Charles' shoulders. He then started to weep. Jim looked at Chrissy. She had turned away and had started to make a drink. He glanced back to Charles. He was swaying side to side, the man clung on. Charles began to tenderly stroke his hair.

A few minutes passed, the man let go and made his way to Chrissy who had a drink waiting for him. Charles watched on.

Jim turned away, out of view from everyone for a while. His eyes filled with tears. This time it wasn't his contact lenses. However bizarre what had just happened seemed, he felt strangely privileged to have witnessed it. It was a beautiful moment.

Hearing the sound of movement behind him, Jim took a couple of shallow breaths to regain his composure. He turned around and saw Charles walking towards him.

'Sorry about that Jim. Where were we?' There was no reference as to what had just occurred, nothing.

'Are you OK Charles?'

'Yes Jim. We all need a little hug every now and then.' Again Jim was stopped in his tracks. He really wanted to ask *what the hell had just happened*, but was gradually learning you did not do that in the Broken Land. There was a strict code of discretion to be followed but concerned for his friend, Jim attempted to offer assistance,

'Charles, can we get help for that guy. Can I help, I feel like a spare penny?'

'That is very kind Jim but the only help we can give is what we are issuing. In the past he may have been admitted to an institution to ease his mind. He is delusional Jim, thinks he is the *King of Rock and Roll* no less. The episodes he suffers more than likely instigated by a stimulant of some sort. Glue probably. These places do not exist for us Jim. We are the forgotten.'

Charles rubbed his gloved hands and started to wriggle awkwardly. 'It is getting colder Jim. Would you like to come inside, to my place, it is a lot warmer?'

'No thank you Charles. I had better get back, things to do.' Jim reasoned his senses had undergone enough of a bashing today. Anymore and he might be singing Elvis songs and holding on to Charles as a partner.

Charles nodded, 'Well we have some sort of plan. It's a start Jim. Let's see where it takes us.'

School was over and Jim had his homework. Both shook hands and went their separate ways.

Jim made his way back to the car. As he left the car park he didn't notice the grey walls. The graffiti didn't grab his attention. Ahead he saw a small mound of paper at the side of a waste container. He stopped, collected the damp paper in his hands and shoved it firmly in the bin. Shaking his hands clear of any unwanted refuse he realised he had changed. That same rubbish was more than likely there when he trod the same route earlier but he had not noticed it then. So why had he now? Jim knew the answer. He had been introduced to another world.

The Cheese Plant

It was the day after Jim's visit to the Broken Land. The plan he and Charles had concocted spiralled like a whirlwind in his head. What he was about to do, not only committing him to help find the killer but significantly meant he had to break the law.

Jim rang the police station and left a message for Detective Inspector Rand to return his call. He needed a meeting at the police station. He needed to physically get into the site to obtain the computer networking protocols and gain access to their systems.

Peering out of his kitchen window, he saw the morning was duller. The sky wore a mottled grey overcoat and wisps of lightly battered snowflakes were beating against the wind. It looked cold and not a day to venture out, but Jim was determined in his task and no amount of bad weather would stop him.

DI Rand rang back. Jim explained his concerns in regard to the investigation and asked to meet. He gave a performance Charles would have been proud of. Rand was accommodating to the meeting and both agreed to be at the police station in a couple of hours.

Jim was in. Now did he wear the deerstalker hat or apply a wax tip to his moustache, this made him appreciate how absurd the whole situation was. It would have been easy for him to ignore the problem. He could stay in his nice warm house, cuddled up with Barnstable watching TV, but he knew he had to go. The Broken Land had called and he had to respond.

The car's satnav guided him towards the police station while Jim's mind was consumed by the challenge ahead. He parked his car near to the station and walked the remainder of the way.

The police station was close to the road. Jim looked inside the offices as he approached the entrance. There was lot of activity behind the smoked-glass windows. He saw silhouetted figures bobbing and dodging between desks and wondered what the law and order machine was processing.

Jim noticed that the police entrance sign had graffiti etched on it: an ejaculating penis that had been partly erased. He wondered how many playground points the artist had earned for his effort. He tittered to himself, thinking that Banksy need not be worried by the competition and questioned whether he'd have been brave or stupid enough to have tried something like that when he was younger. Probably not.

Jim entered the building and made his way to the front desk. An officer stood behind the counter, studying a folder. Jim noticed the faint smell of diluted bleach and looked at the customary cheese plant in the corner of the reception area. The plant's green leaves had flopped down, eager for water, with overgrown roots spewing from cracks in the pot's base.

The officer behind the counter disturbed Jim's botanical observations. 'Can I help you, sir?' he said.

Jim explained he had an appointment to see Detective Inspector Rand and he was asked to take a seat.

A couple of minutes later, a side door opened. Jim recognised Rand, who walked towards him holding out his hand.

'Hello again Mr Thomas,' Rand said.

'Please, call me Jim.'

'Of course, no problem Jim. Please come with me, we'll go to my office.'

Jim followed as Rand led him through several security doors, using a smart card. Each door they passed through closed behind them with a heavy thud. Finally, Rand opened the door to his office. *Clunk*: it closed behind them.

They sat opposite each other at a desk covered with the usual office junk including, importantly for Jim, Rand's computer. To his left, Jim noticed a couple of large windows that looked into a larger office containing several people milling around.

Jim was ready: questions and actions he had ready to be released. Most of all, he didn't want to appear nervous, anticipating that Rand would pick up on any signals. He was more than likely trained to spot a fraud Jim guessed.

'Sorry we've not been in touch, Jim. We've been trying to find out as much as we can about the victim. Unfortunately, due to their circumstances, it's proving difficult to get reliable information. Please, ask if have you any specific questions, but more importantly, how have you been?'

Jim, as with their first meeting with Rand, recognised genuine sentiment in his tone. 'I'll be honest; I think I've felt confused. I struggle to get my head around the whole thing. I don't confess to know much about policing methods, but I imagined you would know more by now. Also, I can't understand why it hasn't been in the Press more. I suppose I am looking for some kind of closure to it all.

You have also said victim, so you now believe he was murdered?' Jim replied.

Rand sat back in his plastic chair, which gave a gentle creak in response as he mulled over his reply. He contemplated what to tell Jim. They were getting nowhere fast with the investigation and he needed some allies. At this point all he had were bodies and no suspects. Pressure was mounting from his superiors for a result. Jim watched Rand and guessed he was forming a decision about whether to go with the truth or policy.

'We have details about what happened to the man. You're not an idiot; you knew he could not have inflicted his injuries on himself. We are investigating a murder, but please, I beg you, do not tell anyone. Yes, we are keeping this from the Press. How moral a decision that is, is open for debate? I could argue it is in the interests of public safety. History has shown me, if we involve the press our position in catching the killer would become more difficult.

'Often the people we need to talk to would refuse because they would not want the publicity. Conversely, the people we wouldn't want to talk to would come forward with false information and muddy the waters so much that we would not be able to see the bottom any more. I hope you understand.'

'I do see your point, Detective Inspector Rand. It's just I am trying to make sense of it all. What about CCTV? There are cameras all over the place, isn't there anything on those?'

'I assure you Jim. We are using everything at our disposal. I'm afraid it's not like the shows on the TV. This is the real world.'

Jim felt suitably chastised and fell quiet temporarily. Now it was time to act, 'I'm sorry to ask, but could I get a drink?'

Rand stood up. 'Of course, I should have asked. Coffee, tea?'

'Coffee would be fine, thank you. White with one if that's OK?

Rand left the office: Jim's ruse had worked. *Clunk*. The door shut as Rand's left. Jim peered through a small window pane and watched him disappear down a corridor. He was alone. Jim looked at the rear of the computer and smiled. He recognised the labels with network details embossed on them. There was the police authority logo and a small collection of numbers. To the untrained they may have looked like the worst attempt at *Sudoku* ever but to Jim they were his meat and gravy. Jim knew most large corporates used them. That would be the start of his way in. He took out his phone, activated the camera function and captured an image of the information. Jim then stood up. Pretending to stretch his legs, he moved to the monitor, keeping a tentative gaze on the open office through the adjacent windows. On the front of the computer monitor a username was clearly visible. Stuck to the side of the screen was a dog-eared yellow Post-It note with two lines of characters. Jim guessed that these were passwords. He took another photo and returned to his seat.

Rand returned a couple of minutes later, and Jim continued the conversation for another fifteen minutes or so. Jim lamented the mans' passing; Rand spewed a political response as if he was lobbying for parliament. Coffee finished, Jim thanked Rand for his time and Rand escorted him from the building. The officer on reception watched as the two men said goodbye. Rand went back to his office. Jim turned to the officer on reception who once again studied a folder on his desk.

‘Plant could do with watering.’

‘What Sir?’

‘I just noticed, the plant could do with watering,’ replied Jim.

‘Thank you Sir. I’ll get on it right away.’ The officer said. Sarcasm personified.

Jim walked towards the exit but stopped. He looked outside, he saw people walking past but his mind was elsewhere. Jim turned, looked around the reception area and spotted a water dispenser. It was an inverted barrel, with cups stacked at its side. He made his way towards it. It was about three quarters full. Jim grabbed a plastic cup from the dispenser, the normal thing happened, two came out together, one hid inside the other. He started to fill the cup. *Glug, glug,* air popped up into the dispenser as it dispersed its fluid. The man behind the desk, stirred by the sound, raised his eyes up, looked at Jim and returned his focus back to his book. Jim gave him a casual smile and walked towards the cheese plant with a full cup of water. He tipped the contents into the plant base. Most dripped to the floor; the roots so hard and dry they repelled the liquid. Jim repeated this about three times. The plant base gradually started to stain a darker colour in response to the water. If Jim had stuck it in a reservoir it probably would have drained that dry.

Jim finished, returned his cup to a waste bin and turned to leave. The officer behind the desk had watched Jim perform his ad hoc gardening.

‘Goodbye.’ Jim said. The officer watched him leave. How childish his behaviour was, Jim didn’t care. He wanted to prove a point. Under his breath he muttered, ‘I’ll water your plant and solve your murder, you read your book.’

Skipping down the steps of the police station, he dodged to one side narrowly avoiding two officers passing in the opposite direction. His phone rang. He stood to the side to answer. It was Charles, ‘How’s it going Jim?’

‘Think I’ve got what I need to make a start. I’m still here, just leaving.’

‘Sorry Jim, I’ll leave you to carry on.’

‘It’s OK Charles, how are you?’ The two then exchanged a few pleasantries and small talk.

The two officers Jim had passed, now stood inside the station. The officer behind the desk spoke to them, ‘Morning boys. Have you had a good one?’ One of the officers, PC Jones, replied immediately, ‘Yes Sir all quiet.’

‘Well I’ve got a little job for you.’ The desk officer said smiling.

‘Pick up that plant in the corner and threw it in the skip around the back. It’s started to disturb our visitors.’

‘What sir?’

‘PC Jones, I understand you are new to the force but I trust your hearing is fine. When a senior officer tells you to do something you do. Do I make myself clear PC Jones?’

‘Yes sir.’ PC Jones walked to the plant and picked it up. The large leaves wrapped around his neck. It looked like he was wrestling with the “Swamp Thing” from one of the late night B movies. PC Jones’ colleague sniggered, the desk officer responded quickly.

‘Don’t just stand there PC Hepworth, get a brush and clean the mess up that plant has left. I am not having my station looking like a shit hole.’

PC Hepworth shot into life. He went to turn left, then right, then realised he didn’t know where the brush was kept. Behind the desk, the officer watched on. He had now been joined by a colleague. They both watched the calamity unfold.

‘What are you looking for PC Hepworth?’

‘The brush sir’

‘It’s behind you. The door marked “Cleaners Room”. Oh dear PC Hepworth, I would not apply for CID yet.’ The man stood with the desk officer burst into laughter, patted him on the shoulder then left.

PC Jones backed into the main station door to open it, his hands full of cheese plant. Outside he headed towards the skip. Jim was still talking to Charles. He spotted the officer and noticed his cargo.

'Sorry Charles. I'll ring you later, got to go.' Jim scurried after PC Jones. He soon caught up, 'Excuse me. Sorry officer, excuse me.'

PC Jones stopped and faced Jim, 'Sorry sir I'm a bit busy at the moment.'

'No, sorry, it's nothing really. Is that plant from reception? I have just left the station. I have seen DI Rand.'

'Yes sir.'

'Are you throwing it away?'

'Yes sir, apparently it is disturbing visitors.' Jim took a breath. Inside he was counting to ten. His natural reaction to open a can of sarcasm was probably best not served at the moment he thought.

'Can I have it?' he asked PC Jones.

'You can for me.' PC jones replied and handed the plant to Jim. Jim clutched the pots base, grappling for the best hold to avoid dropping it. PC Jones stood, brushing soil and cobwebs from his uniform with his hand.

'Thanks for that.' Jim said and started to make his way home again. PC Jones nodded and started to walk back to the station entrance. Under his breath he grumbled, 'Two years of training and I'm a bloody removal man.'

Jim scampered past the station entrance to avoid being seen by anyone inside. He was soon at the graffiti sign he'd passed earlier. He wished he had a marker pen on him, so he could shinny up the post and finish the ejaculating penis artwork. After his recent interaction with the police, he suspected he wouldn't be stopped. He imagined the staff behind the smoke glass windows may simply look out at him and watch whilst they grazed on their lunch.

***

Rand returned to his office. Rather than enter, he moved to the next room along. It was larger, with no windows. The air conditioning was pumping out warm dry air. It was a typical corporate office that promoted dehydration and headaches. There were about six desks set up inside. All faced the same direction. Each desk had a computer, telephone sat on them. A couple looked like they hadn't been used in a while and the others had significant piles of files placed on them. There was a larger desk, which faced the others. The room was set up like a classroom. Perhaps in school days it may have been where the teacher sat. One of the sides of the office was used as huge pin board. It was covered with photographs maps and charts. Scribblings and names were written under various pieces of information. The room was a police incident room. The incident room that Jim and Charles sought entry to. Pictures of the victims adorned the wall. It looked abhorrent, like a wall paper designed by *Charles Manson*. Two detectives were beavering away, one was DC Yates, the other was a newly promoted officer, DC Parson. Both looked up as Rand came into the room.

'You OK boss?' Yates asked his superior. Rand sighed, 'No DC Yates, I'm not really. I have just had a visit from Mr Thomas, the guy who found our last victim. He has pricked my conscience.' All three in the room knew what Rand meant.

'How long have we been after this bastard and we are getting nowhere. Look around you, the situation is getting worse. I only have three full time detectives on the case now with cut backs and budget reviews. I am spending more time arguing for resources than I am trying to catch the killer. We are kidding ourselves that we are making head way. Then there are other issues.' Rand stopped his self from saying anymore.

'Other issues boss?' said Yates. Parson stopped what he was doing and looked towards Rand. Rand's eyes flicked between both their gazes.

'It's something that's complicating matters but I have it in hand.' Rand sensed an uneasy silence in the room. He needed to act, inspire his team, he was the boss after all but this case was a dilemma. It was a car crash of an investigation. It was one that should have been given to a retiring DI not and an up and coming one like Rand. Rand knew this was going to pepper his CV, his standing within the force. All he could do was follow procedures and hope for a break through. He wasn't stupid, he knew deep down the chances of that happening were slim. His meeting with Jim had made him realise how futile their efforts had been up to now and they were out of ideas. They had not just hit a break wall, they had been slammed up against it and partly pulled through.

'Let's look at the evidence again. Are we missing something? Is there something staring us in the face? '

'If we are boss, I don't know what it is? I have gone over and over it until I can recite it in my sleep. My wife thinks I have another woman.' All three laughed. Rand welcomed the slight ease in tensions within the room. Yates continued,

'The evidence we have is so vague, the only credible stuff we have is regarding the details of victim's deaths.' Parson sat, listened and watched his two colleagues. Rand walked to a table directly facing the evidence wall, looking up at the photographs he spoke again,

'The perfect victim's, the bastard is killing the perfect victims.' The two DC's, looked at one another puzzled and alarmed by their superiors' last statement. Then Rand clapped slowly, stopped, put his hands on knees and raised his head, staring at the victim's again.

'Look at them boys, look at the evidence. All of these people were invisible to us. How do we catch criminals now? We use modern methodologies, we use tech. All these were off grid. They have no mobile phones, no bank details, no state benefits, we can't build a picture of them. They lived and frequented places that have no CCTV coverage. They lived a life that we ignored. Isn't that the real reason we are struggling?'

Rand stopped speaking, stood and rubbed his hands through his hair.

'Perfect, they were simply perfect for our killer. Any clues from people that knew them is so tenuous, it's useless. No one knows much about them. When we trace their histories we only get tales of how they all went off the rails, ended up sleeping rough.'

Yates interrupted, 'I have a suggestion boss, let's go public with it. I know we don't want to involve the press but why not. It might be the only option we have of getting some credible evidence. It may tease the killer out, trip him up. Let's put him on the back foot for once. I can't understand how they haven't twigged about the murders already?'

'I have thought about that Yates. Do you know what, I think they already know but it's not important for them. I honestly believe that these vagrant's deaths won't make the headlines.'

'That's a bit harsh boss. These were people, like you and me.'

'I am not speaking for the likes of us Yates. I am talking about people that use others' problems and personal disasters to attract readers. Look at our experiences with the Press. How many times have their actions held up our investigations or delayed them.' Realising his last statement had shocked the two DC's, he looked at both and spoke again,

'Do you know how many people who sleep rough die each year? Last year seven hundred and seventy eight people died in the UK. These are the recorded one's, you can easily double that figure in practice. The lost people who have died, those dropped in skips, canals, never found. Out of these figure's, the worst season for deaths is December. So look at our killers tally it hardly makes a difference. All we have are a few more deaths. Looking at the bigger picture, the real problem is the thousands of deaths of these people each year, not our few.'

Yates rose and stood at Rand's side. He then patted his boss on the shoulder. This startled Rand slightly,

'It may appear I am being pessimistic, I am not lads. I'm assessing our situation. Let's look at motive, what motive has our man. We have all taken statements, what have others said about the victims, good riddance, they are a blight on humanity, they make the place look filthy, they raise my taxes.' The two DC's knew he was right, they had experienced it first-hand.

'Listen, this is where we are. Let's go over what we have again. We are going to get this bastard.'

Deep down he knew this was a futile exercise. All three started to check, re read files and statements again. In the back of his mind, Rand thought, *the perfect victims, you clever bastard.*

***

Jim was eager to get home. It felt like that he was no sooner in the car than he was getting out of it again. He was so preoccupied and excited about the task in hand that he could remember nothing about the journey. He studied the username and Post-It information he had found, hoping that it wouldn't be too easy to access the information: he craved a challenge, a test of his expertise.

As Jim entered through his front door, he made a fuss of an eagerly-waiting Barnstable. He then made himself a coffee and made his way to his study. Jim sat at his desk. It was not elaborate, purely functional. He logged onto his PC. Jim often laughed at theatrical descriptions of nerdy geeks sat in rooms with dozens of computers: in today's technological arena, you could achieve the same results using a smartphone.

Jim got to work and before too long, he was linked into the police network remotely. The programmes and knowledge he had developed during his career allowed him to decipher the organisational firewalls and security measures.

'Damn it, straight in,' Jim muttered.

Rand's username and the information written upon the dog-eared Post-It had worked. Jim quickly scanned the network for security protocols and created an alias account on the system, which gave him full access to all information and the ability to do it all undetected. He turned his attention to analyse the organisational file structure.

Jim was in his element. After a few hours he had completed his initial findings. He discovered files – police cases – linked to individual departments. As he delved further, he found the file he had been looking for: 'Operation December.'

Jim delved deeper and continued to scour through the information. It was elaborately structured and corporately designed. Data was time and date stamped from each of the victims. It included masses of files linking statements taken from various parties.

He scrolled through pages of evidence and as he searched further, the case became clearer. Jim noticed salient points from the police files had been highlighted, cross referenced and rendered as requiring further investigation. Trawling through more and more information his optimism for the police catching the killer began to subside. Worryingly, he noticed there were more questions being asked as opposed to answers discovered: the in-tray definitely overwhelmed the out. Firm conclusions were noticeably absent.

Jim was getting a fuller picture of the task in hand, which seemed as dark and as cold as the season they were experiencing. As he interrogated the information further, he felt liked he had wiped away dirt from long-lost treasure stranded on the seabed.

Jim was getting tired: it had been a long day. He sat back in his chair, took a final swig of his chilled coffee and contemplated what he had found. Operation December had shown that there was a serial killer at large and had been for some years. Each of the victims had received the same injuries: slashed mouths and stapled smiles. Jim's memory was dragged back to his own macabre discovery. *If only he could have talked*, Jim pondered. We might have had a better chance of catching the killer.

There was no doubt that the existence of Operation December confirmed Charles' story. Jim had not doubted Charles. He had only met him twice, but had already grown attached to him and had no reason to doubt Charles' honesty or integrity.

The murder case appeared to have stalled for one reason or another. There was little doubt that the train carrying Operation December needed to start moving again. Was Jim's purpose to drive things forward?

Countless times in his career Jim had waded through reams of data to cherry-pick the relevant facts. He knew the world of today was holding more and more information electronically. It took a particularly perceptive reader to decipher the content, and he had been recognised among his peers as one of the best. In a bygone age, Jim would have definitely rubbed shoulders with Turing's lot at Bletchley Park.

Jim needed to verify his findings. A conversation with Charles was the next step. As he shuffled the virtual files in his mind, he noticed something else: a separate folder hidden from the rest. It was not contained in the Operation December folder on the network but linked to it. Jim questioned why this would be? He looked at the privileges linked to the folder. There was only a certain few who could see this folder. It had been restricted to a select number of people. Scanning the content, he recalled Charles' comments on the ethical nature of the Broken Land. As he read on, Jim felt embarrassed to be running in the same human race. He needed to relay what he had found to Charles. There was one thing Jim recognised with absolute clarity: the police had lied to him.

Jim woke early the next morning. As with all winter mornings, seasonal darkness shrouded the land. Other workers might, like the sun, rise later but not Jim, not today. He felt like a shaken soda bottled fizzing with information that was bubbling to get out.

As he got ready he glanced at Barnstable. 'Don't worry boy. I will always have time for our walk,' he said.

Even at his ripe old age, Barnstaple still had enthusiasm for his morning walk. Dog lead in hand and friend in tow, Jim ventured out.

When they returned, Barnstable headed to his bowl for water while Jim had a quick cup of coffee before heading to the Broken Land and a catch-up with Charles.

Jim stepped outside and headed towards his car. In the air he smelt an acrid, pungent stench and recognised the aroma of rubber burning. He could see plumes of black smoke stretching across a grey winter skyline. 'What the hell?'

Jim got into his car. By now the vile odour was stronger and caused him to choke. His eyes began to itch and stream. 'Shit, shit!' he shouted.

He fumbled for the sun visor in the car and using the inbuilt mirror, removed his contact lenses. Blinking rapidly, the pain from the lenses his eyes weakened as his tears flushed out the contaminant. He squinted into the visor and stared at his reflection. As he looked he questioned what he was doing. Had he considered the consequences of what he had done? He had hacked police files. What about the Broken Land – should it be left as it was: broken? Jim closed his eyes and the pain started to ease. A few deep breaths later, he replaced his contacts. A sense of calm and purpose returned. As he turned the ignition of the car, he had another look in the mirror. Any questions that had been raised where now just for reference: his path was chosen and no atmospheric pollutant would change that.

A short while later, Jim pulled up in the Broken Land. What if Charles wasn't there, he pondered? He decided he would wait anyway. The information he had found needed an audience. His findings needed sanity checking. He knew from experience that key data always need verifying.

Looking around the main area where the people congregated. He could not see Charles but spotted Lizzie. Chrissy wasn't on duty and there was a different lady manning the food station. Lizzie turned, saw Jim approaching and smiled. She noticed tension rising from the woman serving the food as Jim got closer.

'It's OK. He's with us, our saviour no less,' Lizzie said to the lady.

'You know him Lizzie? Are you OK with him?' she asked.

Lizzie laughed, toying with a loose chain around her neck.

'Hmm, I think I'll manage. He's a looker, and beards do tickle if you put them in the right places.'

The woman shook her head and wondered how long her blushes would take to disappear.

Jim approached. 'Hello, remember me?'

Lizzie threw her arms around him and clutched him tightly. Jim returned the expression of affection but with less vigour.

'It's OK Jim, you won't break me,' she said, turning her head to whisper in his ear, 'My advice, the lesson I live by is, don't do anything unless you mean it. Now give me a proper hug, one that means something.'

Jim obliged. He felt the warmth of her body. Her figure was remarkably toned for her age. Lizzie pressed her bosom closer and gently kissed his ear. He could smell her perfume. It didn't smell tainted or strong, like those used to disguise, but sweet and compelling. Jim felt comfortable and although the embrace seemed like an eternity, it had lasted just a few minutes.

Lizzie pulled back from him. 'Looks like Lizzie can still work her magic and it feels like you have a friend in need. I have Thursdays free if you're interested?'

Jim suddenly realised what Lizzie meant and pulled away too, allowing his erection to subside. Lizzie gazed down at his bulging trousers. 'Jim, just because I live in the Broken Land it doesn't mean I'm broken or unclean. You should be chuffed I have offered you the chance. Think about it. I believe a part of you has already made up its mind.'

Jim was embarrassed, but about what, he considered? Was it being caught with an erection from holding a woman, or was it the stigma, the shame of being aroused by someone that society had cast into the shadows? What he was aware of, though, was that he had enjoyed it. It had been a long time since someone had genuinely hugged him like they meant it. Lizzie's philosophy had some truth in it.

'I could look into those big, brown eyes for a long time, Jim. They look so deep. Like strong coffee,' Lizzie said.

Jim blushed at the unwarranted praise. 'Lizzie, you are just totally real. I feel I am slowly beginning to understand this place. Nothing is hidden here. What is spoken is honest and not hidden by the world's bullshit,' Jim said.

The conversation was interrupted by a distinct voice. 'I tend to use the term, "ocular embarrassment", or "visionary shame".' It was Charles. 'I'm sorry, I did hear your last comment Jim,' he continued, 'Indeed, the Broken Land does have a way of opening one's eyes to the real truth, or life's' authenticity.'

'We were having a lovely conversation and then you have to turn up and spoil it with your literary jargon. Charles, you spew out words like I do orgasms,' said Lizzie. As she walked off, she shot a departing wink at Jim. 'Remember, Thursday nights,' she smiled.

Charles turned to Jim. 'So, what did we find? Was the operation a success?'

Jim briefly thought about the question. Charles had just heard what Lizzie had said to him but did not seem to want to pry. Was that another trait of the Broken Land? Was privacy king? He thought back to what Chrissy had said when they had first met: the importance of not judging. Finally, Jim understood the situation: he was merely a tourist.

'We have a lot to discuss, Charles. Is there somewhere more private we can go? It's probably best that no one over hears us.'

'Yes, follow me. I will take you to my humble abode.'

The two headed deeper into the car park, weaving their way past temporary shelters. Jim's senses were overwhelmed by the garish drapery thrown over frames to form roofs, and by the various pungent smells filling his nostrils. People peered from inside makeshift accommodations. Alarmed by the sight of Jim but reassured by Charles at his side. One stretched out an open hand, 'Any loose change please.' Charles leant and closed the man's fingers with his own and spoke,

'He is a guest here, my guest. You know better than to beg in the Broken Land.'

The man immediately withdrew his hand and avoided Charles' glare.

Carefully avoiding what looked like piles of discard clothing they meandered their way further inside. Jim couldn't contain his curiosity, 'Charles what are these piles. They look like old clothes, are they for collection?'

'No Jim, they are homes for some of our residents. They have no water proof covers for protection so they burrow into the middle of the pile to keep warm as best they can.' Jim stared at one of the piles and thought *I wonder if someone is in there now.* A huge pang of guilt came over him, *would he be brave enough to carry on living if that was his life*, he couldn't answer.

As they continued, Jim noticed a couple of elaborate tents ahead, neater and separate from the others. An adjacent streetlight cast a dull glow over both the structures.

Charles turned to Jim and said proudly, 'This is us. Prime real estate! We have all we need: light and warmth.' Charles pointed to a large heater, its long cable snaking off into the distance.

‘We have all the comforts of home. A former resident hooked us up to the mains. Believe it or not, the council left part of the electricity supply live, so the lifers have taken advantage and have power hook-ups all over the car park,’ Charles explained.

Jim noticed both tents were large, and that their glistening outer coverings were obviously waterproof. ‘Are both these yours?’

‘No, the one near to us is mine and the other is Lizzie’s. We are like brother and sister,’ Charles replied.

‘How come no one has moved nearer to you or invaded your space?’

‘There is an invisible demarcation zone. This area is for the upper hierarchy of the Broken Land. The government.’

‘Does anybody ever test that rule?’

‘On occasion, but they soon understand the laws of the land. You met “the law” earlier: Turnip.’

Jim smiled.

Charles invited him in. Inside, the tent was large. Jim was amazed at how neat and tidy everything was. There was a raised bed covered by a quilt, and two high-back armchairs with blankets draped over them. Between the chairs was a small bookcase filled with heavily thumbed titles. Charles motioned to Jim to sit down, then reached to the roof of the tent and switched on a light. The light was suspended from a wire and a small lantern hung below.

‘I also have an electric blanket for when it gets really cold. However will I pay the bill?’ Charles said, giggling. ‘Now please Jim, tell me your findings.’

Jim had deliberated what to relay on the journey over. What information to pass on. He certainly didn’t think Charles needed to know about the full extent of the victims injuries. In the back of his mind, he could not avoid thinking that Charles might be next and if he was in a similar position, would he want to know? Jim took a deep breath and started, ‘Firstly, I don’t think this will surprise you that the police did not tell us the truth – far from it. You were right, Charles, there have been six victims over two years. They all have individual details recorded in case files. I don't know why, but the police did not link the crimes together until after the third murder. I can't tell you why. When I looked at the relevant information, the key indicators, it was harder to make the wrong decision than the right one. I am not a detective but it was clear to me. Then I remembered what you said Charles, about the Broken Land and if the police genuinely want to find the killer. This supports your theory.' Jim paused, looking at Charles for a reaction. Charles sat staring forward, he seemed deep in thought.

'Please continue.' He said.

'All the victims were discovered in different, remote areas, such as where I found my body. They call the investigation Operation December, as all the murders were committed in December. The killer, or our foe, as you describe him, rings the emergency services and gives the victim's location. It looks as though they use a call box so that they cannot be traced. Well that is what the police have concluded. The result is that the police are normally first on the scene, except in the case of the body I discovered. I must have been in the wrong place at the wrong time and was there before them. That explains the lack of immediate media attention, as there was no member of the public who may have involved the Press.'

Jim stopped temporarily, and then quizzed Charles, 'That part puzzles me? Why call the police and not just let someone find them. If the victims were found, whoever did it would get more notoriety? It's like they want to keep it secret. Doesn't make sense to me.' Charles continued to gaze straight ahead. Jim knew he was listening. He was like a huge receptacle, taking it all in.

'Alarmingly, I found that the victims all had the same injuries. I couldn't look at their photographs in detail – that was a step too far for me – but their faces looked the same as the body I found: mouths cut and then stapled into a smile. They were all males, but there was something else that had led the police to conclude that they were hunting a serial killer. In each of the victim's mouths was a piece of paper with writing on it. The writing contained lyrics from a song – "Smile, though your heart is breaking" – and a mobile phone number written underneath. You won't believe this, but when they traced the phone numbers, each one belonged to current, serving members of the local police force. Each of the six victims had a different police officer's mobile number. Also, when the estimated times of death for the victims were established, each officer who was implicated by their mobile phone number was off duty, meaning that they had an opportunity to commit the crime.'

Jim paused, gulped and gazed at Charles. He took a deep breath and continued. 'The next part is difficult for me to discuss, never mind come to terms with. When I dug deeper into the case files I discovered that some of the victim's details had been made available to just a few senior members of the investigation, including DI Rand. There was a secret file. The details in these files showed that after the first body had been found, they had kept knowledge of the mobile phone numbers found on the victims restricted to a select few. They obviously think the killer is from within their own ranks. You could see how they could come to this conclusion. Who else could have obtained the information of the police officers' mobile numbers and work hours? That explains why they kept it so quiet. Just imagine the shit storm if it got out. Imagine the headline: "Police Hunt PC Serial Killer". I jotted down a list of the victims. But is it one killer or multiple killers?' Jim leant forward and passed the list of names to Charles.

'I wondered if you knew any of them,' Jim continued delicately.

They sat together in silence as Charles' nicotine-stained fingers motioned down the victims' names. At last he paused, and seemed to focus on the tent wall before he said sombrely, 'I recognise four of these men. They were not lifers, but had been here a while. The other two could have been here for a short while then moved on. I'm not sure.'

He paused, and Jim could see that he was deep in thought.

At last, Charles spoke, 'Our foe, however macabre he is, is certainly someone not to be trifled with. If he, she, or they are from the police, we have to tread carefully, and with stealth. We have to outwit the fox. I am amazed at how much information you have obtained.'

'My career has given me a skillset that few have. I seem to have a natural ability for understanding code and identifying the actual problem. There needs to be data there in the first place, of course. In our case, it looks like they have captured everything electronically, which is good. I just manipulated that data to extract information that was pertinent to us. Listen, I am no detective, so a lot of the wild guesswork has come out of their findings,' Jim said.

'Sorry, I forgot to say: Rand interviewed someone in the Broken Land. It was in the file – he called him Felix. He said he had seen the attacker take one of the victims but had been too scared to intervene, and ran. Felix did say that although the attacker's mouth and nose were hidden, he had a distinguishing feature: piercing blue eyes.'

Charles turned to Jim, jolted into life by this last statement.

'Charles, do you know something? What is it?'

Charles leant forward, reached under his bed, uncovered an electric heater and switched it on. The bars soon glowed amber. He kneaded his hands in front of the elements, craving their warmth and motioned for Jim to join him. Not wanting to offend, Jim hutched closer to the fire, his palms facing the heat.

'There was a man here called Felix. He left, but you are becoming familiar to our situation so you know we do not question much. He was only here at short time. A timid man, kept himself to himself. We occasionally spoke. Prior to him coming here, he had been a banker in the city but his deals went sour and so did his life. As our community does, it absorbs the needy. But there is something you said, the attacker's blue eyes – now that's struck a chord.

'You know Lizzie, my Lizzie, our Lizzie.' Jim nodded.

'Lizzie has a craving for sex. She is a nymphomaniac and that is who she is. She has a small string of regular guests to fulfil her needs, all chosen by Lizzie. She is in full control. Currently she has four, and I know all of them. She tells me of them openly. One is a leisure centre manager. He lets us shower there every day, and Lizzie even goes for a sauna. She's not a prostitute. Lizzie just uses any available perks for her gratification.' Jim started to fidget.

'On the odd occasion, things get out of hand. One of her previous regulars liked to be rough and nearly strangled Lizzie during their activities. Luckily, she managed to shout and Turnip ran to her aid. The guy fled, never to be seen again. So, why I am telling you this? Well, when I questioned Lizzie as to what had happened, she seemed embarrassed, said it had just got out of hand. I asked about the man, so we could keep a look-out in case he returned. She seemed reluctant to comment but did say one key thing: he had bright blue eyes. Lizzie also told me later he was a police officer, but with his gait and size she wondered how he was still able to manage his duties.'

There was a lull in the conversation as they both lapsed into their own thoughts. A sudden noise from inside the adjacent tent broke the silence. They both heard something. The sound became louder and rhythmical. Charles and Jim strained to listen as the rhythm quickened. Then they heard a voice calling, 'Turnip, Turnip, Turnip,' then faster, 'Turnip, Turnip, Turnip, Turrrnippp!'

Charles turned to Jim and whispered, 'Oh yes, I meant to say – Turnip is also one of Lizzie's regulars. Apparently, the big feet analogy is true.'

The two men cackled under their breath like giddy schoolchildren. The Broken Land's absurdity had struck again. For a brief moment there last conversation had been forgotten.

Jim cautiously rose and made his way to look out of the tent, careful not to attract any attention. He delicately peered out. Jim watched as Turnip emerged from Lizzie's tent fastening his trousers and made his way out of the car park.

'On his way to patrol now: he watches over us all evening,' Charles said.

Jim nodded. In the Broken Land, everything of value seemed to have a purpose.

From Lizzie tent both men heard a voice singing, it was Lizzie, 'I'm going to wash that man right 'outta my hair. I'm going to wash that man right 'outta my hair.'

She then stopped singing, 'You two boys alright over there. You've not been listening have you? If you did, I hope I put on a show. Turnip seemed to enjoy it. Jim, Jimbo, I am not tired. Why don't you come over? The kettles hot and so am I'

They then heard laughing. Jim sat quiet not sure what to do. Part of him wanted to go over but the other part lay trembling under the covers, with the quilt tight around his next.

Charles interrupted, 'Lizzie leave him alone. We have work to do.'

'Night, night.' Lizzies light in her tent then turned off. Jim let out a gasp of air.

Over the rest of the evening, Jim and Charles analysed and digested the information he had discovered. It was a lot to take in in one sitting. No doubt they would both come up with further questions and using one another as sounding boards made sense. It was the only way forward anyway. They agreed that the task had to remain between them. Involving others could prove dangerous. Jim agreed to provide Charles with a laptop computer and a mobile phone to enable more effective communications. He was quite shocked to find Charles was quite familiar with how to use the equipment, and embarrassed at the same time, that he had thought otherwise. Charles had an email address he used regularly. He got access from one of the coffee shops in town which had evolved into a media hub. For a slightly more expensive drink you got a free spell on their broadband and their computers. The owners didn't mind Charles using there shop. They were liberally minded, a member of the dread locked and free love brigade.

Jim left. He felt embarrassed of what he was going home to. A nice house, a bathroom, warm food and security. Hell of a lot different to what he had left. He was greeted with soft-pawed appreciation from Barnstable. He bent and gave him a cuddle. The dog licked his face and then sneaked passed Jims legs to go outside. He stood at the door step, the demarcation zone, where light became dark and warm became cooler. Sniffing the air, he then scampered onto the garden for his night time wee. Jim watched, holding the door open for his little friends return. Two breaths later Barnstable returned and jumped straight back in his bed. Jim locked the door. For a brief moment he had forgotten the day. He was happy again.

Shadows from the Playground

The sign of the Crooked Shoe swung in the wind, its metal chains clinking as it danced along to the atmospheric orchestra. The Crooked Shoe had been a public house for as long as the locals could remember. Apart from the décor, the only change to the building had been a steady rotation of landlords. It was a traditional English inn: a place that allows wet dogs to warm themselves in front of open fires, doesn't serve food and, when it's just the regulars, flouts the national smoking ban. The regulars were mainly the local constabulary, who were reluctant to fine themselves.

The inn was busy, it was always busy. The older patrons sat near the fire to keep warm. Their faces coloured red, caused by a mixture of the heat from the fire and the drink. Others sat in groups around tables. Familiar faces, it wasn't a place that welcomed newcomers unless accompanied by a patron. The table legs, old and warped with age, were propped level by beer mats. They rested tentatively on threadbare carpet, hoovered within an inch of its life. Heavily trodden and so shiny in places you could see your face in it. It had an old pub smell. Anyone who had spent time in these places knew what that was. You wouldn't want to bottle it and sell it. It would never make a successful splash on aftershave or deodorant. It smelt of beer, woodworm and smoky fires.

The bar was small and functional, offering various beers on tap. There was lager for the younger element and cask ales for the traditionalists and serious drinkers. To the back of the bar there were several optics filled with spirits, inverted and ready to do their master's bidding.

Keeping with the seasonal theme, but not so extreme as to cause offence, several lengths of tinsel were draped loosely over the spirit bottles. There had certainly been no great attempt at festive decoration: the garlands looked like weeds strangling the necks of roses. On the bar, near the collection box for the local air ambulance, was a small furry figure shaped like a policeman. It wore Santa Claus themed garb and its construction, looked like it had been made in some Indian sweat shop. Every year it stood in the same place, trying to inspire some seasonal joy. It failed.

The landlord was a stout man. He pumped beer as requested, joined in the small talk enough to keep everyone happy and tried not to cause arguments. He knew his clients were mainly from the local police force. Experience had taught him to keep those people happy. And he had pulled in several favours from the boys in blue over the years. Their assistance would be rewarded by a few late-night drinking sessions, on the house. It was like a freemason's lodge with reciprocal back-scratching being the order of the day.

A steady mumble of conversation rose from the drinkers around the bar. Glasses sat carefully on bone-dry beer mats, there was no sign of spilt beer. These were experienced drinkers, not your louts who swayed with their pints, spilling the ale on the floor. When these patrons drank, they savoured it. It was a common joke, that if anyone of them spilt their ale it would never reach the carpet, somebodies mouth would be open underneath, ready to catch it.

Occasionally, the door swung open as people entered or left, annoying the people sat near the door. The drinkers moaned in unison when the door opened and they were confronted with a cold draft of air from outside. The door was swinging open again, only this time it stayed open, because a heavily built man in the doorway was keeping it ajar. The toe of his boot wedged, preventing the door from closing. Two men sat at a table near the doorway scowled at him. They were just about to read him the riot act when the man brushed snow off his shoulders purposely in their direction.

'Cold out there tonight boys,' the chubby man said, smiling at the two men seated in front of him, who were now peppered with snow.

Another voice called from the bar. 'Crane, shut the door and sit down,' the voice said firmly, as the room quietened.

The chubby man remained standing in the doorway, looking over to and then recognising the speaker. He smiled.

'Great, he's coming over here now,' another voice at the table said.

As Crane got closer, he said, 'Do you two want a top-up?'

They did not look from their drinks. Accepting a drink from Crane would have meant something. It would have meant friendship and an open invitation for him to join them. They didn't want that.

'We're fine,' they replied.

'Suit yourself,' Crane answered, stepping to the bar to give the landlord his order. The landlord offered little more than a pint, knowing that any attempt at pleasantries would be met with nothing but sarcasm from Crane.

At the table, the two men sat in hushed conversation. One said, 'Boss, why did you do that? We don't want that idiot sat with us!'

His companion answered, 'you could see what he was doing: creating a problem we could do without. I know he's an idiot, but we need to keep a lid on things, particularly with the current situation, these murders. Everyone is twitchy and wound up. If the truth gets out that we haven't got a clue, all hell will break loose.'

'Sorry boss, he just winds me and everyone else up. We all know Crane only got the job on the back of the reputation of his old man. Christ, no wonder his wife left him. Could you imagine having to engage with that idiot on a regular basis? Never mind shag him.'

Both men laughed. Their merriment cut short as Crane pulled up a chair to join them at their table. There had been no invitation, it was just assumed.

'Well I didn't think I would be in such fine company this evening, DI Rand and his lap dog, DC Yates. Shouldn't you be out trying to catch our murderer?'

DI Rand turned quickly and rebuffed him in a quiet but determined manner. 'Crane, shut your mouth. I am not your direct superior but I out-rank you. One more word on this case outside the office and I'll drag you into the cells myself. You know what will happen if the public get a hold of this.'

Crane leant back in his chair and gloated. 'You ask me, they deserve all they get: scum, living like animals. It's almost like a humane cull, hey, perhaps we could get David Attenborough on it,' he said, shrugging his shoulders and smiling.

Rand grabbed Crane's hand and pulled it sharply to the table, pulling Crane slightly off balance causing his shoulder to droop. It was intended to be discreet but a number of fellow drinkers were looking towards them.

'Enough Crane,' Rand muttered though gritted teeth and let go of Crane's hand. Crane pulled it back, rubbing his wrist. The bar returned to the low hum of individual conversations, like a serenade from a beehive.

Crane smirked. DC Yates had seen enough; he had managed to restrain himself thus far, but the pressure cooker lid was rocking inside him.

'Anyway Crane, I thought you would be more sympathetic to those people your talking about. Rumour is you were shagging one of them,' said Yates.

Crane was part-way through taking a swig of beer. He stopped and slammed the glass down on the table, glaring at Yates. 'What did you say?' he spat.

'You heard me,' Yates replied.

It was a Mexican standoff: a gunfight just waiting for the hour to chime before the first shot. The bar quietened once again. All attention was now on the table where two men were sitting trance-like opposite one another. Eye to eye, Crane and Yates were oblivious of anything but each other. The situation needed just one spark to ignite it. One spark then boom, Hiroshima or Nagasaki in the Broken Shoe. The fallout would not have been radiation but reprisals. Questions would be asked, attention they didn't need right now.

Rand acted quickly again to diffuse the situation. 'Enough, enough, the whole fucking place is looking at us.'

From behind the bar, the landlord shouted over. 'Is it all OK over there, Inspector, or I have got to call the police?'

The bar erupted with laughter.

Rand turned to the landlord and replied, 'Sorry, been a rough day.'

The two combatants ended their staring match and continued with their drinks.

Rand smiled at everyone in the room – voyeurs attracted by the fracas – in an attempt to head off any escalations.

'If you pair of fuckers push this any further, I assure you both your careers are over. Now as false as my smile is at the moment, I want you pair to start laughing and shake one another's hands. I mean it, I am not pissing with you,' Rand said, leaning back in his chair and taking a drink from his pint.

Yates acted first, forcing out a laugh. You could tell it was not authentic but the room relaxed. He offered his hand to Crane. Yates had worked for Rand for a while and he knew he meant what he said. Yates was a young DC and didn't want to jeopardise anything for a stupid argument, or for Crane's benefit.

Crane shook the offered hand and just smiled. Crane had not given a jot. He had already achieved all that he'd wanted from the force. There was no future for him and everyone knew it.

Both men sat back in their chairs. The hum of the bar replaced tense silence. Yates gazed around at his fellow patrons, making eye contact with anyone who looked in his direction. They all looked sympathetically back at him. If Yates had swung at Crane, no one would have cared really. It would have just made a mess of things, caused an atmosphere. Fights rarely happened in the Broken Shoe, that's why its regulars liked it.

Everyone knew Crane and his antics. He wore a chip on his shoulder like a general's epaulettes. Unfortunately for Crane, everyone that was familiar with his past was also familiar with the debt he owed his father. Cranes father, Alan, had been Chief Inspector for a long time. A man of morals and dedication, he'd earned the respect of everyone who'd met him. That was until Crane had reached adolescence. Things changed for the worse, spiralled out of control. Countless times he covered up for his son. Alan had tried to dismiss the reports from school of his son's behaviour: the truancy, fights, and reported bullying. It was thanks only to his father that Crane had avoided being excluded. Alan paid the school a visit, begged them to give his son another chance under the proviso he would watch over him. He also made a donation to the construction of a new school sports hall. Ultimately, the building was erected and Crane remained at school.

For Alan, it had been the bitterest pill to swallow. Everything he had fought to resolve in his life had manifested again in his own son. He believed in the law, he believed in his job. If blood was thicker than water, Crane's behaviour had diluted that bond in the eyes of his father.

Crane had left school with the minimum qualifications. His father had paid for additional lessons to boost his son's education and had managed to negotiate a place for Crane in the police force. Later, his father engineered a move for him to come under his operational umbrella, where he could nurture his son. Alan wondered if a bit of discipline was all he needed. At first, the signs were promising: Crane knuckled down and was promoted to sergeant, but it seemed to reignite the worst in him. His arrogance abounded, unable or unwilling to see the hard truth that his father had furthered his career.

Alan had had to retire when the job eventually took its toll on his health. He couldn't remain locally and decided to move to the coast with his wife, leaving Crane his house and a fabricated career. Quite a few people who knew Alan well, argued that he had moved away to avoid the embarrassment of his son.

Crane stood up from the table, pint glass in hand, and made his way to the bar. Yates watched him, leant forward and said, 'Sorry, boss. He's just a prick.'

Rand, with one eye on Crane at the bar, answered, 'I know Yates, but we need to keep a lid on it. These murders, if the great unwashed knew about them, the balloon would go up. So bite your lip a bit harder, do not give him the benefit.'

Yates nodded and watched as Crane paid for his drink. 'I'd better be going anyway boss,' he said, picking up his jacket. He walked towards the door, not looking back to catch Crane's glare.

Crane returned to the table. 'Has the puppy gone home? Nothing I said I hope,' he said, with a tone that capitalised the word sarcastic, and underlined it.

Initially, Rand did not respond. He wanted to, but his position within the force frustrated any knee-jerk reaction. Experience had taught him that a tap on the verbal patella had proven increasingly difficult to redress. Anyway, if he had reacted he would have been playing straight into Crane's hands. He was always trying to force a response. A sniper did not fire a bullet without a target and he had neither time nor inclination to be a victim of Crane's. He knew if he had reacted, Crane would blurt it out like a baby back at the station and he was under enough pressure at the moment with his peers.

'So you guys no further forward catching the killer? You're just sat on your arses while we do all the work, eh?' Crane jeered.

Rand looked at him, mute with frustration. He focused in on Crane's pupils and watched them shrink. Rand remembered stories from Crane's past: of how his father had helped his career; the tales about his school days; the shadows of bullying in the playground. Rand's venom soon ebbed away, though its toxicity flowed around his body.

Crane, unnerved, offered an apology. 'Eh, I am only pissing with you.'

Rand got up and replied, 'Time I went home.'

Crane took another drink from his pint pot. It was not from thirst; it was one of those casual moves he made to avoid an awkward moment. He watched Rand pick up his coat and make his way to the exit. There was no goodnight, no familiarity: Rand's leaving was functional. As Rand left, a now isolated Crane looked around the bar. Eyes peered in his direction, neither welcoming nor warm but observant and dismissive. Crane took a last big gulp of beer and decided that he too would leave.

As he stood to leave a man tapped him firmly on the shoulder.

'Not going yet are we David? What's the hurry, let me get you a drink,' he said.

Crane turned, 'Tom, err. Well I was going home.'

'No you're not David. We need a little chat.' The man took Cranes pint pot from the table and made his way to the bar. Crane sat down, whispering under his breath, 'Shit, shit, shit.'

Within the pub, sets of eyes strained from their corners watching what was about to unfold. Crane racked his brain, tried to remember what he could have done to attract Tom's attention? Tom was someone you did not mess with. If Tom spoke to you, you spoke back. You only started a conversation with him, if he was comfortable with you or you fancied your chances up against him. His language was the fist, and he was fluent in it. Tom didn't care for the law. He had been arrested so many times, he was on first name terms with a lot of the officers but it was strange how no one ever pressed charges against him. Quite the opposite, a lot of his casualties explained how they had started it. *Best to let things go*, they would say. They were all scared of reprisals.

Tom returned back to the table, sitting opposite Crane, he spoke,

'You know my boy David don't you.'

'Yes Tom,' Crane stuttered.

'My pride and joy, like you are to your father, how is Alan?'

'He's fine Tom. He's retired now, lives on the coast.'

'Good man your father, Alan. The only man that bested me, that was a scrap. We must have been at one another for a good hour. If pay per view fighting had been around then, we would be millionaires now. Prime viewing that would have been.' Tom laughed. Crane laughed back.

'Did I say you could laugh David? Your uniform and stripes mean nothing here. They mean nothing to me.' Crane looked at the floor and thought if the carpet's colour might be tinted a little redder shortly.

'Back to my boy David, Carl is his name. He's not like me. He's a quite lad, keeps himself to himself. You know what I mean,' Tom said, pointing a finger at Crane. Crane nodded a reply.

'He came home the other day in a right state. Upset he was, said he had been pulled up for his driving. Now I know him

David, he's a good lad, a good driver, so I asked him what he had been doing. He said nothing. This officer seemed to have it in for him he told me. Well blow me, when he showed me the ticket he had been given, whose name was on it but Sergeant Crane. What do you think about that David?'

Crane's heart, stomach, every internal organ he had, seemed to slump to the floor. Tom was getting on a bit but he did not fancy his chances against him even now.

'Cat got you tongue David?' Tom asked.

'I made a mistake Tom. It was a busy day and I…'

'Oh you made a mistake alright David. It's how you put this right. I want this sorting out.'

'Yes of course, course you do, I would want the same. It was a mistake, a genuine mistake.' Crane whimpered.

'You see David. I could knock you about a bit in here. No one would mind, no one really likes you. Or I could tell them some home truths of your past David. I like the past David. I think it makes you appreciate the future.'

Crane took a drink from his pot. The ale left a beer moustache.

Tom laughed, 'Hey, it's Santa Claus.' Crane wiped his lip with his sleeve.

'Yes, the past is a lovely thing. It holds happier times for me. When my beautiful wife was alive, Nancy. She was a looker. Far too good for me, she had a kind nature and a body to die for you. But you knew that didn't you David.'

Crane sat in a state of total shock. He understood what was coming. There was no way he could engineer is way out of it.

'How old where you, when I caught you watching her get undressed through our bedroom window. David Crane the peeping Tom.'

'Twenty two,' Crane mumbled.

'And what did you have in your hand David?' Tom asked intently. Crane shook his head and glanced around the bar. No one was looking but plenty were listening.

'I said David, what did you have in your hands?' No response.

‘I’ll tell you. It was little David, your cock. All swollen and ready to explode it was. Good thing I got there in time. You might have drowned if it had gone off.’

Cranes chest raced. He didn’t know what to say. It was true, all true. Tom continued, ‘When I told your father. He wasn’t best pleased but one good thing came out of it, the fight of the century.’

Both men fell quiet. Tom emptied his drink with one huge swallow.

‘I’m sure you will sort out my boy’s ticket David.’ Tom stood, looked around the bar, ‘Merry Christmas everyone.’ Everyone replied and watched as Tom left.

Crane sat wondering what to do next? He decided to finish his drink and let Tom get on his way. A couple of minutes had passed. Crane thought the coast would be clear now. Picking up his coat, he made for the door.

As the door closed behind him he could hear voices start to talk and laugh inside. It was as though the room had been given a voice again. Crane pulled his jacket tight and said, ‘Screw ‘em all.’

The car park was pitch-black, the only change in light coming from the paint of the paler coloured cars. The clouded sky hid the moon and the atmosphere was cold. Crane walked to his car, took out his key and placed it in the lock. The car was a hand-me-down from his father too. Crane had no appetite for the latest and greatest: he needed something to go, stop and peep its horn, which got planet of use. He was an arrogant, unforgiving driver. The door lock had started to freeze and the side window had an opaque sheen of frost forming on it. If it had been clear, he would have noticed a figure reflected in it, standing behind him.

Crane was forced forward, his arm shoved tightly up his back by an all-too-familiar a grip. The pain caused him to squeal out. His assailant just exaggerated the action, increasing the pain. Crane spoke excitedly, ‘Tom, I’ll sort it out. I told you I’ll sort it. Do you know who I am? Have you any idea who I am?’

There was no response, just a more powerful hold. Crane felt like a seal in a nature documentary, held in the serrated teeth of a shark, one instant away from oblivion.

Crane tried another approach with his attacker. 'I have a bit of money. Take it,' he burbled nervously.

His assailant replied, 'I don't need your money you wanker, and I know who you are.'

Crane instantly recognised the voice. It was Yates, but it couldn't be: he was his drinking buddy.

'Yates, what the hell? Come on. If it's about what happened in the bar, it was just a joke,' Crane muttered.

Yates spun Crane around and punched him firmly in his stomach. Crane doubled up, his doughy physique unable to cope with the violence. Yates still had him held up and moved away slightly, to avoid the vomit pouring from Crane's mouth.

'You'll pay for this,' Crane spat, and offered a cursory giggle.

Yates hit Crane in the midriff again and he gasped. This time there was no flippant remark, as the last one had failed to de-escalate things.

'How am I going to pay Crane?' said Yates, 'There's no CCTV here; just you and me. Who you going to tell at the station? No one can stand you – you're slipping off your fathers' shirt-tails. Time is running out for you, Crane.'

Releasing Crane, Yates threw him to the ground, the gravel scattering as Crane's knees made contact with the floor.

'Watch your back, Crane,' Yates hissed. A dampening patch was spreading across Crane's trousers. 'Uh, the big man pissed himself. Sgt Crane, you know your place – you're nothing,' Yates sneered, as he turned and walked away.

Crane sat up clutching his stomach. He could hear the sound of people leaving the pub but he did not raise the alarm. He just stooped and hid from view. Crane's reputation, as tarnished as it was, was all he had.

He clung to the icy metal of the car door, his fingers pressed along its metal contours as he tried to form a silhouetted mass with the vehicle. He couldn't afford to be seen, not like this. The sound of the revellers soon diminished. When Crane felt comfortable enough, he climbed into his car and began his journey home. He adjusted his urine-dampened crotch and noticed the pain from his stomach had started to subside. He needed to regroup, think things through.

Crane looked around as he drove away from the car park to see if anyone had noticed his delayed exit. He was in the clear, so he set off on his short journey home, pulling away from the car park steadily to minimise attention.

The rear lights from Crane's car shone cherry red, obscured temporarily by the vapour from the car's exhaust then disappeared down the road. As he left a second vehicle jumped into life, its headlights ignited like a dragon waking from a slumber. The driver had witnessed everything but there had been no offer of assistance from the solitary voyeur: DI Rand.

He had been waiting for Crane, having resolved to address Crane's arrogance himself, but his fledgling detective had done it instead. As Rand had sat in the dark, he had forged a plan similar to Yates' actions. Luckily for him, fortune had smiled and he had not needed to lift a finger. As Rand pulled away from the car park, there was no pang of guilt or responsibility, just a sense of job done.

The journey home was a short one for Crane, and he used the time to rehearse his grievances. He twisted the drivers mirror so he could talk to his reflection.

'So they think I am a fool do they? They will all pay. Yates will be the first, then that old fuck, Tom,' he muttered with emotion. 'This is still my playground, I earned "Crane the Pain": no one fucks with me.'

Before long, he was home: the family home. It had been left as a gift to Crane and his wife, but it was now a solitary abode. Crane's wife had left years ago. His childhood sweetheart apparently had had enough of him. She had simply gone. There one day, gone the next.

He entered the house using the same door key his father had used, all those years ago. Crane recalled his pride when his father had placed it in his hand on his wedding day. *I hope it gives you as many happy years as it has me and your mother.* Not quite, Crane thought.

The lights were already on; automatically set by timers to relieve the gloom of the waning evening. Crane hated returning home to a darkened house: it just emphasised his isolation. He passed into the kitchen, took a meal for one from the refrigerators and started to cook it in the microwave. The dinner turned in the microwave as the fan whirred. The cooker's light illuminated a less-than-impressive depiction of the packaging of the meal that was being heated. Crane was used to such dinners: they were his staple diet, along with takeaways. He did not get his physique from salads. The refrigerator would need a spiritual medium to remember when it last had contact with a lettuce.

The microwave pinged. Crane took two plates and two sets of cutlery from the kitchen. His side still ached, he grimaced slightly. He set the crockery on his dining table, beside each other. Placed perfectly on table mats, he creased the table cloth with his hand as he went past and rubbed out any imperfections. Next, he brought the meal in glove-handed and spooned it onto one of the plates. The food slopped on the plate and steam billowed upwards. If he had took a bite now the meal may have scold his tongue or at the least burnt the top of his mouth, causing one of those awkward injuries that seems to take an age to heal and makes you to drink liquids cooler than you normally would have. Waiting for his nuked dinner to cool he took a box from the cabinet in the dining room and placed it alongside the empty plate. It was a wooden box, its edges rounded by use. There was no lock but the lid fit snuggly. Crane lifted the lid and laid the contents on the table in front of him, alongside the empty plate.

'Crane the Pain – if they only knew. No one leaves me. There's a reason people use only my surname: that's out of respect.'

He picked up a fork of steaming food from his plate, blowing on it before carefully putting it into his mouth. The food stuck to his teeth and he chewed monotonously trying to extract any flavour. As he ate, he stared at the box's contents on the table. It was a single finger: dried and almost mummified. The severed joint was covered by hardened skin. There was no clean cut or a demonstration of surgical amputation; it looked as if an animal had bitten it off. Its edges torn erratically. The severed finger sported a gold wedding ring. The ring was worn but highly polished. White residue stuck on the side of the finger indicating it had been cleaned recently. Crane recognised the ring, he knew its owner. He had placed it on the same finger he had promised its owner to worship and obey in the eyes of God. As he munched through his overheated food, he reached deeper into the box and pulled out a tatty piece of paper. He unfolded it to reveal a list of names, some of which had been inked through. He took a pen from his pocket and added a new entry: *Yates*.

He looked at the scrawled-out name at top of the paper: *Wife*.

The Daffodil

Jim's attention was fully focused on the task in hand. He had to try to catch a serial killer.

He mulled over his latest conversation with Charles. Jim recognised that sometimes the most ominous thing you can face is the consequences of your own actions. He had started on a path he couldn't veer away from, even if he wanted to. There were people depending on him and he couldn't let them down. Amid all the darkness, however, there was a chink of light he could aim for: the Broken Land and its inhabitants. His mind wandered towards Lizzie and curiosity overwhelmed him. She stirred something deep within him. He didn't know what it was. It was something he couldn't reason. Was it sexual, yes, but there was more than that. In olden times, he imagined her sat on a rock, enticing sailors like a siren. It was the enigma of Lizzie he wanted. How had she become 'Lizzie of the Broken Land'? Jim needed to know, but trepidation tempered his enthusiasm. He felt like he was peering under a dimly lit door and seeing people inside when he'd thought that the room was empty. But Jim knew he had to act: his hand was firmly on the doorknob and he had to enter the room. He wanted Lizzie, he needed Lizzie.

Jim made his way to the Broken Land hopefully to arrange an impromptu date with her.

Arriving, there were just a few people at the food station. The weather was freezing and damp. The cold clung to your face. He remembered his uncle used to say, "days like this, were colder than a witches tit." Jim had tried to use the saying at home once in front of his mother and father. Let's say it didn't go down to well and a family argument ensued with a kangaroo court held to try and find out where young Jim had heard that sort of language. He never fessed up, Jim loved his uncle. He was one of the wrong sides of the tracks guys but had a good heart. Jim admired him, nothing bothered him. He loved it when he baby sat him. Nothing was off limits. He showed

Jim his first Playboy, even let him keep a copy. Good times Jim thought. Jim looked around for Lizzie. He couldn't see her anywhere and knew not to ask for her whereabouts. He was now familiar with some of the residents, but he was also aware that a code of contact existed in the Broken Land: nothing was ever passed on to strangers. This community's family album was only visible to the affiliated.

Jim scoured around, trying to look for a familiar face, but he didn't recognise anyone. Even Charles was absent, which was strange, as he was so predictable in his movements. Should he give him a quick call, see where he was, no, he decided against it. Charles needed his own time. Jim didn't want to intrude too much. He wondered what to do next: he didn't feel comfortable straying deeper into the car park alone, to where Charles and Lizzie lived. He thought it would be rude and insensitive. The Broken Land had already taught him to respect everyone's privacy.

He checked his watch. He had been out for an hour and decided to make his way back home. As he started to stroll away, he thought about his visit. Why had he assumed that Lizzie would be there? Just because these people lived in the Broken Land, it didn't mean that they had no purpose, or lacked appointments to fill their days. Jim felt embarrassed. He wondered if he had learned anything at all from his conversations with Charles and Lizzie. Head bowed, as if judged, he made his way to his car.

A few brief steps later, he became aware of the sound of scampering feet behind him. Before he could turn, an arm passed through his. He did not have to look around as he recognised the fragrance: it was Lizzie. His heart raced, his body seemed charged with electricity.

She rubbed her cheek against his arm, cooing excitedly, 'Hello handsome!'

Jim turned, smiled, and blushed.

'Are you going to take me for something to eat? I could do with a change of scenery.'

Jim laughed at her directness. 'My pleasure, madam! Where to – the Ritz or the Savoy?'

'I know a little place not far away. Nice food,' she giggled. 'You never know, if your luck's in later I might let you walk me home. Perhaps even invite you in for a cup of coffee. My tent is lovely and cosy. If it's not we can soon warm it up.'

He felt like he was being laired into a beasts cave. It was like a vampires love scene, with the victim purposely prolonging the bite.

Jim burst out laughing. There was something about Lizzie that he adored. As they walked along the street arm-in-arm, he didn't feel the slightest bit awkward: quite the contrary. He could have been anywhere and everywhere, me and my gal.

They soon arrived at a small café.

'Here we are. This will do nicely. We can talk in here.'

'Talk? I didn't come to talk, it's just– '

'Jim it's OK,' Lizzie interrupted, 'I know people. I understand them: men in particular. I know when a weight needs lifting.'

Jim's eyes softened. He wanted to hold her tightly; kiss her. Lizzie recognised the sign and held out her hand, grasping Jim's palm.

'Come on, let's go in. Maybe later,' she whispered.

Jim didn't blush: he felt privileged to be in her presence.

A waitress steered them to a table. They sat down and ordered drinks and a meal from a list of items chalked on a small board. It was an intimate café. The décor hinted at a bygone age, with reclaimed furnishings placed about the room, intended to tug at memories and start conversations.

'This is really nice Lizzie, have you been here before?'

'All the time, it's a familiar haunt. I have a loyalty card,' Lizzie replied raising her eyebrows.

'How did you come across it then?'

'I bring all my men here on our first date.' Jim, shocked, looked for an answer. He had none.

'Honestly Jim, you are so gullible. Chrissy, told me about it.'

Phew, Jim thought. Another potential bullet dodged.

To the outside world they looked like a couple enjoying a day out. Lizzie was slightly older than Jim, but she wore her age well, and dressed and held herself with style, so there were few suspicious glances. No one would have guessed at the truth of her existence.

'Are you going to tell me what's going on? You and Charles seem to be thicker than thieves.'

Jim looked around the room to avoid eye contact with Lizzie. He did not want to have to reveal their plan and realised that Lizzie would be able to see straight through him if he looked her in the eye.

'It's complicated Lizzie but we have it in hand.' He had to change the subject. 'If I am honest, I came today to find you. You intrigue me. I have never met anyone like you before'

Lizzie chuckled. 'Intrigued? Or do I make you nervous?'

'Both,' Jim replied. 'I'm really interested to find out how you came to be here. You don't need to tell me, of course,' he continued. He glanced at Lizzie: her gaze seemed pained and her brow furrowed slightly.

'I'll tell you Jim, because I trust you, and Charles trusts you. I couldn't wish for a better judge of character than him. It's not easy for me to tell you my past, but sometimes it helps, I suppose.'

'Lizzie, if it's painful then please let's leave it and let's enjoy our lunch,' Jim replied.

'No Jim, let's do it,' Lizzie said firmly, 'Just one thing you can do for me though.'

'Anything Lizzie, of course.'

She smiled, her eyes focused on his. 'I want us to make love when all this is over. Not just sex Jim, to make love. I want to look into your eyes whilst you touch me. I want you to want me, not just my body.'

Jim spat out the tea he'd just sipped across the table. His face blushed again. *Jesus*, Jim thought, *I'll be going behind the bike shed next and playing doctors and nurses*.

Lizzie just went about her business. She took gentle sips from her drink and used her serviette to mop up Jim's brown spittle stains from the once pristine table cloth.

'Dirty boy. I see I need to teach you some manners,' she said.

Giggle, giggle, giggle, from the couple on table seven. Lunch arrived and they ate as Lizzie told her story.

'As you can guess, I wasn't always like this. I have always liked sex, though. Well, not *like*: I *love* it. It's an obsession with me: a craving, an addiction. I could honestly have sex all day and still want more, just orgasm after orgasm. It's OK Jim, you can blink now,' she laughed.

Jim sat transfixed. He didn't know if it was the narrative or the honesty that held his attention. There was no doubt about it: he had been truly slam-dunked.

Lizzie continued, 'I didn't always have the confidence to talk or even act like this. I was married quite young, at twenty-one to a lovely man. We had been courting for two years and life seemed rich and fulfilled. Our families approved. To the outside world we were like ripe grapes hanging from vines, we just needed picking and tasting. We both had steady jobs and had set up our first home: a new house, a forever home. The aroma of fresh paint often sent us to sleep, when we did sleep. I never let him have a minute and when he was too tired I sorted myself out. You see Jim, masturbation is an art: prodding around only gets you so far, you need to respect your body to maximise the climax.'

Jim looked around the café to ensure that the conversation had remained out of earshot. It would have been easy to identify anyone listening in, as their chins would have been swinging from their jaws, like Christmas lanterns swaying in heavy winds.

'After about two years, the cracks started to show. We had been trying for a child. Nothing happened and tests showed that it was me who had the problem. After that, my husband's attitude changed towards me. I believe I no longer appeared like a woman to him anymore. My body was of no use and my mind refused any kind of solace. I tried so hard to make it work. I was a dutiful housewife: I quit my job; I cooked; I cleaned. Our friends eventually stopped visiting. They grew tired of our awkward conversations. I just existed: I didn't *live* any more. I was an empty vessel.

Then one day I packed my bags and left. I moved to a nice flat on the edge of town. I had quite a bit of money saved and tried to get back to enjoying life. I started going out, socialising. Exploring the things I had missed getting married so early. That's when I found out my true vocation. You would be surprised, the power I wielded through sex and being able to deliver the ultimate orgasm. I chose my partners sensibly, and honed my ability. Men came and went, literally I mean. Tall, short, fat, thin, for me it was a huge experiment. It wasn't prostitution: far from it, I was in control. But in the end my money ran out and before too long I ended up on the streets. It's ironic that people think that becoming homeless is a calamity that's easily avoided. The truth is, there are thousands of people just one payslip away from my fate. I know that too well living as I do now.

'I had no idea what to do, what to expect. I was a broken-heeled woman walking down dark streets, dragging a small-wheeled suitcase behind me. Luckily, I came across a kind, articulate man. He helped me and we have been the best of friends ever since. There is a significant chunk I have left out, but my rollercoaster life is probably not any different to anyone else's.'

The waitress interrupted to ask for if they wanted anything else and they both ordered dessert. Jim thought he would need all his strength if he were to make good on their bargain.

'Tell me Lizzie, did you love your husband?' Jim asked.

Lizzie cocked her head to one side and replied, 'I thought I was in love initially: when we first met he was all I could think about. Now I don't think I was. I think it was infatuation.'

'Have you ever been in love?

Lizzie paused again, her silence making Jim feel like a stand-up comedian whose joke has gone bad.

'I'm sorry Lizzie. That was a question too far.'

She leant over and grabbed his hand. 'No Jim, not a question too far but an answer I had chosen to forget,' she replied, taking another drink to moisten her lips. 'I was in love once: with a woman.'

Jim was now on the canvas of an imaginary boxing ring and the referee was counting him out. He wasn't conservative in his attitude, far from it. He believed in live and let live and all that. He'd just had not expected this new revelation. There was no doubt it, he had been 'Lizzied' again.

Quite proud of the fact he had managed to keep his composure, he listened as Lizzie elaborated.

'It was a chance meeting. I remember it was a beautiful spring day and I was walking through the gardens in the centre of town. Nature seemed to be at fever pitch: plants and flowers bursting open against a blue sky and a crescendo of colour from the trees. Bees danced from bloom to bloom. Fields of bluebells carpeted the ground, so delicate that even wild rabbits cautiously weaved their path through them. The gentle warmth of the sun softened the air. There was an old man dozing on a bench. His head rested on his chin as he trumpeted deep breaths of sleep from his cheeks. That's when I saw her.'

'She was sat alone and looked like she had the weight of the world on her shoulders. She was slumped and was trying her hardest to mask her tears. I sat down at her side and watched her. She did not even realise that I was there, so consumed with her situation. Concerned, I asked her if she was OK. I will never forget the shock on her face when she heard my voice. It took my reassuring hand to stop her from leaving.' Lizzie took another drink of wine and continued.

'We started to talk. It was an open conversation. You know the ones women have? Well you probably wouldn't. I find men when they talk, are direct, straight to the point. A woman's language is deeper, meaningful. Basically, you sound brutal as though you are speaking German or Russian; we are the flowery French or Italian speakers,' Lizzie tittered.

'Think I'm getting a bit tipsy Jim.'

'So what happened with the lady you met?'

'Whoops sorry, yes my lady, lovely lady,' Lizzie spoke slightly slurred.

'I listened to her intently. It was what she wanted, someone to listen. Something as simple, as that. She was so sad. Her story sounded similar to mine. Her life revolved around her husband. She was secondary in their relationship. A partner, she made up a duo when they went out and became accomplished at small talk. Her friends had long gone, left to build their own lives, she was alone, isolated, not even a text buddy to converse with. She told me of her past, explained how they had both met at school, got married early and that she became a maid to the sink and a whore to a husband. As we talked Jim, something clicked. It was as though our lives were either side of a mirror and our faces and features, although different, resembled the same person. We talked of sacrifices. In the eyes of the Church we had both vowed to serve in sickness and health, but at what cost to ourselves? How many more martyrs would fall along the wayside? We talked for hours, only stopping to move positions on the bench to shield from the sun. We laughed and put the world to rights. People walked past and smiled, happy to see two friends enjoying the day.

'Then an alarm went off on her watch. She had set it to remind her to go home to prepare her husband's dinner for that evening. An alarm Jim, she lived her life to an alarm. Not to get her up in the morning, to accomplish her duties.' Lizzie shook her head.

'She had to go. Her life called her and she became uncomfortable. Before we parted, we exchanged mobile numbers and agreed to stay in touch. I remember she called out to me as she left, and said thank you. She then said something I will never forget: she said I was like a daffodil lighting up a kerbside. A daffodil Jim.'

'As I walked home, the sun felt even warmer and brighter, and the birds' chorus sounded more melodic than I had ever heard before. I knew then that I had fallen in love.' She took another sip of her drink as the desserts arrived and they both started to munch away.

'Have you ever been in love, Jim?' she asked.

'I don't think I have Lizzie, no.' Secretly, he wondered if that situation would change as he spent more time with Lizzie. There was something about her frankness that stimulated his soul. 'What happened then Lizzie, with the woman you met?'

Lizzie spooned up the last of her dessert then picked up her story again. 'Nothing, initially: I didn't want to call her straight away. Everything was telling me to, but I didn't wish to add to her burden. After a week or so I got a call from her, and we agreed to meet again. We just sat and talked, and soon it became apparent to us both that we felt the same way about one another. I had never kissed someone of the same sex before that day, never have since. The excitement, anticipation and overwhelming trepidation of the next steps, made it more special. We kissed, one thing led to another and the passion, Jim, the passion. I can remember the first time we made love: making love, it's different to sex. You see, you men think that your penis is a gift from God to move us along the orgasm highway. Oh, how wrong you are! A same-sex partner knows the places to touch, to kiss: it was amazing.'

'Should I get us another drink? I think I need cooling down a bit,' said Jim. He ordered a couple of glasses of wine from the waitress.

'Getting a bit warm are we Jim?' Lizzie whispered, leaning across the table.

'Hmm, you could say that.'

'I've told you, Jim – all good things come to those that wait.'

Jim didn't just feel like a fish inspecting an angler's hook; he had taken the bait and was climbing the line to the reel. He did not care about the Broken Land; did not care about Lizzie's promiscuity. He wanted her.

The waitress returned with the drinks. Jim scanned the café: people were deep in their own conversations: *A good job too*, he thought.

Lizzie sipped her wine then continued. 'We met regularly for a while. It was difficult for her to avoid her husband's suspicion. I am not keen on subterfuge; I'd much sooner be open about things, but I was scared for her, as she'd told me that her husband could be violent. After a while she decided to leave him and asked me if I would go with her. She had money in her own right – an inheritance – and we agreed to find somewhere new together. It was to be a fresh start for us. So we made plans for our future. We would lie together, talking of new horizons and watching sunsets, of moisturising each other's wrinkles, as we got older. Both agreed, it was decided, it was time to act. A date was chosen. I said my goodbyes to Charles and waited. I'm still waiting now.'

Jim noticed Lizzie's lip quivering. She put her head down, only lifting it to take another gulp of wine. Her eyes had teared up. He pulled a handkerchief from his pocket and offered it to her. She smiled and wiped the corners of her eyes. It was the only time he had seen her vulnerable, and he wanted to hold her.

'So you heard nothing. Do you think she had second thoughts?'

'I didn't know what to think. I got angry, frustrated. I didn't even know her address. Maybe I wouldn't have gone there even if I had known it. I didn't want to cause more trouble for her. Time moved on. Weeks soon became months and I was left holding a lottery ticket I couldn't cash.'

'Then I came up with a plan. She had told me her husband was a policeman, so I set out to try to find him, and test the water for answers. I just wanted to see if he could help me find my Abby.'

Stunned, Jim tried to stay calm as he asked, 'Sorry Lizzie, you said her name is Abby?'

'Yes Jim, Abby Crane,' she replied.

Jim squirmed, as if a cold shard had pierced his spine, while he wrestled with his emotions.

'Jim, are you all right? You look flustered – do you recognise the name? Do you know Abby?'

'No, but I do know her husband.'

'You know David Crane?' Lizzie said, with a hint of venom in her tone.

She lifted her half-filled wine glass and emptied it one gulp. She sat the glass back delicately on the table and began to rub a fingertip slowly around its rim, lost for a moment in thought.

'I was lost, you see Jim. I needed to try and find my Abby,' she stammered.

'What did you do?'

Like a scolded dog or a repentant schoolgirl, Lizzie avoided eye contact as she spoke. 'It didn't take me long to find out who he was. Police in the Broken Land are well known. So I introduced myself and, well let's say, "worked my charms" on him. I had to find out about my Abby and I only knew one way of achieving that. Pretty soon he became a regular thing, but I had one purpose only: to find my Abby. Believe me Jim, it was the only time in my life I have prostituted myself. I hated it every time we had sex – his body, his breath . . . but I needed my Abby back. Until one day, we had just finished the deed and I couldn't take any more. I asked him where Abby was. He went crazy, pushed me around, attempted to strangle me. I told him Abby and I loved one another. He said he had suspected his wife and called Abby "a fucking dyke". I dived at him. We struggled and he threw me to the ground. Luckily, Turnip arrived and "escorted him off the premises". As he left he smiled and said to me that she had gone and that she wouldn't be back. I guess she couldn't handle all the shit. I probably kidded myself I was worth the trouble.'

The tornado of life that was Lizzie had just ripped through Jim's land. Everything she seemed to do was extreme to him, or was it? Jim was more and more confused but sleeping with Crane, Crane the pain. Was that a step too far? In Jim's life he was still there, an eternal thorn in his hoof. He needed the biggest Swiss Army knife attachment to remove him, once and for all. Jim realised he was still sat with Lizzie and did his best to keep his composure. His initial revulsion at the idea of Lizzie having sex with Crane soon melted to sympathy. He speculated what it would be like to truly love someone enough to allow yourself to be used in that way. Jim reached out for her hand, saying gently, 'So what happened next?'

'Nothing: nothing at all. I haven't seen him or Abby since,' cried Lizzie.

As he watched her, Jim felt they were like fish trapped in a bowl, but in their case the bowl was moral rather than physical. Lizzie's dilemma frustrated and angered Jim. He felt compelled to find answers to Lizzie's questions but was constrained by the greater needs of the investigation that he and Charles had already begun.

He excused himself and made his way to the bathroom. As he opened the door, the sanitised fragrance filled his nostrils. The room was small with just a single basin and toilet. He locked the door and stood with hands pressed down on either side of the basin as he stared at his reflection in the mirror. His eyes burned: he squeezed them shut and tears started to flow down his face. He smothered his mouth with his hand to gag his whimpering voice. He cried. The situation was too much. His mind bounced from side to side, as if pitched into a fun-fair ride, spinning faster and faster. He thought about Lizzie, her life, and what she had experienced to get her to where she was now. How can someone be in that position? How many more are like this? His stomach turned, he felt sick, and nausea began to overwhelm him.

Questions, questions: he had been charged with finding answers and solutions but when faced with finding the ultimate answer, who was the killer, what would he do? He leant forward and teased his contact lenses from his eyes. Squeezing his eyes tighter, he felt a subtle relief and caught his vision in the mirror. What about Lizzie's attacker - was Crane the killer too?

Jims mind raced. *You bastard Crane! You fat fuck! Could it really be you, you fat fucking murderer?* His heart was thumping in time with his exaggerated breath. *Calm, keep calm, get back to Lizzie, she is your immediate priority*. He replaced his lenses, which felt slightly more comfortable, rinsed his hands in the sink, and made his way back to the table.

There was no sign of Lizzie: her seat had been pushed in tightly under the table and the waitress had already started to clear away. On the table there was a saucer with a spent mint wrapping and a few coins left as a tip.

'Excuse me, the lady who is with me, has she left?' Jim asked the waitress.

'Yes sir, said she needed to go,' she replied.

Jim grabbed his coat and started hunting for his wallet. He pulled out some notes. 'There you go, thank you,' he said. Forcing the money into the waitress's palm.

'It's OK Sir, the lady paid,' the waitress replied.

Jim was left perplexed again but smiled at his ignorance and arrogance. Why wouldn't she pay?

'When did she leave?'

'Just a few minutes ago Sir.'

He tossed some more notes on the table. 'Please, keep it – Merry Christmas,' Jim said hurriedly, as he raced to the door. The waitress's surprised thanks rang in his ears as he exited. 'Merry Christmas to you too, sir!'

He looked left and right. It was dark and it had begun to snow and the vibrant street decorations were already laden with their winter burden. Neon Christmas street decorations depicting presents and brightly lit stars lit his way. He set off, hoping to catch up with Lizzie, as he walked briskly along the street. Snow slushed around his boots and falling flakes clung to his cheeks. Periodically, he raised his head, searching for his target. At last he thought he saw her. He hurried on and shouted, 'Lizzie, Lizzie, please wait!'

The woman looked over her shoulder at him then quickened her steps, slipping slightly as she tumbled towards an alleyway.

Jim shouted again, 'Lizzie, Lizzie, please!'

The alley was dark and narrow; snow had slightly covered one side of its brick wall. The other side was heavily shaded. Jim finally caught up with the woman and grabbed her by the shoulder. There was no cry: she just stopped in her tracks and slowly turned round. Jim shuddered to a halt: what if it wasn't Lizzie, he thought? *Shit!* How would he get out of that one? Relieved, he was looking into Lizzie's face, now dusted by snow. Her eyes flickered, fighting against the weather. He gently lifted up her chin with his hand. 'Lizzie, why did you go?'

She stifled a sob. 'Jim, as sweet as you are, I'm sorry. I shouldn't have told you about him, I'm just a whore.'

Jim looked into Lizzie's eyes. It shocked him, to see her like this. She looked like a fragile vision fractured by society. 'No

Lizzie, never say that. You told me not to judge, and I won't,' he said firmly.

'Your world, you. Charles, all of this. I don't seem to recognise anything anymore Lizzie. I am lost or have I been found?' Jim shook his head.

All they could hear was their breathing. As absurd as it seemed, Jim was still holding Lizzie's chin in his hand. He moved his face closer to hers and kissed her. He felt the contradiction of her warm lips against the cold of her cheeks. She responded and flung her arms around Jim's neck, pulling him closer towards her. Jim could taste the wine on her mouth as their passion developed. She pulled him closer then moved her hands to his crotch. She slowly unzipped and felt for his manhood then raised her coat and skirt, revealing her nakedness underneath. Jim lifted her up against the wall, with Lizzie's legs clasped around his waist, they made love.

Under a galaxy of stars shrouded by clouds, two lovers embraced, winter's confetti covering their bodies. At that moment, neither of them wanted to be anywhere else, lost in an embrace that would have earned jealous looks from Antony and Cleopatra. As their passions finished, they held one another. They felt as one, whole, no need to be separate from one another. The alley had welcomed them as individuals and watched them leave as a couple. Like an impromptu church, both walked hand in hand along a virtual aisle.

The journey home was a pleasant experience for both of them. Lizzie clung tightly to Jim's arm as they strolled in step together. Looking at one another, they didn't speak. They smiled. A genuine smile. The information Lizzie had passed to Jim just sat as reference for him now, to help him forge a way forward in helping to uncover the killer. Before he had met Charles or Lizzie he would have never contemplated such an evening. Now he was not just comfortable with the encounter, he wanted it more than ever.

When they arrived back at the Broken Land, Lizzie turned to Jim and spoke, 'Do you want to come in? The night is still young and I'm not tired!'

Jim grinned and whispered, 'You may not be Lizzie, but I am. It has been quite the evening for me.'

Lizzie leaned over, kissed him on the cheek, waved delicately and made her way to her abode. She hummed a song quietly, twisting her way through the various makeshift beds to her home. Getting closer home, she noticed a light was still on in Charles' tent. Stood outside, she said quietly, 'Knock, knock.'

'Entrée,' Charles replied. Lizzie crept into the tent. Inside was warm. Charles was sat with his feet up in front of his electric fire. His boots were off and his feet wriggled enjoying the heat.

'Had a good evening?'

'The best ever. Lovely, just lovely.' Lizzie then got up and swayed her skirt, twirling around.

Charles clapped, 'Who's the lucky man?'

'That would be telling. I'll give you a clue, you know him.'

'I know him. Have I known him long?'

'About the same time as me. He's quite the looker.'

Charles stopped, realising who her partner was. 'I guess it's Jim?'

'Yes, my Jim. He is different Charles. There is something different about him. He listens, he is so kind.'

Charles kept his council. Lizzie had no idea how important Jim was to them both. She sat at Charles side and pulled his arm towards her. 'I think we have good times ahead of us. Something to look forward to at last.'

Charles remained steadfast in his chair. Both looked at the orange bars on the electric fire, almost hypnotised, deep in thought. Lizzie imagined walks in the park, arm in arm with her new lover. Charles had more pressing thoughts. He simply wanted them to still be there, to exist.

Jim had returned home. His euphoria quelled by the task in hand. He returned to the conversation with Lizzie and deliberated as to the whereabouts of Abby Crane. It had been an age since he had last seen her. If she stood near him now, would he recognise her? There was only one real person who could answer those questions: Crane. Jim hated him, but could he really be the killer? If not, Jim was still sure that Crane had a part to play in the story. All those years ago, memories forgotten, brought to the fore once more. The playground was back. Time taunted him again.

Light the Touchpaper

A couple of days had passed since Jim and Lizzie's rendezvous. Absence from the Broken Land gave Jim some sorely needed space for thinking. Where did he fit in with it all? He needed some head room. What the hell had happened with Lizzie? He tried to think of other things, distractions, but his mind wandered back to his walk home with her. It had been more than a walk home and it was playing havoc with his conscience and his heart.

There was no doubt he had feelings for Lizzie. He wanted to see her again, and not just as a friend. Jim knew what her life involved and, taking all that into consideration, he decided he would gladly accept all that baggage.

Then he considered Charles. He had become a friend and a mentor. If you saw him in the street you would pull up your coat collar higher and ignore him, but Jim knew differently.

One thing he knew for certain: this drama still had several acts to play, and it involved Jim continuing on his path to expose the killer.

One question led to another, specifically around Crane's involvement in everything. Could Crane be the killer? There was some evidence to support that idea but to progress in his investigations he realised that he would have to speak to Crane. That in itself created a problem. Speaking to Crane was not something he was looking forward to. Any meeting which involved Crane was going to be difficult to digest.

He would have to try to tease information from him, tread cautiously. Failing that, he would have to try and find his wife, Abby. Where on earth do you start? You couldn't go to the police and even with his talents for data manipulation, what source of information would you work from? Abby might night want to be found?

His options were limited to say the least. He had to act and fast. If he did that, then hopefully he could start to unlock the puzzle. It would be a starting point, like finding the corner squares in a jigsaw. Speaking to Crane, this had to be the next move, but in the back of his mind his psyche advised caution. Jim did not have a clue as to what he might unearth and he wasn't keen to start a domino chain of chaos. Crane was unpredictable.

Jim was at home. He paced around his living room, trying to work out a method of introduction. Jim held a mug of coffee, analysing options available to him. He stared at the carpet and noticed that its plain design was disturbed by his weight. Looking closer, he thought about the change that had been temporarily caused in the design of the weave. *Change was that it*, Jim thought. *If I can find out when his shift change is, perhaps I can catch up with Crane*. Most of the police went for a drink after work. That was well known about town. Let's get started. Jim made his way to his study. Barnstable watched his master leave the room from the sofa until tiredness overwhelmed his curiosity.

Jim logged back into the police system covertly using the alias account he had created. He browsed around until he spotted the personnel files. Various folders held information on obligatory courses staff attended. Then he found it, Crane, D. It was Crane's personnel folder. It contained everything. A one-stop shop of his time within the force and bingo, his shift patterns for the next six months. He made a quick copy for reference. Curiosity got the better of him, he searched around the system reading Cranes work reviews by his peers. There was an abundance of box ticking and corporate compliance. He looked at older files. These can't have been long after he had left school. They were in a different format, just scanned in, probably a drive to reduce paper records about the place.

The information was only just legible, not due to the writing but the quality of the scan. Back in the day, they did not have the equipment we have now. One particular file immediately grabbed Jim's attention, *Commendation.* He read on and then sat back in chair. Not in a million years did Jim expect to uncover what he had just read. Crane had been commended by the Chief Constable for an act of outstanding bravery in apprehending a criminal. An armed man had held up a bank in town and taken hostages as the situation turned sour. Crane attended the scene and apparently offered his life in return for the hostage's release and I quote, "with little regard for his own life managed to subdue the criminal and bring about a peaceful resolution," end quote. *Crane a hero, you must be joking*, Jim asked himself. He searched through more of the records. Again, all the records spoke well of him. He passed his Sergeants exam first time and started work locally. A three striped, hero, Crane. Jim found this more and more bizarre. So what changed? When did his life fall off the wagon? Jim scanned more files. 'Wait, here's something,' he said, talking to himself. These files were easier to read and written electronically, they were only a few years old. Jim mumbled his findings under his breath, 'Sgt Crane, blah, blah, blah. No nothing there. Hang on, what's this?' He looked closer. It was a return to work schedule for a long period of absence. It looked like Crane had undergone counselling after his marriage break up. Drink issues, substance abuse, he'd done it all. He performed a phased return to duties OK. Jim gradually checked the files, working towards the present. There was a noticeable change in Cranes personal assessments. Complaints after complaints, *a reluctance to change* one of his peers wrote. Jim logged off the system.

If he hadn't been suspicious of Crane's potential involvement before, he was now. It was time for a face to face. He examined Crane's shift patterns rigorously and mapped out the time he thought Crane might visit the Broken Shoe.

Luckily, Jim discovered that there would be an opportunity that very evening. Even though Jim's demeanour suggested otherwise, he was determined to instigate his plan. At six pm an hour before Jim expected Crane to arrive at the Broken Shoe, he made his way to the pub.

As he approached, Jim could see the Broken Shoe's sign swinging in the wind. It was an image of a red stiletto, heel cracked. Frozen ice stuck to the sign's façade, which was dimly lit by a tube light that had long been in need of replacing. Jim peered in through the small, square windowpanes. The windows were steamed up inside, moisture clung to the edges of the panes. He could see the shapes of heads through the opaque glass.

The inn door was adorned with stickers. One warned against underage drinkers while others advertised events whose sell-by dates had expired, rather like the enthusiasm to keep the posters up to date.

As Jim entered, a few people turned to look at him. He acknowledged them with a nod of his head. Some returned the gesture while others just ignored him and turned away. He didn't take offence. He knew these people, and understood you needed to be familiar to get a proper welcome.

Jim wandered over to the bar, dodging tables as he went. Finding a vacant space, he perched with his hands on the round brass hand rail that curved around the bar's front. Its surface had been polished by the touch of countless palms of past patrons, and held a host of fingerprint records of their visits.

A nostalgic malaise came over him. The aroma of beer and the slow hum of conversation cast his mind's eye back to lighter times, from his youth. He could remember his inaugural drink with his father on his eighteenth birthday, and his first taste of beer. It had been a coming-of-age ceremony like so many other young men's down the years. His first proper drink was served in a large pint pot and Jim had tried to make his grip look comfortable around it. He recalled watching his father talking and laughing with his friends, while Jim had scanned the room for tips to help him acclimatise to his new environment. He sort of understood then what going to the pub meant. For some it was solely drinking, servicing a requirement but for others in meant much more. It stood for comradery, social acceptance and for having a good time in different company. For many men it was an escape. An escape from chores at home, finishing jobs that wanted doing and importantly a place where swearing was practiced, not shunned.

'Can I help you sir?' a voice said from behind the bar.

Jim was stirred out of his temporary sedation, induced by his recollections of the past. 'Sorry, yes please. Could I have a pint of lager please,' Jim replied. As he looked up he saw the barman smiling at him.

‘Of course sir – any particular one, we have a few to choose from?’ the barman asked.

‘No, any local brew will do,’ answered Jim.

The barman started to pour the beer and Jim watched the frothing beverage fill the glass. *I wonder how many times he has done that, pulled a pint*, Jim thought as he watched the pot fill up.

‘There we go sir,’ the barman said, passing Jim his drink.

Jim placed a crumpled note in his hand and replied, ‘Please, keep the change.’

‘Really? Thank you, sir!’ said the surprised barman.

Jim smiled and turned looking around the bar area again. How long ago had it been since the barman had last received a tip, – perhaps so long ago it would probably have been a brace of pheasant or rabbits. Although a town pub, the Broken Shoe still had village charm, and its regulars the same village mentality: its patrons were careful with their purses. Potential landlords who looked to turn any profit into a lucrative retirement fund would be disappointed there.

Jim sipped his drink steadily. He turned cautiously every time he heard the door open, in anticipation of Crane’s arrival. He occasionally looked at his phone: not out of need but purely to disguise his isolation. Jim recognised it was not unusual to see people indulge in such behaviour. He had seen people scan their phones and watches, or thumb newspapers for articles and information that would not normally hold their attention. They were tools to mask a purpose or self-consciousness, the same as an actor whose artistry is liberated only after putting on face paint.

He glanced at his watch. Jim had been in the bar about an hour. He thought Crane should have been there by now. His drink was nearly finished and rather than order a fresh one, he reluctantly decided to call it a day. Placing the empty pint pot on the bar he made his way to the door. As he grabbed the handle, the door was pushed towards him. As Jim stepped back for the new arrival he said, ‘Sgt Crane!’

Crane held the door open, then replied,

‘Jimmy! Sorry, I didn’t see you there. Are you leaving?’

Jim, surprised by this stroke of luck, acted quickly.

'Yes, I just popped in for a Christmas drink. With everything going on I thought it might help.'

Crane just smiled, looked at Jim and said, 'Yeah, tell me about it. Listen are you in a rush? Come on, let me buy you a drink – after all, it's the season to be jolly!'

Jim smiled back and nodded. They stepped back into the pub and sat at a vacant table. Fate or fortune had intervened and given him his prize, Jim accepted.

Crane bought a round of drinks and they settled to chew the cud. The conversation was innocent enough: they reminisced about schooldays and their pasts. As Crane drank more, he started to open up. He talked of his childhood: the pressure to succeed that had come from his father and the admiration that Crane had sought, in return, from him. Jim listened: Crane had his full attention. Jim thought he was starting to see Crane in a new light and questioned his opinion of the man.

Crane paused suddenly: Jim wondered if he was supposed to do something – clap? Cry *encore*? He had certainly been surprised by Crane's frankness. In a weird way, he felt privileged to have been taken into the man's confidence.

'Anyway Jimmy, enough about me: how are you? Finding that tramp couldn't have been easy,' Crane asked, as he took a long swig from another pint of beer.

Jim looked at the beer froth as it tide-marked the inside of Crane's pint. He cautiously pondered his response. Jim understood the power of language and knew that, when accompanied with the correct delivery, it could be as cutting as a slash from the sharpest blade.

Crane's previous conversation and any sympathy Jim had felt had been diminished by Crane's 'tramp' reference. Literally, there was nothing wrong with the word. It probably described the victim Jim had found correctly, but those people meant something to Jim.

Jim answered, 'I am not going to lie. It has been difficult. The poor man: no one deserves to go like that.'

Crane shook his head then looked Jim squarely in the eyes. 'Jimmy, they're better off dead. You have no idea of the shit they bring: begging, drugs, stealing, leaving crap everywhere, and we have to deal with all of it,' he said, slurring his words slightly.

Jim returned his gaze, deliberately softening his look. He was conscious that his true reaction to Crane's last statement might show. The pain of Crane's poisonous words charged hurt Jim. He was doing everything he could to avoid reacting. He felt like little Jimmy again, back in the presence of Crane the Pain.

Jim doubted he could physically tolerate this encounter a great deal longer: his best intentions had been blown out the window and his composure was waning. He tossed Crane's comments about the Broken Land's inhabitants around his head. He had noticed that Crane had missed out one word, a significant one, relevant to both of them, prostitution. Should he bring up the subject himself, or would that show his hand? As he mulled over his next actions, his concentration was interrupted.

'Come on Jimmy, you look like you're in a trance. Is this stuff going to your head? Crane laughed, blissfully ignorant of any upset he had caused.

Jim smiled a dutiful smile, perfectly hiding his true feelings. He had heard enough: any cares for caution had been glibly destroyed. 'Yeah, its strong stuff,' he smiled. 'Looking back to our past, I think our schooldays were the best. I remembered you had a girlfriend: Abby Yes it was! Abby Merrymen. She was pretty . . . how did that pan out?'

Crane stared down at the table and thumbed his pint pot. 'Yes she was pretty. Believe it or not, we got married. We had great times, but this job takes its toll: working too many hours. It impacts on your home life and we split up.'

Jim taking the opportunity, questioned Crane further. 'You didn't have a family? No kids?'

'No, we tried, oh boy we tried. I think we wore out two beds trying, if you know what I mean, but it didn't happen. It was her problem, something wrong down below,' Crane muttered, rolling his eyes, looking for acceptance from Jim. He got none.

Jim pushed on. 'So it just ended then? She just left you?'

Crane sat back in his chair and laughed while simultaneously stroking his ample stomach. His chair rocked forward as he spoke. 'Left me, no. Oh! no, no. She didn't leave me Jimmy; nobody leaves me.'

Crane's steely-blue eyes focused intently on Jim's, as if there were an atmospheric charge passing between them. If they had been in a hardware store, Jim wondered if batteries would have started popping from their sheaths or if tills would have started ringing randomly. For the first time since they'd met that evening, Jim felt scared and he averted his eyes.

'Come on Jimmy, let's have one for the road,' Crane said.

Jim shook his head, trying to regain his composure. 'No thank you, time I was making tracks.' Jim got up and put on his jacket.

Crane rose also and grabbed Jim's hand, clasped it in his own and said, 'No doubt I will be in touch with you again, Jimmy.'

Jim mirrored Crane's smile: it was about all he could muster at that moment. He slowly made his way to exit the Broken Shoe.

Jim stood outside, the door closed behind him as he stopped to button his coat. He heard the door open again and moved to one side making room for whomever to pass. The door shut again, Jim turned and saw a man copying him in fastening his jacket. The man then spoke, 'Do you know Sgt Crane?'

Jim shocked at the intrusion replied, 'Yes is there a problem?'

'No, it's just I haven't seen you around here before. This place is not on a popular route. I asked myself, what is a fine young man like that doing here?'

'I was born here. I moved away but now I'm back.'

'Born here, what's your name?' Jim looked at the man again. *I haven't got time for this crap.*

'It's Jim, Jim Thomas.'

The man stopped talking and peered closer towards him. He withdrew and spoke, 'Jim Thomas, Gwen's boy, I remember you as a kid. You've shot up.'

'Yeah, you tend to, when you get older. It kind of comes with the turf,' Jim was in no mood for chit chat, he had work to do.

'How well do you know David?'

'David, you mean,' Jim stopped himself from completing his response with the default "the pain", 'sorry, David Crane.'

'Yes son. That's the one.' The word son threw Jim off guard. His father used it and he hadn't heard it in a long time. The man then pulled Jim to one side of the entrance. Looking around, seeing if he could be overhead he whispered in Jim's direction.

'He's a bad penny that one. Always has been, always will be. His father, he was a different kettle of fish. I used to work with him. He was my Chief Inspector. I worked in the records department. I got to know everything that was going on and I know is father paid the ultimate price for his sons' antics.' Jim's attention was heightened, 'What do you mean,' he asked.

'When David's wife left him. David sort of cracked up. According to form, I don't think there was any love lost between them and a lot of his colleagues said it was because she had left him that upset him the most. He's an arrogant man, brim full of self-worth and importance. When he returned to work he attacked one of his colleagues, a woman. All hell broke loose but his father intervened.' The man paused.

'But you said the ultimate price. David's father paid the ultimate price, what was it?' Jim questioned.

'Chief Inspector Crane is a man of morals. This hurt him, he had to cover it up so his son didn't go to jail, never mind keep his job. That's why he left the force because of his son. All he had worked for, gone. Only a few of us were aware of the truth.'

'Why tell me all this. A moment a go I was a total stranger.'

'You look like a good soul. Not many people sit with David unless it is work related. It wouldn't be proper for you to get mixed up with the likes of him. When you said you were Gwen's boy, then that was enough for me. I was quiet sweet on your mother when I was younger. He was a lucky man your father. She was a lovely woman, your mother.'

The door opened, another man appeared. He looked at Jim and then spoke, 'Alright Dan.'

The man at Jim's side replied, 'Yes mate.'

'Load of bollocks this is.'

'What's that?'

'Having to go outside for a smoke, I'll freeze to death before I die of cancer, never mind give it anyone else.' All three laughed. The man ventured out into the cold, lighting a cigarette. Jim turned to the other man, 'you're name is Dan?'

'Yes son. Now you be on your way and remember what I've told you. He's a bad penny.'

Dan returned back into the pub. Jim set off for home. He was even more confused: the entire episode had thrown up yet more questions. There was no doubt in Jim's mind that Crane was involved somehow. As for Abby's whereabouts, Jim was beginning to have grave concerns. He certainly had no intention of telling Lizzie what he had discovered.

***

Back at home Jim collected further information from the police network. He noticed that up-to-date findings were sparse and once again questioned the ambition of the police in solving the case. He searched through recent case files and managed to locate the names of officers whose mobile phone numbers had been used by the murderer. Immediately, Jim recognised two of them: PC Roper, whose number was found on victim number four, and Sergeant Crane, whose number had been found on the last body; the one that Jim had discovered. This posed a problem for Jim, if Crane was the chief suspect. *Why would he implicate himself*? Jim thought – was it a ploy to divert attention from himself?

While Jim had been analysing and extracting data, Charles had been busy trying to trigger renewed police interest in the investigation. It would have to be done delicately, so as not to unleash havoc or unwanted attention on the Broken Land.

Charles scoured the internet. Was there another source he could use? A way of applying pressure, turning up the heat without causing the pot to boil over? Internal escalations directly within the police had been ruled out. Charles and Jim both agreed that the focus may move to the handling of the case and not to solving it. Then Charles had come up with a perfect solution. He had been looking at chains of command within the local government structure and stumbled upon a way to get things moving, the Crime Commissioner. This was an elected role whose main duty was to hold the Police to account. Surely a gentle nudge in their direction would get things moving. Charles set to work gathering as much background information as he could on who held the role locally. It did not take long to find out. Jim invited Charles to his house to discuss his findings and work out the next way forward. He picked up Charles from the Broken Land and drove him home.

Barnstable greeted Charles with a tentative sniff. Whatever his fragrance was, it had his attention. Jim invited Charles into the living room. Charles accepted and sat down on the sofa.

'I'll make us a drink,' Jim said.

Returning to the living room, Jim recognised Barnstable had joined Charles on the sofa. He lay on his back, his head resting on a pillow. Charles was stroking the dog's chest.

'Some life he has?' Jim said to Charles. Charles smiled politely. Jim passed Charles his drink but noticed he looked uncomfortable. He looked tense, not his normal relaxed demeanour he was used to seeing.

'You OK Charles?'

Charles peered at Jim out of the corner of his eye. Jim had already made up his mind that if Charles said he was OK, he would immediately challenge him. This was his home. He didn't want anyone to feel nervous about being there and certainly not Charles.

'It's strange being here Jim. I am surrounded by nice things.'

This stopped Jim in his tracks. He had not considered how bringing Charles home might affect him. Here he was surrounded by a lot of things he had not. Jim had visited Charles in the Broken Land and yes, he had heating and a roof over of his head, however good that was. But in his house, it was different. His house, his heating, the TV, it meant one significant difference, it was permanent. It would be there tomorrow and the next day. Jim recalled what Charles had told him when they met in the Broken Land, *we don't plan in weeks or months.* He had to try and make Charles feel more at ease, how do they release caged animals into the wild?

'Charles, how can I help?'

Charles looked to the fire place. A few photographs sat pride of place on top. 'Are those your parents Jim?' Jim followed his gaze, got up from the sofa, collected the picture and passed it to Charles. Charles examined the photograph. It was an image from the past. A younger Jim sat in the middle of his parents. All wore the customary smiles.

'You look a happy trio Jim. How old were you here?'

Jim glanced at the picture, 'I think about eleven or twelve. We were at the coast. We went to the same place every year. My father was only allowed a couple of weeks off over the summer. That was our holiday.'

'You look different.'

'Yes, I was a lot chubbier then.'

'No, theirs is something else. I can't put my finger on it.'

'You know what it is Charles, I look happy. Back then, like most kids. I had no worries. I just wanted to run around, play on the beach, splash in the sea. We always stopped on the east coast. Have you ever been to the east coast Charles?' Charles shook his head.

'The sea is a brown colour. It has a lot of sediment in it. Even when it's calm, it's the same colour. You didn't need your snorkel and mask. You wouldn't be able to see the end of your nose. You couldn't buy one locally if you wanted one. The local shops sold buckets and spades, animal themed air beds and plastic windmills. It was a fond experience that had serviced many generations before us and will continue to for many to come.'

Jim glanced back at Charles. He seemed more relaxed, and then spoke, 'This reminds me of my other self.'

'Your other self?' Jim asked.

'Yes Jim, before I became Charles of the Broken Land.'

Jim hoped Charles would explain his past. He wasn't being nosey. He had a genuine interest in who he was. Charles obliged,

'I had a family. Not the two point four children government model. I had a wife and a little girl, Portia. She was named after the character in Shakespeare's, *Merchant of Venice*. She was a beautiful child, like her mother. I worked as an actor, that's how I met my wife, Isabella. We worked together in a play in London, not in the West End, a smaller affair. We were young, carefree and loved life. We cherished every day, every moment together. The more time we were awake, the more we could embrace our time with one another. Sleep was merely an obstacle, it got in our way, we welcomed each morning with so much anticipation. Do you know what the feels like Jim?'

'I don't think I do Charles, no.' Jim humbly answered.

'We travelled around the UK, performing in plays, some bit parts for TV. For a year or so, we lived in an old camper van. It was all we could afford. An actors pay was slim pickings. The Hollywood salaries you see on the big screen are few and far between. Most actors live hand to mouth, particularly mediocre ones. We were free as birds Jim not knowing what one day to the next might bring. Ironically, similar to my situation now.' Jim noticed Charles' enthusiasm wain slightly.

'What happened then Charles? When did you have your daughter?'

Charles placed his hand on his chest. The same action you might perform if you were going to pledge your allegiance to the flag.

'Isabella fell pregnant and along came Portia, she clipped our wings alright but we wouldn't have changed anything. Her arrival wasn't planned. We honestly did not ever seem to plan anything. In our lives, things always seem to fall into place as if we were guided by some fairy god mother. We often looked at our friends sat in their mortgaged houses, driving their shiny new cars and pitied them. They would talk of pressures of work, the latest fashions and how they hated the idea of "keeping up with the Jones'" but actually they ran within the same circles. Their eyes would swell grey with responsibility, unaware the treadmill of the nine to five slowly killing them.'

Jim struggled to understand the pressures of marriage or serious relationships, he had not had to deal with that in his life but recognised the shit storm that can be generated by work. He wanted to know more of Charles' life but didn't want to keep prompting him to continue his story. He need not have worried Charles obliged,

'When Portia came along, we lived in a rented house. Isabella got a job as a waitress. I was left literally holding the baby. I performed in the evenings. We fitted child care between us. We had no family or friends we could call on. We were our own little bubble. I loved it, me and my little girl. I practiced my lines before her, she was the perfect audience. I was the first to notice,' Charles stopped. He went to take a drink from his cup but it was empty. He put it back down.

'Should I make us another Charles?'

'No, thank you. I'm OK. I needed to pause a moment, sorry.'

There was a temporary silence.

'I like this. I like the silence. It is noticeably absent in the Broken Land. You can think, you can remember. It allows your mind to absorb.' Jim did nothing, reluctant to disturb Charles.

'My Portia started to fall ill. We first thought it was just a juvenile malady and we were initially reassured it was nothing to worry about. Two years later, she was no longer with us. She had a brain tumour, inoperable. We went to private specialists, tried to put off the inevitable but all they did was strangle an already exhausted bank account. As for Isabella and me, it was as though life had been pulled from our very bodies. We slept more, started to grow apart. I went out frequently with my fellow artists. I partied like a rock star for a while. It was no life for a couple and my beautiful Isabella left. I remained in an empty flat, blurry eyed, watching the world go by. Excess became a norm for me, drink, drugs, sex I experienced it all with a vitality instigated by loss. But we all have to balance the books and I lost every remaining possession I had. Here I am now, Charles of the Broken Land.'

Another silence hung between them, less comfortable for both.

'I'm sorry Charles, your life has been. I haven't the words to say what your life has been. My own life seems so shallow compared to yours.' Jim placed his hand on Charles' shoulder.

'I'll tell you one thing Charles. I am going to do my damnedest to find our killer.' Jim got up, 'I think we need another drink, perhaps a little tipple inside to keep us going.'

Jim went to the kitchen. Charles remained cuddling a sleepy Barnstable. Out of Jim's sight Charles picked up a cushion from the sofa, pulling it close. He rubbed the velvet cover to his cheek and breathed in its fragrance. It felt warm and smelt fresh. It reminded him of home. Unaware, Jim watched from the kitchen and felt humbled to be in Charles' company. Re-entering the living room he purposely made a noise so as to warn Charles of his impending arrival.

'There we go,' He handed Charles his cup. He had put a healthy tot of brandy in. 'That'll keep us going.'

'Thank you Jim.' Charles smelt the drink, instantly recognising the fumes of the brandy.

'Now, let me tell you my plan, let me tell you what I have found.'

Charles pulled a small notebook from his pocket. It was bound shut by an elastic band which he expertly removed. Referring to the notepad, he explained to Jim his idea,

'Our local Crime Commissioner is a chap by the name of Gabriel Ambrose. He has been in the role for the last two years, his tenure running out next year. They serve three years unless things go south. There is lots of bumf about his achievements. I cannot find anything negative about him, so, he is either really good at his role or he has a good publicity campaign around him. He absolutely courts attention. He is a photo op. dream. There are more pictures of him holding babies and supporting local charities than a little. He is without doubt a networker. If we can get him involved without causing merry hell, I believe he is our escalation point.'

The room went quiet again as both deliberated how to light the touch paper. Cogs whirred, options were considered. Jim was sat in a comfy chair to the side of Charles, leaning back he smiled,

'Think I have got it. It may be a double win for us.'

The break in the silence startled Charles, he flinched and Barnstable, who was still at his side, shot up. Charles stroked his head to calm him.

'What if Gabriel received an e mail from a police officer voicing their concerns over the failing investigation?'

'You can do that Jim?'

'Easily, I will log back into the police system, hack an e mail account and send the mail. If I delete the message from the officers e mail sent box, they will not immediately know what has happened. It could be traced through the messaging system if scrutinised but it will only lead back to the email sender not us. It would only implicate the person sending the e mail and I have the ideal candidate, Sgt David Crane.'

'Genius my boy!' Barnstable flinched again. 'I'm sorry little chap, I keep making you jump.' Charles then put his face to the dogs and he promptly licked his cheek.

The two put their head together and concocted a story saying that Crane had been made aware that his mobile phone number had been found on one of the murder victims. Crane was writing to Gabriel because he was scared he would become a scapegoat for the murders, as the investigation was faltering.

In reality, Crane knew none of this, but it didn't matter to Charles and Jim. The email contained all the evidence, including descriptions of all the blue-eyed killer's victims and their injuries.

The email was sent. It was now a waiting game. Jim and Charles having to pause for a while, hope for a reaction.

There was nothing more they could do. 'Do you want to stay tonight Charles? I have a spare room and it's getting late.'

'Thank you Jim but no. You have experienced the Broken Land. You know what a fragile ecosystem it is. If I am not within it, I fear chaos may reign.'

'OK Charles. I tell you what, have a hot shower. I'll make us something to eat and I have some clean clothes you can have. Now you'd be a fool to turn that down. I know you're not that Charles?' Jim hoped Charles accepted his offer, he hoped he hadn't overstepped the friendship mark.

'That would be excellent Jim. You really are our saviour.'

They had pressed the send button together. Jim felt as if an exorcism had been completed. Catching the killer was paramount, but revenge for years of school abuse maybe just as sweet.

The Smoke Alarm

The alarm clock sounded. The early winter's morning meant it was still dark. On the digital display of the clock it flashed 06:00, in what seemed the blink of an eye it showed 06:12. A brief doze pushing time on in chunks not nibbles. He felt like he had no sleep at all. It certainly did not help being awoken at daft o'clock by the smoke alarm telling him that the battery was low, then repeating it, again and again until he had no alternative to get up. It was only ever going to be his job. His wife slept at his side but she was dead to the world, a mixture of wine and prescribed drugs saw to that. If a real fire had been blazing away, she probably wouldn't have noticed 'till the flames were licking around her nether regions. Not that he recognised what they looked like now. It had been a while since they had had any sexual interaction. He laughed, querying if the flames might be extinguished by the dust on her privates anyway.

It wasn't the fact that the smoke alarm had gone off, it was that he had to deal with it. By their nature they are sited on the ceiling, so stumbling around for a step ladder with your eyes trying to get accustomed to the bright artificial light so you can locate the damn thing is a great way to start the day. If it had been Christmas morning and he had heard the big red fella' *yo, ho, hoing*, he would have knocked him out, bugger the kids. They get enough anyway, he thought. Now, he felt tired. A fantastic start to the day. He got out of bed, headed straight to the shower. It had to be a quick one. He was already late.

Getting ready quickly he managed to claw back a few minutes. He had an early morning meeting he couldn't miss. Outside, he pressed the button for his automatic garage door. It started to rise slowly. Bobbing down, to get under before it was fully opened, he caught his shoulder on the metal edge on the bottom of the door. 'Fuck!' he shouted, as he stood inside the garage inspecting the shoulder of his suit. There was a slight bit of dirt which was soon removed by a bit of spit and the rub of his hand. He looked at his car. It looked like he had driven it through a farmer's field. He had meant to put it through the car wash but then again he had meant to do a lot of things. Time always seemed to be against him or has a consultant might say, "you are not managing your time correctly". He had been to a few of those lectures and come away with the only opinion that the lunch was nice. He got in the car, turned it over. It started sweet as a nut. You didn't pay out that sort of money on a car for it not to. He argued that his accountant advised him to spend some money, get a nice car. Bentley's are good, he'd look good in a Bentley. So he bought one. The accountant hadn't advised him to buy a personal number plate, that was all him.

He reversed out of the garage and headed off. The radio was advising of "No current traffic problems" so he anticipated arriving on time.

The sun was starting to rise. Ask any driver and they will tell you that a winter's sun is tricky at best to drive in. He flicked the windscreen wipers to clear his screen, they made it worse. Dirt smeared his view, he activated the jets. No water shot on the screen, he only heard the noise of the washer pump trying to strangle the last droplets from the water reservoir. Another job he had ignored. The car had notified him a couple of days ago. He had been to see a business contact which involved driving some serious motorway miles, hence the state of his car. Even if it appeared dry on main roads in winter, it was never the case. Salt, dirt, all kinds of crap stuck to the car. As he drove, he peered through the gaps of dirt on his windscreen. He felt like a tank commander, looking through slits in the armour, negotiating their way over the battlefield.

Slowing the car he joined a line of traffic. As he squinted forward looking for his best viewing position, he glanced to his side. It was a police car, with two officers in the front seats. The officer nearest him had been watching him closely. He acknowledged him with a smile. The officer turned, said something to his colleague and looked forward. The line of traffic started to move. He drove forward, watching his speed. The police car didn't move forward, it indicated to follow immediately behind him. Driving for about half a mile, he was greeted in his rear view mirror by the blue flashing lights from the patrol car.

'Shit. This is really what I need,' he blurted.

One of the officers walked to the passenger door, he had already lowered the window. The officer bent down to speak, his high visibility coat crumpling as he did, 'Morning sir. Nice car, have you thought about getting it cleaned?' The officer put his head into the vehicle slightly, just enough to get a view from the cockpit, through the windscreen.

'Can't really see a lot sir, can you?' He had remained quiet up to that point.

'Can I see you're licence please sir?'

Pulling out his wallet, he passed the licence to the officer.

'Mr Gabriel Ambrose.'

'Yes officer, that's me. I am the Crime Commissioner.'

He hoped that might win him some brownie points. He was wrong. The officer did not look impressed.

'Morning Mr Ambrose, Crime Commissioner, you still have a windscreen you can't see through. It is dangerous for you to go any further. I am guessing your car washer reservoir has run dry.'

'Yes, only just. I was going to fill it up at the next garage I came to.'

The officer stood back from the car slightly, looked it up and down, spoke again, 'Car like this. You'd have thought that the alarm would have given you a bit more notice.' Gabriel shrugged his shoulders to agree. Both knew the truth.

'Have you anything to clear the screen Mr Ambrose?' Gabriel looked inside the car randomly. He thought to himself, *what on earth does he think I am going to find, a fucking water butt.* Luckily he spotted a bottle of spring water on the floor behind the passenger seat. A litre bottle, there quarters full. He hadn't notice it rolling around. Stuff didn't roll around in a Bentley. Picking it up, he showed the officer,

'I'll try this.'

The officer nodded. Carefully getting out, negotiating passing traffic, Gabriel tipped the contents of the bottle on the windscreen. It trickled down, evaporating as it did. He'd forgotten he had activated the heated windscreen. The water made little difference. Gabriel resisted trying to wipe the screen with his hands, other than standing on the bonnet and pissing on the screen, he was out of ideas. The officer peered over to the look at the screen again.

'That's not worked as it Mr Ambrose.' Gabriel looked at him. He restrained his response, inside he was saying, *no shit Sherlock.*

'No officer sorry, think I am out of ideas.' He replied, biting hard on his lip.

'Can you see enough to follow us Mr Ambrose? We will get you to the nearest garage, you being the Crime Commissioner and all. I bet you're a busy man?'

'Yes. Thank you.'

The two men got back in their cars.

'Sarcastic twat,' Gabriel uttered. Looking in his rear view window, he saw the officer laughing as he spoke to his colleague. The patrol car drove away slowly, Gabriel followed. About fifteen painful minutes later, they reached a garage. The bright orange advertising sign hung outside, displaying the price of the fuel. His escort waved him into the garage courtyard, then waved him good bye. Gabriel waved back in acknowledgement. Spotting a space, clear of the fuel pumps he parked up. A young boy spotted him getting out of the car, 'Nice car Mr?'

'What?' Gabriel replied.

'Nice car, what is it a Bentley?'

'Err, yes, sorry I'm a bit busy.' Gabriel headed towards the forecourt shop, wallet in hand.

'Could do with a clean though.' Turning towards the lad, Gabriel contemplated, *is he taking the piss*. Ignoring the last comment, he carried on towards the shop. A short while later, his car was topped up with washer fluid and he was on his way to his meeting, late.

He screeched into the car park. Everyone else was already there. He knew as he recognised the cars in the car park. They stood out like a sore thumb. A Rolls Royce, an Aston Martin, a Maserati and now his Bentley joined them. It looked like a successful footballer's garage. Grabbing a small wash bag, he ran to the entrance. He slowed to allow the automatic doors open, entering he recognised the elaborate reception. Behind the plush reception desk, the logo stood proudly, *James Leisure*. It was an exclusive health spa for the select ones that could afford it. The receptionist spotted Gabriel straight away,

'Morning Mr Ambrose. The others are already in there.' Gabriel forced a smile, rushing past her. Dashing into the changing room, he emerged robed up and made his way to the sauna. The sauna was the meeting room. He opened the door to the sauna entrance. It was a small area that contained showers before you actually went into the sauna itself. He was instantly greeted by the goliath that was Paddy. As his name suggested he was of Irish descent, an ex-boxer. If you spoke to him, that is if Paddy allowed you to speak to him, he was ex-everything. You only had to look at him to see he had lived an interesting life. He had a face that looked like it had been towed behind a truck for a few miles, let heal and towed again. After a few short words with him, one thing was obvious; you did not mess with him.

'Morning Mr Ambrose, they're waiting for you inside. You'll probably be in the naughty corner.' Paddy moved out of the way to allow him through. He went to open the sauna door, removing his robe and wrapping a towel around his waist to cover his modesty. As he did, he heard the outer door open behind him. Paddy jumped into action, 'Sorry Sir, this is a private party.' A man in the doorway looked Paddy up and down.

'Private sauna's, there's no such thing. Let me bye.' The man spoke firmly. Gabriel cringed. He understood this was not going to end well for the unwanted visitor. Paddy spoke again, 'Go to another sauna while you can still walk. I'll rip your fucking legs off and watch you eat 'em.' The man moved back, 'I'll be letting Mr James know about this.'

'Don't worry. I'll tell him, I work for him.' The outer door closed, the man left. Gabriel thought best thing for all. Paddy just giggled, 'Some people Mr Ambrose, you try and be nice to 'em.'

Gabriel entered the sauna and was greeted by a round of applause. The heat was oppressive. Blowing out air through his mouth, he made his way further in and sat down on the pine slatted seating. He looked around, the usual suspects sprawled around. These were the people that actually ran things in the area, the important stuff. They were door openers and significantly, door closers. These were men of influence. To his left was Sir Stephen Richmond, or Stephen to his friends, a retired high court judge. A man of great social standing and who still held great sways in the corridors of justice. He was seventy seven, not bad for his age. A portly man, someone you may associate with the finer things in life. A guy who ate quail's eggs and caviar, not for show but he actually liked them. He mixed with the select people. Those folk that got things done with a phone call or a wave of a finger, their actions outside of authority but embedded secretly within it. His towel stretched tight around his waist, always hung low under his belly. When he moved he had to hold it in place or his size burst the thing open wide and a game of spot the Willy might begin. Sweat congregated in the folds of his stomach. If he ever had a six pack, it had long gone. His body was covered with grey hair, apart from his head which only sported coiffured tufts either side of his ears. Gabriel often thought he looked like a new born chick, covered in down.

To his right and who persistently threw water on the coals to raise the internal temperature was Aubrey James. He was a man you kept close. You needed him on your side. If you crossed him, Paddy would take you for a swim in the local canal. He was the closest thing the area had to a gangster but Aubrey hated that word. He convinced himself he was not part of the underworld. As far from a Marlon Brando or De Niro, depiction of a Don as you could get. Aubrey told you he was a businessman. He owned this place and several others. His other places accommodated more than a sauna, you got anything in them. Women, men, drugs, whatever your little heart desired. He was a tall man, slender built, mid-sixties. He looked after himself and wasn't a bad chap to get on with. Gabriel liked his honesty, what he said he meant.

Behind Gabriel laying in the hottest part of the sauna, was Henry Smythe-Fraser. Gabriel daren't turned around, he would have been face to face with his penis. He didn't wear a towel, he was completely starkers, proud of his body, He worked out regularly and it showed. If you passed him in the street you may have mistaken him for a reality TV star. Perfectly tanned skin, pearly white teeth and groomed to within an inch of his life. Paddy hated him, he was his polar opposite. Gabriel and the others didn't like him either. He had a natural arrogance but he was probably the most important man in their group. He provided a key service to the area and to them all, he provided product, drugs. Henry was Oxford educated. A silver spoon upbringing ensured he operated within some exclusive circles. His father was one of the biggest import, exporters on the south coast. That's where Henry made his first contacts. He now had a resilient network that imported and distributed drugs throughout the country. The main difference that singled Henry from any other drug dealer was his intellect. His actual business was running the family one. His father handed it down when he retired to live on a beach somewhere hot. Henry ran it and operated his other affairs under its shadow.

‘Nice of you to make it old boy,’ Henry commented, ‘can we crack on, I have a facial booked in an hour?’

‘Sorry gents. I have had a bit of a morning,’ apologised Gabriel.

‘No worries Gabby old boy. To business, I have a supply coming up from the coast this weekend. Is that going to be a problem?’

Gabriel answered first, ‘I was at a meeting yesterday with the Chief Constable, they are concentrating on disturbing the operations of the county lines over the next month. There’ a big push from the home secretary to get it sorted. So, the towns should be clear. Does that seem OK?’

‘First rate old bean, I don’t bother with the county line thing. It’s too messy, employing kids to sell product, too unreliable. It would be like letting them loose in a sweet shop. No, the towns are fine for me. I can’t keep up with demand as it is.’

Aubrey piped up, ‘my delivery still OK, same price?’

‘Certainly Mr James, anything for a pal. I presume our arrangement for my executive entry to your establishments is still gratis?’

‘You scratch my back Henry. You know the rest.’

‘Indeed, indeed I do.’ Gabriel understood the undercurrent of their conversation. As perfect as Henry seemed physically, he was twisted sexually and needed bizarre interactions with partners to fulfil his whims. Gabriel deliberated if it wasn’t the Oxbridge educational system that created his deviance.

Stephen spoke next. ‘How are we fixed with getting Gabriel re-elected? I have got my people on side. Are we aware of anything bubbling about that might prevent it?’

Gabriel replied, ‘Things are tidy enough my end. No one seems out of sorts. The crime statistics have gone down. The chief seemed happy enough.’

‘What about the competition, this other fellow, somebody Tucker or something like that?’

‘He’s going to withdraw shortly,’ Aubrey commented, whilst throwing another cup of water on the coals. The heat was instant and migrated quickly across the room.

‘Nice one Aubrey. Little Smythe-Fraser has nearly turned inside out.’ Henry said, staring down at his penis. ‘I’ll be in need of his services later. That’s enough for me.’

Henry promptly jumped from his bench and walked to the front of the sauna door, as left he turned, ‘Oh yes, I have left a little gift for you all in your lockers. A little white envelope with a pick me up inside, toodle pip.’

Henry left the sauna, walking naked past Paddy towards the door, stopped and started to put on his robe.

‘Ready for our big fight my Irish friend?’

‘Anytime, I have told you that. Don’t worry I won’t mess with your face.’

‘Hmm, shame I can’t say the same, looks like plenty have beaten me to it,’ Paddy watched him leave.

Inside the sauna, conversations continued.

‘He’s annoying,’ Stephen commented.

‘No doubt it,’ Aubrey replied, ‘but he knows what is doing. I have never had a supply of product as reliable. It makes life a lot easier for me.’

‘I’m old school but I recognise that product has become a big part of our normal world.’

‘Stephen, if you saw my client list, it would shock you. It’s no longer exclusively for the young, the party goers. It’s made up of people from every walk of life. From the normal worker to professionals, you would not believe how many police officers pay me a visit. The pressure of today means they need a release. In this place alone, I can clear five hundred thousand a year easily. Everybody wants it. If I don’t supply it, somebody else will. It’s everyday life now.’

Gabriel sat listening. He recognised what was going on. It was not even that hard to spot anymore. Shady deals down alleyways were a thing of the past. Stephen looked at Gabriel,

'All things as they are, it looks like you will get another three years. You just need to keep your head down. There are no skeletons in the cupboard likely to derail us, are there? I have got a land acquisition going on. I have the council on board and I need you're influence to get it through.'

'No, all fine on my side.' Gabriel understood what he meant. He could provide leverage at the right meetings to make sure things happened. Big building projects needed police clearance and Gabriel was adept at making sure this was realised. This was to the benefit of all his friends. Gabriel stood up, 'I have got to go folks, things to do. See you in a couple of days and before you say anything, I will not be late.' The other two raised their hands as he left.

Paddy looked at him, 'Did you get your hands slapped?'

'No my arse cheek,' Gabriel replied, lifting his towel up at one side.

Paddy laughed and spoke, 'Good job you didn't do that to that posh twat, he would probably be balls deep into your arsehole like a flash.' They both erupted into laughter.

'Nice one Paddy.' Gabriel patted him on the shoulder. It felt like he had tapped a slab of concrete, 'See you later this week.'

'Don't be late Mr Ambrose. Remember your bum hole.' Paddy chuckled. Gabriel made his way to his locker.

Back in the sauna, the conversations continued between the remaining two.

'Have we a plan B if he doesn't get re-elected,' Aubrey asked.

'I always have a plan B. I have a man in the wings if needed,' replied Stephen. The entire sauna group were aware that he was the governor. He was like an octopus, with each tentacle in a host of pies.

'If it doesn't go to plan, Gabriel will be become a problem, he knows too much and he will not be of much value. He might need to disappear. Is that a problem?'

'No Stephen, if it has to happen, it can be arranged.' Aubrey threw another cup of water on the coals. Stephen got up to leave, 'I'll look like a prune if you carry on. I've had enough.' Holding his towel around his waist, he shuffled from the sauna.

Gabriel was getting dressed. He scanned the insides of his locker and noticed a folded white envelope had been left in the top part. Instantly, he knew this was Henry's gift. He took it out, slid it into his jacket pocket and made his way to the toilet. The toilets were private, independent booths with wash basins. There were no communal toilets in this place, well not in the member's area. The place had been designed for optimum privacy. He took out the envelope and his wallet. Rolling a twenty pound note into a straw, he tipped the contents onto a credit card. It was an American Express Gold Card, *that'll do nicely* he recited in his head remembering the old advert from the TV. He took a deep snort of cocaine. The buzz immediately hit him, that's better. He stumbled backward and sat astride the toilet. Allowing a minute or so to gather himself. As his heart beat steadied from the initial hit of the narcotic, he tidied up. A quick check in the mirror, a wipe of the white stuff from under his nose and he was good to go.

Gabriel left the building, making the way to his office. He was in a far better place than when he arrived at the sauna. A lot less stressed, ready for the day ahead. The nose candy had made the day seem rosier and he could also see through his windscreen, what could be better than this?

It wasn't long before he was at his office. He parked his car in his parking spot, everyone knew it was his, it had his name printed on it, G. Ambrose, CEO. The CEO meant he was the big cheese. Gabriel didn't mind his work. The sauna group was extreme and his home life was desolate. Between these two poles he at least had work to exist within for a while, he had normal human interaction with people. Making his way to office, he said the customary good mornings to the receptionist and a couple of his staff he passed along the way. He wasn't a tyrant, far from it. So long as his people did their jobs he didn't give a monkeys. His staff turnover was negligible and as work environments go, it was OK.

Entering his office, he hung his coat on the hangar, shaking his head. He recognised he was still quite heady from the cocaine. Deciding to sit down to let his body recover from this artificial stimulation he thought about the mornings events.

As well as being the local Crime Commissioner, he also had to run his local businesses. When he took the Crime Commissioner role on, he promised his employers faithfully that there would be no cutting corners, he would divide his time efficiently between his roles. He promised to give the position the respect it deserved. Two years later in reality, it proved to be different story, with more time spent feathering the nest of his own business and others, at the expense of his role to the public. No one was the wiser. He was well schooled in the art of deception and politics. A few well-orchestrated photo ops' and private donations kept people on side. His speeches persistently spouted about reduced crime figures in the area and the difference he had made since being in post. These were verified by the police authority but if they had looked a little closer they may have discovered another story. Although the areas under Gabriel responsibility showed crime had reduced, the suburbs out his jurisdiction had increased. With the help of the sauna group they moved the problem for the better of them all. The drug addicts disappeared or moved out of area, which meant burglaries, other theft and public disturbance moved with them. The role worked for all interested parties.

Gabriel loved his role of Crime Commissioner; adored the voice it had given him. When he spoke, people listened and the circles he moved in as a commissioner provided opportunities to bolster his own businesses. Doors opened and the provision of extended liquor licences to business contacts eased his entry into the local Masonic lodge.

Gabriel was a confident character, perhaps viewed by some as arrogant, but he didn't care. The eighty-twenty rule of decision-making did not apply to him: things tended to swing towards one hundred per cent in his favour. There was little doubt that if you challenged his argument or point of view, you needed to have your heals dug in pretty deep to withstand his retaliatory volley of opinion.

It was time to get to work. He needed to login to his computer, check his calendar and his e mail. He hated this part of his day because he knew what he found had a huge potential for controlling his day. He loathed the hold the digital world had over him.

There is little doubt that the twentieth century moved technology on at a pace. The information superhighway swamped businesses with new media, particularly email systems, in the ceaseless drive for efficiency and accountability. Nevertheless, ask anyone who has worked in a large organisation or conglomerate, and they will tell you that managing a corporate mailbox is a thankless task. In the good old days of paper messages and faxes, you could always plead ignorance – 'I never received that message, sorry, could you send it again?' – but with the advent of email you had a duty to act. There was no escaping accountability. In society it is one thing to influence people verbally but to do so literally is another thing. It certainly was not a skill familiar to Gabriel. Good old-fashioned intimidation and bullying were his tried and tested methods for getting what he wanted.

He sat in front of his computer and sighed before finally powering on his PC. *Let's see what we've got*, he thought, little knowing that his inconspicuous action would set in motion an important sequence of events.

Gabriel's' secretary, Mary, came into the room with a cup of tea and placed it on his desk, 'Crikey, straight into your emails! You must be desperate,' she said, smiling

'Haha!' Gabriel grinned back, 'I'm an upstanding pillar of the community, don't you know!'

'Yeah of course you are,' Mary tittered.

Gabriel sat legs crossed, clicking through his emails as his secretary tidied about the office. She loved his presence and maturity. If there had been any chance of an affair, she would have grabbed it, but his focus was elsewhere. He might have felt the same towards her at one time, but he knew that a fling would cost him too much and so locked any such thoughts away.

He clicked his way down the list of emails. 'Boring, boring,' he sighed, trawling through the messages. Then something pricked his attention: a subject line that begged investigation: 'You Need to Know'.

Gabriel looked at the sender's name: *Crane, Sgt*. It was a police authority email address. He opened the email and started to read. Fascinated, he began to read faster, scrolling down the page. Mary looked up, noticing a change in his mood.

'Gabriel, are you OK?' she said. No answer. 'Gabriel?'

Gabriel stared at the desk, then back to the computer screen. 'No, it can't be,' he muttered.

'Gabriel, what is it, what's going on?' Mary asked.

Gabriel stood and started to move around erratically in front of the desk, casting a glance back to the computer screen. 'No, no, no, this was dealt with.'

'Gabriel . . . Mr Ambrose . . . you're scaring me. What is it?'

This startled him. He hadn't been called Mr Ambrose by his secretary in a long while. He answered,

'It's OK, it's OK, I've just got some work to do. If you could leave me for a moment, please.'

On leaving, Mary peered through the frosted glass of the office window. She could just make out Gabriel was sat at his desk with his head in his hands. This was unusual behaviour for him. He was a bit eccentric at times, a bit up and down but in all the time she had known him, he had not reacted like that. He looked like he had seen a ghost. Everyone was aware of his past, his loss and Mary wandered if a memory had prompted his response. Gabriel rose, made his way to his coat and pulled the white envelope from his pocket. He rubbed his finger on the inside of the open envelope to try and pick up the remnants inside. His finger showed a slight dusting of white powder. Moving out of sight of his secretary, he rubbed his finger across his gums and then licked them with his tongue. He recognised the bitter taste of the drug. It wasn't enough but it might help him, he needed something.

A couple of minutes later he had calmed, only slightly. Sat back at his desk he picked his phone and frantically created a text message.

'He is back!' He sent the message and waited.

***

Before the advent of mobile phones, it was the cry of a baby or a shout of alarm that roused our senses. Nowadays, it's the ringtone or constant ping that demands our instant attention. *Ping*! Another message alert had Edward Moffatt scrambling in his coat pocket, trying to locate his phone. *Got it! Now swipe, enter your pin . . . no that's not it! Try again . . . wait put my glasses on . . . try the pin code again.* At last, he was in. Edward read the text from his old friend Gabriel Ambrose. He was perplexed by it: *He's back!* Then another *ping*, and he read: *We did not succeed, blue eyes is back!*

To any other person, such cryptic messages would prompt further questions, but not Edward and Gabriel.

Edward had been strolling in the park, trying to make the most of a mild winter's morning. The text message from his friend had brought a sudden stop to his walk and he had sat down on a nearby bench to think through a myriad of possible consequences. He needed to compose himself and contact Gabriel. The pair often talked as friends, not conspirators but now they would have to discuss past deeds.

Edward's concentration was briefly interrupted by a passer bye. 'Hello, Dr Moffatt?' a young woman said.

Edward squinted up into the low-lying sun. Straining his eyes to see who had spoken.

'Yes . . . I'm sorry you but have me at a disadvantage,' he replied.

'Please, don't apologise. I wouldn't expect you to remember me, but you might remember the birth of my son in the surgery. I had only visited for an ear infection. My waters broke in the waiting room and then that was that. He came early and you delivered him in your consulting room,' the lady giggled.

‘Ah yes, I remember! How long ago was that? Are you both well?’ Edward asked politely.

‘We’re fine. You won’t believe it, but he’s eight now,’ she continued, ‘What about you, are you still working?’

A man of manners, Edward stood to continue the conversation. ‘No, I retired a year ago – taking it easy now.’

The lady stroked his arm and said warmly, ‘I don’t blame you – you deserve it. Enjoy the rest of the day, and thank you for all you did for me and my family.’ She gave a brief smile and disappeared along the frost-covered gravel path, her footsteps crunching as she walked away.

Edward watched her leave. He felt the warmth of gratitude envelope him. All in all, he had enjoyed his time has a GP. During his childhood, it was all he wanted to do and his ambition had been realised. He grew up with a vision of wanting to help people, becoming a doctor seemed the natural choice. He often believed he got this outlook from his parents. His mother was a nurse in the local hospital and his father a psychiatrist. Both had passed away now and he only had fond memories of them.

He would never forget their faces when he became a doctor. It wasn’t just their smiles; it’s how they looked at Edward and themselves. It was as though they had accomplished their task as parents, they had achieved their end goal for their son. Edward never forgot them. On their birthdays and Christmas, flowers or wreaths decorated their headstone. They had been buried together as they wished.

Edward was an only child but never felt lonely in his youth. He had plenty of cousins to play with and family occasions were always elaborate and involved him. His childhood had been beyond happy. He was nurtured by their parents to become what he was today. As a child all he saw was happiness in the world. It wasn’t until he became older that is parents introduced him to aspects of the darker side of life, preparing him for the real world. Edward’s father, Vincent, was all set to become a doctor in his own right until his father returned from the war. His father had been an officer in the Second World War. His battalion was one of the British regiments that landed on Sword Beach on D-Day. He survived, well physically he did. Mentally he returned a different man. Vincent later explained to a mature Edward, that before he went to war, his father was scared of nothing, a man who loved every second of life. He returned a man who only wanted to live in the shadows, scared to venture out anywhere. Seeing such a change in his father, forced Vincent's hand, he wanted to understand his father's behaviour, so he became a psychiatrist with a hope to help others potentially suffering the same fate.

Whilst Vincent had been on placement in a hospital he came across a beautiful young nurse, Mellissa, they courted and soon married. A few years later, Edward was born. They were so proud of their son, so proud.

As Edward reminisced, his phone pinged again. He was brought back to the present with a sudden bang. He didn't need to look at the text, he realised who it was from. Gazing at the phone screen, he was right, the sender was Gabriel. He did not open the message. He guessed it was related to the previous ones. *How proud would his parents be now, if they understood what he had done*, Edward reflected.

His attention was swiftly drawn back to the text. How on earth could the text message be right? It didn't make sense. They had to meet. Edward needed to speak to Gabriel to understand what had happened. He typed a short reply: *We need to talk.*

A few texts between them later and all other appointments for the day had been re-arranged. An urgent meeting in their favourite local coffee shop had been set up.

Edward was sitting in a large leather chair in the corner of the room when Gabriel arrived. The coffee shop was retro-themed and its hefty prices meant that it was always not busy. Both men liked the place's lack of custom as it meant they could have quiet and avoid having any delicate conversations overheard.

Gabriel looked flustered. Edward had noticed his behaviour had become more erratic lately but he was aware that his long term friend had been under increasing pressure. He realised how much Gabriel wanted to retain the Crime Commissioner's role and put it down to that.

After the normal cordial handshake Gabriel described the email's shocking details regarding murder victims and related evidence. Edward, for the most part, sat listening and quietly absorbing what he was being told as he stared into his oversized coffee mug. The chocolate sprinkle stains clung to the sides of his mug like mountain peaks cutting through clouds of frothy milk. Gabriel noticed his friend apparently captured in a trance.

'Edward are you listening, did you get that?' said Gabriel, testily.

Edward looked up. 'Yes, I did. Believe me I did. God, I thought we had dealt with this. I don't want to jump to conclusions Gabriel but these crimes are too similar. Have you replied to the sender – Sgt Crane, is it?'

'Yes, I've asked him to keep quiet while I investigate his concerns covertly, so I can find out what is actually going on.'

'Do you think he will go with that?'

Gabriel frowned. 'Not sure, I think he might. There are other avenues he could have followed before coming to me, so I can't see why not.'

Little did they know that Crane would not be the recipient of Gabriel's reply: Jim had set a filter to delete any email replies to Crane, so Crane's mailbox would never see the reply message. Crane would remain blissfully ignorant to it all. Jim and Charles did not underestimate the size of the task in hand. They grasped the fragility of the situation, they needed to proceed carefully and hope the plan worked. If Crane was the killer, when would he strike again and to who? Jim secretly held growing concerns and worries if poking the bear might lead to grave repercussions, particularly for Charles and Lizzie.

Back in the coffee shop, the sombre mood drowned out the faint sound of Christmas songs playing in the background. Bing Crosby was doing his best to wish everybody, *a merry little Christmas*. He was far off the mark with Gabriel and Edward.

Their concentration was interrupted. A young women with a homemade bauble head dress butted in, 'Excuse me gents, would you, take a photo of me and me mate.' Gabriel twisted to look at the women and then the phone. He really wanted to say, *piss off* but couldn't. It wasn't in his nature.

'OK sure, sorry we are a bit busy.'

'Aw thanks, me and me mate 'r on our works do. A bit lonely tho' only two on us.' Gabriel stood, took the woman's camera and shepherded the women together for the photo.

'Say cheese!' Click, click.

'There we go. I have taken two just in case.'

'Thank you, you're a star.' The woman then lent over and kissed Gabriel's cheek. Awkwardly, Gabriel moved away, 'That's ok.'

The woman left and Gabriel sat back down near Edward. Edward took a hander kerchief from his pocket and handed it to his friend.

'You might want that.' Gabriel looked at Edward puzzled. Edward pointed to Gabriel's cheek where a bright red coloured lipstick kiss was tattooed. Gabriel wiped it off, checking the hanky for smudges of cherry red until no more appeared on it.

'I'm surprised it's come off. She was classy. Her perfume reminded me of the first aftershave I received as a teenager. It was called, *MAN*, obviously from a market stall. The only hair I possessed when I was younger was under my lip. I shaved it off, applied my *MAN* aftershave liberally. I went to school looking like a red moustached Adolf Hitler for a month until my skin healed.'

Gabriel sniggered. Edward's shoulders juddered as he joined in the muted laughter. Gabriel leant forward, the heavily padded chair sighing as he did. He studied Edward and gently spoke, 'This young woman with her own unique aroma has made me realise something. We must get on with our lives. This morning neither of us were aware of the e mail. We have to make sure that from this point going forward we can forget about it once more.'

The brief interruption had been a light hearted distraction but it quickly disappeared as both men considered Gabriel's narrative. Edward regained his composure, looked at Gabriel and asked, 'So what do we do next?'

Gabriel swirled the last of his coffee around the sides of his cup and answered, 'We haven't much of an alternative. I have got to find out if a ghost from our past has returned to haunt us'. In his head, he pondered, *could this day have got any worse, bloody smoke alarm, you started it off.*

Edward watched Gabriel recognising the severity of the situation they were both potentially in. If the details contained in the e mail sent to Gabriel proved correct, Edward dared not contemplate the consequences.

Gabriel rested back in his chair, hung his head and began to recall painful memories he had chosen to lock away.

Porcelain

Thirty years earlier

Gabriel had set up his first recycling business at a time when local government and national policies were changing in response to the 'Green Vote', which had been gaining momentum. He had spotted a gap in the market for corporate scrap and waste recycling and within a year, he had become a millionaire. A luxury house, a few fast cars and one well-heeled wife later, he had become a happy man.

He had lobbied his long-term friend Edward to join him in his venture but Edward had been determined to follow up on his medical education and set up as a General Practitioner in their town.

Gabriel and Edward had known one another for a lifetime. They grew up together, friends at school, only parting briefly when they attended different colleges. Edward went to medical school, Gabriel studied engineering. But they still kept in touch regularly and once their formal educations came to an end, they naturally drifted back towards one another. They felt comfortable together and valued each's company.

Edward had been Gabriel's best man at his wedding, and godfather to his daughter, Tabitha, known as Tabby to her friends. Tabby was the sun in Gabriel's universe: everything revolved around her, and her warmth seemed to cast a light on even the most distant planet.

Tabby loved her uncle Edward. He was young at heart and Tabby talked openly to him about most things. The things that were not for parent's ears. Edward adored Tabby and along with his children, she became part of his extended family. Anyone who spent time in Gabriel's and Edwards company, realised that was always going to be the case.

Like most proud parents, Gabriel kept a video diary of all the happy events of his daughter's young life. Gabriel and his wife, Jessica, would often replay the tapes in front of Tabby, much to her embarrassment.

Today was special, it was Tabby's birthday. Gabriel returned home from work early, intent on surprising her. He and Jessica had arranged to go indoor bowling with their daughter and for a meal afterwards as a birthday treat. Tabby loved indoor bowling. She loved any family competition because Gabriel always made it fun.

Jessica greeted Gabriel with a welcoming smile, partially hidden by her finger pressed to her lips. She lowered her hand and whispered, 'Tabby's upstairs getting ready.' They both giggled like naughty schoolchildren. They loved family time and cherished the opportunity to be with their daughter. It was Tabby's seventeenth birthday, but in her parents' eyes she was still their little girl. Most parents would agree that although your children physically grow, they will always be infants in their eyes.

Gabriel called up the stairs, 'Tabby, I hope you're ready for a whooping! Get a move on and we'll get on our way.' There was no response.

'Tabby, I hope you're not catching five on duty!' Again, there was no answer. Gabriel climbed the stairs and opened Tabby's bedroom door. He could hear water running in her bathroom.

He knocked on the bathroom door. 'Tabby, hello, Tabby.' There was no sound, other than the running tap. 'Tabby, I'm coming in.'

Images can change your life, but what Gabriel saw next tattooed a picture on his very soul: Tabby lay naked in a half-filled bath of bloody water, her arms slashed with deep cut marks that ran up along her veins. The plug had been left out, allowing the water to drain away, but its path had been partially blocked by Tabby's flaccid leg. Gabriel saw, looking at his pale daughter, that there would be no need for an ambulance: she had passed. He reached over, turned off the tap and sank to his knees, too overwhelmed to cry. At the side of the bath was a note in Tabby's handwriting:

Sorry Dad, Sorry Mum.

I tried, I really tried but I could not live with the shame. I cannot be Tabitha any more, or your little girl. Please don't think badly of me.

Love Tabby XX

Gabriel, stared at the note; at his daughter's blueing face, and then he cried. He knew exactly what the note referred to but there was no time to think about that now. His body jolted as the bathroom door was pushed against him. It was Jessica. She tried to push the door open. 'Jess, stay where you are!' Gabriel shouted

'Gabby, what is it? Tabby are you OK?' Jessica cried out frantically. She shoved at the door harder and began to claw at it.

'Stop it Jess, please stop it,' Gabriel cried.

She backed away from the door, and braced herself against the bedroom wall, staring at the partly open bathroom door. Gabriel quickly got to his feet and squeezed out of the room trying to hide the awful sight of the bath from his wife. He grabbed Jessica and pulled her close to him. 'She's gone Jess: Tabby is gone.'

'Gone? What do you mean, gone? Tabby's gone? What do you mean, Gabby? My baby? Let me see!'

'No Jess, please.'

Jessica tried to shrug clear of Gabriel but he held her all the more tightly. He needed to hold on for both of them.

'Let me see my baby, Gabby!' Jessica screamed.

'Jess no . . . no.' The realisation slammed into Jessica like a speeding train. She looked into Gabriel's tear-filled eyes and went limp in his arms. Gabriel lowered her to the floor, gently cradling her head. 'I am sorry Jess,' he crooned softly.

***

Tabby was dead, leaving a void in Gabriel and Jessica's lives that could not be filled. The days seemed a lot longer and nights darker and colder for them both. Their hopes and aspirations had been tossed in the garbage, like yesterday's newspaper. The responsibility of being a parent hung heavier now, even more than when Tabby had been alive. In Gabriel's eyes, her death had forced him to question if he could have done more to prevent it. Why hadn't he seen that things had become too much for her? She'd seemed fine, even accepting of her situation. She'd received counselling and had managed to convince everyone that she was coping. Jessica had taken her to support sessions and Tabby had appeared as well as anyone could have expected, under the circumstances. She had said repeatedly that she had not been the first person to be raped and that she would not be the last. 'At least I'm still alive,' she'd said, but now . . .

Tabby's rape had fuelled in Gabriel an overpowering need for justice – not the kind administered in a courtroom by a judge, but old-fashioned revenge: the rapist, whoever it was, had to suffer.

Gabriel had seen the physical reminders of the rape, the bruises inflicted on his daughter heal and slowly disappear, but the psychological scars had remained etched in both his and Tabby's minds. He had tried to forget, to pack the images away, knowing that he was expected to be strong. He was the man of the family, after all. But Gabriel had started to feel fragile and vulnerable. The quiet times, when he was alone, had been the worst. Dark images would overwhelm him. He would put on the radio, the TV, anything, to serve as a distraction. But it never worked: any short period of solace was soon replaced by the memories of Tabby's injuries. She had been his baby; he had cradled her as a child. How could he live with the thought of her brutal violation? How had they managed to live with that thought? He knew the truth now: Tabitha hadn't managed at all.

The investigation into the rape had seemed as intrusive to the family as the actual crime. Empathy and sympathy had appeared in short supply. The questions from the police had infuriated Gabriel: Could Tabby have unintentionally incited the attack, they had asked? Tabby had answered all the questions with composure, her calmness arising more from being in a state of shock than through any conscious effort. Gabriel had felt nothing but rage and anger. Someone was out there who had dared to touch his daughter. His seemingly perfect life had been torn to pieces. All he had worked for in his life; his personal sacrifices to create his suburban Utopia – it had all gone. There had been nothing he could do and all his wealth had counted for nothing.

The investigation into the rape had progressed. The police had had a clear suspect: a vagrant who'd been sleeping near the college that Tabby had attended. The college had not been Tabby's first choice for her studies: Gabriel and Jessica had convinced her that the one closer to home was the better choice. They had come up with a case for her staying locally; she would still have their support if needed. Not that she needed any help. Tabby had always seemed a tough cookie and she had been a bit of tomboy in her youth. While her friends were playing with their dolls, Tabby would be in the park kicking a football with her father. Cut knees and scuffed arms had meant nothing to her. She had been a wipe-your-nose-on-your sleeve sort: definitely not a handkerchief carrier.

Reluctantly, Tabby had agreed to study at the local college. She could have argued a case to go further afield, to flee the nest, but she had hidden her desire for freedom, knowing how much her parents had invested in her, and not wanting to disappoint them.

Tabby had known the police's main suspect. She passed him regularly and had often given him any spare change she had while on her way to college. He had always seemed grateful, never rude and was appreciative of her charity. A witness had spotted him following Tabby on several occasions, including the day of the attack. Tabby had not noticed and had remained unaware of any threat.

Investigating the incident, the police had found a vital piece of evidence. When Tabby's clothes had been inspected, forensics had found a small piece of checked cloth that did not match any of her attire. It had been torn off something and had lodged in the shoulder of her dress. When the police questioned the vagrant, they had noticed that his gloves looked like they were made from the same material. This heightened their suspicions concerning the man's involvement with the rape.

Tests positively concluded the material was a match. Furthermore, under pressure his account of that day had been questionable. When asked directly about Tabby he had become agitated, particularly when asked about why he had followed her.

The authorities had believed they had enough to detain him for further questioning, hoping that he would crack while in custody, and he had been arrested.

This did not happen. The vagrant had an answer for everything put to him. He stuttered his answers at times but they were consistent. He always maintained he had not raped Tabby. This had intensified police suspicions, but there had not been enough evidence to prosecute him. In his defence, the vagrant said that he had seen a man on top of Tabby attacking her. He helped fight him off but ran scared as Tabby's attacker had fled.

She had been raped in an isolated alleyway and when asked why he had been there, he'd replied that he had been looking for food, scavenging. As absurd as this sound to the police, they understood that this was a regular act for a lot of the street dwellers. He remained steadfast in his account of what had happened with no deviation in his story. The police became more and more frustrated with their lack of progress.

Tabby's account of the attacker was also inconclusive. When interviewed, she explained to the police that she had not seen her assailant, as she had been knocked unconscious. When she had come round, her clothes had been ripped off and she knew she had been raped. Tabby was not a virgin but was not promiscuous; she only slept with partners she wanted.

Time ran out for the police, they had to let the vagrant go. Eventually, he was released. Did the police believe he was innocent? It didn't matter: they couldn't prove it either way.

Following Tabby's death, the lack of a conclusion to her rape fuelled Gabriel's anxiety further. He needed an answer and someone had to pay for his daughter's death. Someone had to be held to account: you don't get to snuff out the candle flame without getting burned, he had reasoned.

***

Tabby's funeral was delayed because of the need for an autopsy. Gabriel and Jessica fudged their way through life meantime. Edward visited regularly, listening and offering advice where he could and when he felt comfortable to do so. They all found small talk was not so small when bigger, scarier topics needed airing. Edward had been unsure of how best he could support his friend. He had been Tabby's godfather but had been confused as to what that role had meant. In the end, he'd had the distinct feeling that he had failed.

The day of the funeral arrived. Tabby was finally laid to rest amid many tears. The vicar stood at the pulpit and spoke with clarity and authority. Gabriel and Jessica sat at the front of the church, an arm's length from their daughter's coffin. Gabriel resisted placing his hand on the casket's side, to see if he could feel warmth or movement from within. He clenched Jessica's hand within his and could feel her trembling palm. 'You OK?' he asked. His wife just nodded unconvincingly. Edward tried to comfort Jessica too as he sat at her side, but he was also in a daze. As a GP Edward had plenty of experience of death, but nothing could have prepared him for this loss and he tried to hide his anguish by thumbing through the hymn book.

The vicar tried to deliver a sermon that celebrated Tabby's life but the mourners' attentions were focused elsewhere. A hundred pairs of eyes seemed to watch Gabriel and his wife intently, questioning what would they have done if faced with the same situation. The service finished. Gabriel and Jessica led the procession of mourners from the church, the clicking of shoes on the flagstone floor echoing around them as they exited.

Gabriel, Jessica, and Edward drifted through the rest of the day in a trance-like state and found themselves huddled together at the wake, cups and saucers in hands, watching the funeral guests pick their way through the buffet. Occasionally, friends came over to shake their hands and to sympathise over their loss. Jessica thanked them but Gabriel recoiled at the word *loss*. In his mind he had not *lost* anyone: Tabby had been *taken* from him. He wanted to reach out to everyone and shout, 'Come on! Let's form a posse! Let's get the bastard who raped my daughter!' But he kept his peace. He was still the man of the family and had an image to maintain. Edward watched his friend as he chatted to some of the guests, always keeping an eye out for his life-long wingman. Noticing Gabriel's change of demeanour, he made his way over to him. Edward grabbed Gabriel's hand and he started as if woken from a deep sleep. He gazed at Edward.

'You looked miles away their Gabriel,' Edward said softly.

Gabriel forced a smile, 'Just thinking.'

Edward placed a hand on his friend's shoulder. 'I don't think today is a day for thinking my friend. It's about remembering.'

'No Edward, it's not. You see I am thinking that I am going to find the bastard that raped my daughter and when I do I will kill him. I will force open his eyes and let him see my pain. I haven't got time to remember anymore.'

Gabriel turned away from his friend and returned to Jessica's side, sat next to her and placed his arm around her shoulder. Only then did he look back at his ever-watchful friend.

When the black-coated mourners left the building, Gabriel watched the caterers as they cleared away the crockery and emptied the waste bins full of tear-stained handkerchiefs and paper plates. The hum of muted conversation had been replaced by the sound of brushes sweeping across the floor. Life had started again. Normality had already begun to replace the sorrow of the day. Gabriel envied the departing guests. He wanted to follow them, go home with them, turn on the TV and forget.

As they left, Gabriel looked at his exhausted wife. He had been blind to her emotions during the whole episode and felt ashamed. Putting her coat over her shoulders, he found he could not to talk to her. He felt broken and cracked, like a china doll knocked from its shelf. It felt as if his whole body was made of porcelain, not flesh.

Alone with Jessica in the house, he noticed that it was no longer a home. He watched as his wife poured herself a glass of Merlot and walked to the lounge. He heard the click of the TV and then the sound of conversations from the set. Gabriel remained in the kitchen. He looked down at his shoes: black brogues. He'd bought them for that day. Carefully, he took them off. He opened the back door and made his way to the shed. He picked up a spade and started to dig a hole in the garden. His stockinged feet felt cold but he ignored them. He placed his shoes in the freshly dug whole and filled it in. Finally, he tapped down the mounded earth with his hands and begun to sob. The day was over.

***

Gabriel returned to work soon after Tabby's funeral. The distraction of business helped to dilute his grief. Months passed, but his daughter's absence weighed heavily upon him, as did the manner of her death. The textbooks said to talk and work through it all, but the circumstances of her death made Gabriel wonder how to proceed: how would he ever be able to grieve?

Besides, a conversation needed at least two people and Gabriel and Jessica would sooner avoid each other than face talking about their daughter's death. *Time is the great healer, wasn't that the great fable*? Gabriel thought. He wondered if the author of that phrase had ever been in need of healing himself. Gabriel felt like a fraud and was consumed by guilt, like a hospice visitor embarrassed at being able to walk away and leave the pain behind.

For Gabriel and Jessica, life had taken a nosedive into despair. Neither had any idea how to handle their daughter's death. There was no *today* any more, only memories of the past. Life's vital current had slowed to a trickle.

One day, sometime later, a man in his late teens arrived at Gabriel's office, asking to speak to him about Tabby. Gabriel, intrigued, promptly met the visitor. The young man was well dressed, unassuming, nothing out of the ordinary.

'Hello Mr Ambrose, my name is Josh Temple, I am sorry to disturb you,' said the visitor as he entered the office and sat down.

'I studied at the same college as Tabby. I attended some lectures with her. I am so sorry for your loss. I can't imagine how you must feel.'

'Thank you,' Gabriel replied, surveying his visitor. His words struck a chord with Gabriel and he welcomed the opportunity to talk about his daughter again. He had tried to consume himself with work but Tabby's death was never far from his thoughts. Sometimes, he felt ashamed and embarrassed if he caught himself not remembering his daughter. Josh's introduction was a gentle reminder of his loss and in an absurd way, he welcomed that. Gabriel, distracted momentarily by Josh's vivid blue eyes and their piercing gaze, recovered himself and asked, 'You say you studied with Tabby?'

'Yes sir, we were not on the same course but we frequently shared lectures. That's how we met. Tabby was wonderful; so kind and caring. We were quite close. I wouldn't say boyfriend, girlfriend close. I could have only wished for that. She was a beautiful woman inside and outside.'

Gabriel sat back in his chair and smiled. *That was my Tabby.* They reminisced about Tabby, though mainly it was Gabriel who talked, while Josh listened. Josh did not judge, nor did he appear uncomfortable: quite the opposite, he seemed to enjoy the time spent with the older man.

After a brief lull in the conversation, Josh fixed Gabriel with his blue eyes once more. 'Mr Ambrose, I'm not going to lie: I came here for a reason. I need your help.' Gabriel, jolted out of a comforting reminiscence, replied stiffly.

'What sort of help?' He felt betrayed. Had Josh come to gain his trust and then ask for money?

'What I am going to ask, Mr Ambrose, is not something I do lightly and I have given it a lot of thought. It has to stop.'

'What has to stop?'

Josh explained his request, 'Tabby talked to me a lot about her ordeal. She told me details of what happened. It was cruel, vicious, a violation. I have no idea why she confided in me? I was pleased in a way she did. Listening to her it was obvious that she craved for someone to talk to. An outsider, who she could trust and would not judge.'

Josh peered up at Gabriel, hoping he hadn't offended him. Gabriel sat quiet, eager to hear more from Josh. 'This is more difficult to tell you Mr Ambrose. I am sorry but it needs to be said. I know quite a few people at college. We often meet in small groups, talk about our woes and who's seeing who, the regular teen stuff. I hate to say this but Tabby and what happened to her, was the hot topic for a while.'

'Everyone knew I was helping Tabby. They saw us together often enough. Then a friend suggested I speak to a couple of fellow students. I asked why? I was told, they would explain. So I found them out.' Josh stopped temporarily. Coughed uncomfortably, and started talking again, 'The two told me they had also been raped. These two people, a man and a woman both said it had been the same person. It resembled the same person Tabby had described to me.' Gabriel spun his chair towards Josh, 'You said Tabby described the attacker to you.'

'Yes Mr Ambrose,'

'But she didn't tell me. She told the police she didn't see the attacker.'

'She was scared of the outcome if she told anyone Mr Ambrose. She told me she wanted to forget the whole thing, move forward. If she had told more people, then she worried the whole thing would have dragged on. Tabby didn't want her ordeal made even more public. I understood Mr Ambrose. The other two people told me exactly the same. They said although they would always have to live with the tag of *raped*, the less people that were aware the better. It meant there were fewer people to forget it ever happened. How could I question what they said Mr Ambrose? I couldn't comment. It hadn't happened to me.'

Josh ceased, his lip quivered, 'I have a huge regret Mr Ambrose. I will take it to my grave. Had I acted earlier, perhaps Tabby would still be alive.' Josh said, wiping away tears.

Gabriel recognised the pain in Josh's voice and thought how it mirrored his own emotions. 'Josh, there is no need to blame yourself. I have questioned my part in the whole thing many times and probably always will until the day I die, but I understand it will not change anything now.'

'We can't change the past, Mr Ambrose, but what about the future? What about any future victims? Don't we both owe it to Tabby? We cannot fail again.'

'Future victims, what do you mean Josh?' Gabriel had listened to his rhetoric but not contemplated any other victim. He was consumed by his own situation.

'These people confided in me. Your Tabby confided in me. I didn't ask them to but I don't want to talk to anymore. I have to close the conversation.'

Gabriel understood what he meant. Josh wanted an end to it all.

As Josh talked, Gabriel focused on a photo of Tabby on his desk. Fuelled by anger but tempered by pity for the young man, Gabriel asked, 'What help would you need from me?' At that moment Gabriel saw a change in the blue eyes: a new glint of steel.

'He's got to be stopped,' said Josh.

'Stopped: that's easier said than done. How? Without the other victims coming forward, the police wouldn't have a case. Believe me I know; I know how hard it would be to get him to trial.' Gabriel replied, remembering his own recent experiences with the law.

'It has to be us.'

'Us Josh. What do you mean us?'

'Me and you Mr Ambrose. We have got to act. We can't let this be repeated. We owe it to Tabby and the others. I assure you Mr Ambrose I am determined to see this through. If needed I will do it on my own.'

Gabriel, shocked, interrupted the young man. 'What, exactly are we to do? You keep saying do something. What Josh?'

'I'll kill him,' Josh replied calmly. 'For my friends. To avenge Tabby's death and to save any future victims.'

Boom, just like an atomic bomb exploding. The shockwaves from Josh's reply seemed to shudder around the room.

'Kill him? Really Josh, you are deluded. You need help. You can't just kill someone; take someone's life. You are asking me to commit a murder!'

'I have one question for you, Mr Ambrose. What is your idea of murder? In my opinion, killing an innocent is murder. I am asking you to help me kill someone who is guilty of your daughter's death. Our Tabby's death.'

Gabriel then spent time trying to dissuade Josh from doing anything rash, but finally agreed to think things through. He hoped it would at least give him some head room. 'Can you come back in a few days,' he said. Josh agreed. The young man left without another word.

Alone in his empty office Gabriel deliberated upon their conversation. What had just occurred? He had been asked to help commit a murder. He had no intention of executing such a plan but what about Tabby, his poor Tabby. He never wanted another parent to experience what he had. He realised his next step, he needed to seek advice from Edward.

Gabriel met Edward later that day and told him everything concerning his impromptu meeting with Josh. They agreed that the suggestion of committing a murder was ludicrous, deciding instead that Gabriel would talk Josh out of the idea and see if they could persuade one or both of the witnesses Josh had revealed to come forward.

It was evening when Gabriel returned home. He did not have to ring to say he was going to be late: family dinners had passed with Tabby. As he walked into the living room, he saw Jessica sitting in her usual armchair staring at the TV, a glass of red from a half-empty bottle perched at her side. Josh's words – 'future victims' – were echoing in his head and Gabriel wondered how many more victims there might be. If there were more victims to come then there would be more people grieving. He did not want that. Josh had set a seed within Gabriel. However immoral and illegal that seed was, it had settled in. Out of tiny acorns great oak trees grow.

Gabriel met Josh several more times at his office, but the outcome was far from satisfactory. Josh explained at length that the other victims would never come forward. They had too much to lose. It was easier for them to keep that skeleton in the cupboard. As a result, Josh's argument for removal of the vagrant became more compelling. Then Josh announced that he was going to do it alone. He had decided that he had to. To Gabriel's own astonishment he found he had become interested in the plan. Josh explained how he had tracked down the vagrant, found a place for the deed to take place and had even fabricated a story to lure him there. He was determined to follow it through. Finally, Josh told Gabriel that if he would not help, that would be the last time that they would meet. Josh then asked Gabriel not to think badly of him.

Gabriel felt caught between a rock and a hard place. Was committing murder the only way to get justice for his daughter's death? For a while, he struggled with the situation. The voice of reason argued strongly against any plan for retribution, but the pain of the loss of his daughter gagged it.

Gabriel awaited Josh in his office. He had wrestled to a conclusion and had decided he would not let Josh act on his own. As Josh entered the room, Gabriel spoke, 'Josh please don't sit down, I have to tell you something.' Josh stopped in his tracks. 'I won't let you do this on your own.'

Josh smiled in a way that suggested he realised all along that this would be the outcome. 'It might seem wrong now, but I do not believe we should be judged by anyone. This *thing*; this so-called man, this destroyer of lives, should not grace our world any longer.'

'We will do it for Tabby Mr Ambrose.' The two shook hands. Josh left smiling. Content he had an accomplice.

Gabriel's feelings danced about: he felt excited, invigorated but also scared. He felt scared of being caught, of being held responsible for murder, but there was a new consideration. He now felt scared of Josh. He started to wonder, as he gazed at the blue-eyed young man chatting away in front of him, just what Josh was capable of.

After agreeing to Josh's plan, time became meaningless to Gabriel. He almost looked forward to the deed. Josh's plan, the plan, was cold and methodical; designed to achieve a purpose without sentiment or concern, just like a general asking 'the boys' to go over the top one last time. Gabriel shuddered at Josh's complete lack of empathy for his intended victim, but revenge was foremost in his mind from that point onwards.

The evening of the planned execution arrived and Gabriel met Josh at the agreed place. Josh had done his homework. He had met and convinced the vagrant to sleep in an alley he had already ensured was fit for purpose. Josh had explained to the vagrant that he knew of a safe, warmer and out-of-the-way place he could use.

Gabriel had spent the day in an ethical stupor. He felt like a voyeur. There was no doubt in his mind that Josh was chauffeuring him. However wrong it all seemed to him, however illegal the act would be, he could not shake the image of his dead daughter from his mind. He wanted revenge for her death.

As the hour grew closer, so Gabriel's enthusiasm for the task waned. Perhaps, he thought, he might take one last shot at dissuading Josh. Could *he* talk to the other rape victims about coming forward to the police? That might work, he thought. At the appointed time, Gabriel left his office wanting a truce, a postponement.

Gabriel felt sick as he arrived at the designated spot and time. He entered the alley and heard a noise from behind a large refuse container. The bin shuddered and moved as if something was trapped inside. Gabriel peered around it to see Josh dragging a man along the floor by a tourniquet wrapped around his neck. The noise of clothing being tugged and pulled filled the air. The man's legs kicked out and his fingers clawed at his assailant's grip. His boot heals rubbed against the cold floor, skidding due to the lack of grip. The two twisted side to side. Josh remained steadfast with his task. He used his weight to force the vagrant to one side to reduce his struggle.

Josh looked up at Gabriel and hissed, 'Grab his legs!'

Gabriel stood looking in shock at what was unfolding. Josh gritted his teeth and blew air out of his cheeks repeatedly while maintaining his grip on the vagrant. He shouted again. 'Gabriel, think of Tabby. Think of our Tabby.'

Gabriel complied automatically and pulled the man's writhing limbs towards his chest. The man's body twisted and turned, while Gabriel held on and thought of his daughter. He pulled him tighter towards him, Gabriel recalling the past to summon the conviction to continue. He remembered finding his daughter in the bathroom and reading the note she'd left behind. Gabriel had no intention of letting go of the vagrant or his daughter's memory. The man's struggling weakened, until there was no need for Gabriel's assistance any more. He looked up at Josh, who was still pulling the strap tightly around the victim's neck. He would never forget Josh's steely-blue expression at that moment: devoid of emotion, he seemed more mechanical than human.

As he held the vagrant's limp and lifeless body, Josh said, 'It's over now. Let me finish up.'

Gabriel did not object: he moved away from the dead body, backing away until his back rested against one of the large refuse containers in the alley. He rubbed his hands up and down his chest, trying to wipe away the deed. What did Josh mean by *finish up*? Nothing meant anything anymore: he had helped commit a murder. He watched in disbelief as Josh began to create a macabre work of art. Josh sat the man upright, holding his limp head in his hands, he slashed each corner of his mouth into an exaggerated smile. Blood oozed from the freshly opened wound. Josh stood back slightly, scrutinising the victims head with the detail of a sculptor.

'Hmm, that looks even,' He uttered. Josh then reached into his pocket, pulled out a staple gun and pressed it across the freshly opened wounds on the man's face. Gabriel choked at the perfectly crafted smile Josh had created.

'God almighty, what is he doing?' As Josh worked on his grotesque creation he sang quietly, 'Smile, though your heart is breaking, smile even though it's aching . . .'

'Enough!' Gabriel grabbed Josh but the young man just brushed himself down. 'It's all done now,' he said, as he walked away calmly from the body, Gabriel following behind. At the front of the alley, Josh turned to face Gabriel and held out his hand. Gabriel refused it, shaking his head. Josh shrugged his shoulders and walked away. Gabriel wanted to run after him and ask what was that? What was that all about? Gabriel looked back to the scene of the attack: everything looked just the same, but for Gabriel a tare had appeared in the universe. He watched Josh disappear into the distance, trying to come to terms with what had happened but still in a state of shock. Then he left quickly, as the gravity of their deed started to sink in.

Back home, he passed his wife in the living room with her bottle of Merlot. He removed his clothing and placed it in a bag then showered and scrubbed his hands. To hide any evidence, he decided to burn his clothes the next day in his workshop wood burner. He'd seen such a tactic played out in many a crime show on TV. He hid the bag containing his clothes in his wardrobe. The crumpled shirt had been a birthday present from his wife and before Tabby's suicide she would have noticed if it had gone missing. Gabriel's wife had always bought carefully considered presents but after Tabby's death she preferred drinking wine.

As Gabriel stuffed his jacket into a bag, he recognised the logo. It had been a Christmas present from Tabby and had been Gabriel's favourite brand. She'd have saved hard to be able to afford it. As he shoved the jacket into the bulging bag he began to feel his actions were justified.

Weeks passed without any news on the murder at all. The media remained as quiet on that subject as the proverbial mouse. And there was no word from Josh. He had no visits from his partner in crime.

Gabriel hadn't been sleeping well, but then he'd not been sleeping well since Tabby's death anyway. His time on the planet was edging further towards a difficult phase. His latest adventure certainly did not help. He questioned his involvement with the murder, what had he done? He'd decided not to tell Edward. Even though Edward was his trusted friend, it wasn't really the sort of thing you brought up in conversation. How could he tell him?

Gabriel's part in the murder continued to leave its mark: In quiet moments, he remembered the victim's kicking legs as he'd pulled them to his chest. He continued to try to justify the killing. It had not been a murder but a sacrifice to save others, hadn't it? He wondered at the ability to manipulate one's own version of events to justify the outcome.

Gabriel became more and more anxious. This wasn't right. What he done, it wasn't right at all. He had to talk to someone; not to confess, but for release. He desperately wanted a graveside to sit beside. For someone to hear his part in the story and not respond. And where was Josh? His absence and his involvement in the execution of the murder were far from right. It was ghoulish. The sort of thing you might watch in a modern horror movie. Gabriel decided to try to find Josh. He needed to confide in someone. But how to find him?

He thought a stealthy approach would work. He remembered that Josh had said he attended some of Tabby's classes, he spent a lot of time with her. Gabriel had kept hold of a few phone numbers for Tabby's college friends after the funeral. A couple of calls and a few white lies later, he had arranged to meet a couple of them, claiming he wanted to dedicate something in Tabby's memory and needed ideas. They met in a coffee shop. Tabby's friends all arrived. Gabriel greeted them, bought coffees, 'We are so sorry Mr Ambrose. Tabby was wonderful,' they said in unison. Gabriel wondered if they had practised the speech outside but then calmed his cynicism. They talked, they all shared their sorrow at Tabby's passing. Her loss had left a bitter taste for them all. An uncomfortable silence settled and Gabriel noticed his guests' twitchy discomfort. He manoeuvred the conversation to his agenda: finding Josh. After a few covert questions to focus the girls' thoughts, Gabriel asked, 'I recently met another student who knew Tabby. A young man who was at college with you all, he said he was close to Tabby, his name is Josh.' The girls looked confused. Their replies rattled him like stones in a can rolling down the street: 'Sorry, we have never heard of him.'
Gabriel described Josh to them, but not even the steely-blue eyes were recognised. Nothing prompted a response. What was going on, Gabriel wondered? He ended the meeting soon after, his mind already elsewhere.

Gabriel's curiosity was now moving towards anger. What was Josh's role in all of this? Whatever it was, he had become part of it and he needed to find Josh. But to uncover the truth about Josh, his investigation needed to be subtle, to avoid drawing attention to their deadly pact.

He found Josh more by luck than judgement. Gabriel remembered that security cameras would have filmed Josh's first visit to his office, so he examined the historic CCTV. He watched Josh arrive and spotted that he had been on a motor scooter with corporate branding. The advertising was for a local takeaway, its name labelled on the rear pannier. Gabriel found the business address online and decided to visit the takeaway.

The takeaway sat in nest of other shops. As he approached Gabriel peered inside. There were a few customers stood at the counter. One was being served, the other waiting in line. Manoeuvring for a better view, Gabriel spotted Josh was serving. Gabriel moved away from the shop front temporarily, gathering himself. He hadn't seen Josh since the murder and struggled to picture him performing anything normal, particularly after he watched him mutilate the vagrant. Plucking up courage, Gabriel entered the takeaway. Josh reaction was alarming. He acted as though spotting an old friend. Whispering to a colleague to be excused, he beckoned Gabriel over to a table and they sat opposite each other. Smiling, Josh said, 'Mr Ambrose, it's great to see you again. How have you been?'

'As well as can be expected, I haven't seen you for a while. You don't come and visit me anymore.'

'I've been busy Mr Ambrose. Lots of tidying up to do.'

The words took Gabriel back to the scene of the murder.

Small talk between them soon subsided. Forced along by Gabriel, the conversation's focus turned, he wanted answers and no bullshit this time. Gabriel was tired of being played. 'Who are you Josh? How did you know my Tabby?'

Josh leaned across the table and looked deep into Gabriel's eyes. 'The fact that you're here leads me to be believe that you have been doing a bit of detective work. I'll tell you the truth. I never met Tabby in my life.'

It was then that the perversity of Josh's intent became apparent. Josh spoke to Gabriel at length. He explained how he'd never had any real information about the vagrant's involvement in Tabby's death; he'd just read that a vagrant had been mentioned in the papers. The man they killed might not have even been the man the police interviewed. He just picked him at random and had made up the story of the other rapes to promote the murderous act. Josh had read about Tabby's death in the local paper and suspected that Gabriel might be seeking revenge. Gabriel listened, his stomach turned over as he interrogated himself as to how he had been so easily duped. Josh leant across the table to grab Gabriel's hand. Gabriel pulled his hand away, 'What are you doing?' he belched.

'I'm sorry Mr Ambrose. For using Tabby's death, I had to have an accomplice for our little escapade. It would have been lonely doing it by myself,' he smiled. Gabriel felt the nausea rising as he realised that Josh was a deranged psychopath. He got up and left, leaving a smiling Josh behind. As he exited he glanced over his shoulder and saw Josh staring back at him, his head twisting from side to side. Gabriel felt his whole body twist with guilt. Josh returned back to the counter. His colleague asked, 'You OK mate?'

'Yes thank you. You know what it's like when you have to end a relationship.'

'Oh, err, OK.'

Gabriel tried to come to terms with the sense of isolation as he walked home: the loss of life, the loss of dignity, all parcelled together with the loss of morality. How could he resolve such a situation? Confession and suicide were not considered options. He understood if he did that a torrent of undeserved attention towards his remaining family might follow. Gabriel decided to speak to Edward. He had not wanted to get him involved but the situation now left him little choice.

Edward was working as a GP locally. It had always been Edwards's intention to practice where he had grown up. He loved it there and wanted to give something back to the community. Reluctantly, Gabriel called to his house the same evening. He told the story to Edward, warts and all. Edward sat and listened, but he wanted to press his hands to ears. He craved temporary deafness. Edward knew what he had just heard carried huge consequences.

'Gabriel, how could you?'

Gabriel held his head in his hands and mumbled, 'I don't know Edward. The world is so much darker since Tabby died. I struggle to see through the darkness. There is no light any more to guide me. I am so lost.'

Edward had been Gabriel's best friend forever, but now he felt betrayed. His felt sick to the core, nauseous. How could Gabriel have done it? His friend had committed a murder. There was no hiding the fact Gabriel had become a different person, someone he no longer knew or recognised. The correct response would have been for Edward to report him to the police. But how could he do that to his best friend, a man consumed by grief? And he could never forget the fact that he had been Tabby's failed godfather.

The pair remained trapped in their private dilemmas for a while, running scenarios through in their heads as they tried to engineer a way out of the situation. Then Edward arrived at the only option that was open to them, 'Gabriel, we need to act and quickly. We need to remove Josh from the picture permanently.'

'Remove Josh, what do you mean Edward?'

'We have to kill him.'

'Edward I am telling you, this is wrong, we can't. I can't again. Not again.'

'You can't again. You shouldn't have done it in the first place. Tell me Gabriel, what's your idea? This Josh, whoever he his, is a psychopath anyway. He is not normal. What you did is not normal.'

Gabriel pulled at the shirt around his chest, blowing rapidly. Edward watched his friend, 'Gabriel we have no alternative. You have no alternative.' Gabriel burst into tears, Edward comforted him.

The two talked on and off for the next couple of days. Edward became increasingly worried about Gabriel's state of mind: he seemed ready to give himself up, believing there was no way out of his involvement in the murder. So Edward took the driving seat and came up with a plan. There was no doubt there had to be another murder or, as Gabriel and Edward conspired to label it, *a mercy killing.*

The details of the plan soon became a reality. Gabriel met Josh again and managed to persuade him to meet out of work under the guise of wanting to understand why Josh had acted as he did. Without hesitation Josh agreed, buoyed by the attention and keen to impart his point of view, and totally ignorant of the murderous redress that lay in wait for him. Gabriel picked Josh up in his car, a short distance away from the takeaway. He drove to a quiet lane and they started to talk.

'It is nice to talk again Mr Ambrose. I didn't know if we would meet again. I miss our chats. How you talk about Tabby, I think I would have liked her a lot. We could have been friends.'

Gabriel kept his peace. Josh's twisted words just confirmed what he needed to do.

'A friend to my Tabby? You sick, murdering psychopath,' he thought.

Josh continued, 'I liked our evening out together. Perhaps we could do it again sometime. I didn't wash my hands for hours after. I could still smell our friend upon them. His sweat, it was like the most fragrant cologne to me. Hmm, happy days indeed.'

Gabriel allowed Josh to spew his rhetoric, though he wanted to vomit as he listened.

The next part of the plan came to the fore. Gabriel offered Josh a coffee. It was laced with a sleeping draft Edward had made. The drug didn't take long to work and Josh passed out. Gabriel drove further along the lane where an expectant Edward was waiting. He had no feeling other than malice for the man tethered by a seat belt at his side. Josh's unconscious body lolling around in the passenger seat as the car rolled on.

The execution of Edward's plan was as prescribed and as deliberate as the murder of the vagrant. Gabriel drove the car to a quiet pull in off the beaten track. Edward injected a lethal dose of cocaine into Josh's arm. The narcotic had come into his possession via a colleague who had asked him to dispose of it to avoid professional reprisals. He had decided to keep it, and had placed it in his own version of Pandora's Box, never believing it would be used as it was now. Edward struggled to find a suitable vein through his quivering, gloved hands. Eventually he hit a blood vessel and they both watched Josh as the drug coursed through his blood stream. The conspirators then drove to a chosen site, where Josh's flaccid body would be dumped. The site was one of the refuse centres Gabriel owned. He had carefully chosen it. It was one of his newer acquisitions and had a distinct lack of security and monitoring.

They both covered their clothing with disposable overalls before getting rid of Josh's body, to minimise any incriminating evidence that might lead back to them. The site was barren. Piles of refuse mound about them. As the pair carried Josh through the rubbish, the vile smell of decaying refuse rose up around them.

'This will do,' Gabriel said, as they stumbled for footing. Refuse moving under their weight. The rubbish had formed a hole and piles of paper banked its side. Josh was tossed in and the couple covered him with other refuse. Gabriel realised the site would be compacted in the next few days, committing Josh's body to the trash. There was no formal grave for this man, just an overcoat of yesterday's possessions and the distant serenade of disturbed seagulls. Gabriel thought that the absurdity of a sea bird on a refuse tip was amplified by the arrival of a corpse without a coffin.

The drive home was quiet. Both men heady with what they had just done. It had started snowing making the journey slower. They didn't want stopping by the police so they kept to the speed limit. The Christmas season meant more officers were on the road to catch drunk drivers. They had already de-robed, their overalls wrapped up, in bags in the car boot. Edward was disposing of them. He would place them in the incineration bin at work. There would be no chance of discovery and it wasn't unusual to be used for a non-business purpose. All his colleagues did.

Days later the men hardly talked to one another. Gabriel drove by the takeaway but there was no sign that Josh had been missed, apart from a 'staff wanted' poster in the window. There was nothing on the news, either, about a body being discovered. The status quo of the world remained the same. It was as if nothing had happened. From that moment, Gabriel and Edward were two men bound by more than friendship.

Allies & Conversations

The Present

Edward had been analysing their current situation. How could Josh be back? They both recognised the gravity of what they had done. The memory of the murder had been buried away but now it was headline news for them again. Edward rang Gabriel, 'Have you any ideas what we do now? How we approach this? We are older and have more to lose.'

Gabriel, paused on the other end of the phone and replied, 'I have thought of nothing else. I feel we are trapped in a corner. How does the killer know exactly what Josh did to the vagrant's body? Does the killer know what we did to Josh? Josh couldn't be alive? We know that, don't we? Could he have had an accomplice that we didn't know about?'

Edward said firmly, 'Josh is dead. The drug I gave him would have killed him. His body was never found because the refuse tip was filled in. I think that sick individual had a helper. Someone he didn't tell you about, but why would that person resurface now?'

Gabriel ran his hands through his hair. 'I think we are asking the wrong questions. We need to try and bring whomever it is out in the open. Then we can make a decision. I am not visiting the officer, I think that wouldn't work at this point and he wouldn't thank me for it. Exposing him for his what he has done. I'll visit the location where the victims came from – the old car park where the homeless live. Try and find out about the victims. It will be easy for me to ask questions. After all, I am the Crime Commissioner – I can say what I want if it ensures that the people there are safe and feel assured in their community.'

Edward answered. 'That might work, tread carefully Gabriel. We have no idea who this person is or what they are capable of. The one thing we do know is they are a killer. I am not thinking of ourselves, we have our families to think about.'

‘I will Edward. Let me see what I can find out. I’ll be in touch.’

Gabriel racked his brain for a solution. He didn’t tell Edward he had other things to consider, namely, the Crime Commissioner role. This could not have come at a worse time, not that this would be convenient at any other time. The whole thing had to be kept quiet; nothing had to get out about the e-mail from Crane and its potential consequence. His reputation had to remain intact and what about the sauna group? He dared not even consider how they might react.

Stumbling around, Gabriel then had an idea that might work, it could clear all this up. Walking about his room, he started to speak out aloud to himself, ‘What if he found the killer first, without the police? Then I could remove the problem. *That would work*. That could be the only way to clear all this sorry mess up.’

Gabriel nodded, accepting his own plan he had conjured up. He started to talk again, ‘How would I get this person removed if I found them though. Got it! The sauna gang, Paddy, I need a quiet word. I’ll make up a story to convince him. I could do with a little pick me up to help me anyway.’

The second weekly meeting of the group was tomorrow. Gabriel decided to go their first before visiting the old car park.

The following morning Gabriel arrived early to the James Leisure Complex. He could have been there from the early hours for what sleep he had managed to get. He said his good morning’s to the receptionists and stood in the sauna area, gowned up, waiting for the others. Paddy was usually the first to go into the room, he checked it, made sure *it was clean* he would say. Clean in Paddy’s world did not mean scrubbed within an inch of its life, or so sparkly you could see your face in it. It meant no bugs or people listening in. The group were business men remember, not gangsters, yeah right, Gabriel pondered.

True to form, Paddy entered, ‘Mr Ambrose, you’re early. You after making some brownie points up?’

Laughing, Gabriel replied, ‘You’re right Paddy. I don’t want another black mark against my name for being late.’

'You're OK Mr Ambrose, they like you, I like you. You're a good man Mr Ambrose.'

'Thank you Paddy.' Gabriel stopped, debating how best to broker his intentions to his friend. There wasn't time to faff about. The others would be there shortly.

'Paddy, I have a problem.'

'Really Mr Ambrose, what's that? Can Paddy help?'

'You can but it has to remain between us two. I need someone getting rid of, permanently.'

'Are they causing a problem Mr Ambrose?'

'They have been threatening my wife Paddy. I can't do anything or I'll end up in trouble. This man he has a reputation, for doing these things,'

'Should I have a word with him Mr Ambrose? I can be very persuasive.'

'I think it's beyond that Paddy,'

'You let me know Mr Ambrose. I am sure I can help.'

Gabriel patted him on the shoulder. He wanted to hug him but Paddy wasn't a hugger. If he hugged you, you probably wouldn't recover.

'Can we keep this between us Paddy?'

'Keep what between us Mr Ambrose?' Gabriel smiled.

The others turned up and the meeting was held as usual. As they were leaving Gabriel pulled Henry to one side, 'I could do with a pick me up.'

'No problem Gabby, I'll leave a bit in your locker.'

'Can I have a bit more, just a bit stressful at the moment.'

Henry stopped, scrutinising Gabriel, 'Everything OK Gabby. The product is not becoming a problem for you is it? It has a way of getting hold of your life if you are not careful.'

'No, I'm fine. It's the crap from this Crime Commissioner job. I need something to keep me going. There's going to be some long days, late nights.'

'Anything for a friend Gabby, you know that. Just keep an eye on it.'

They all left the meeting. Gabriel happy he had a plan to remove his problem and at top of nose candy to keep him happy.

***

In the Broken Land, Jim and Charles awaited a response to the email they had sent to Gabriel Ambrose. Their main concern was that there appeared to be a complete lack of action from the recipient. It had been four days. They'd both thought that something should have happened by now. Surely receiving that e-mail would spur you into doing something, to prompt some kind of reaction. If not, why not? Jim wondered if Gabriel had actually received the email. The only way to confirm it was to hack another IT system. He didn't have the appetite to try that. As good as he was, he understood all too well, that every time you accessed a system there was a chance of being discovered. Was it something else? Could Gabriel be on vacation?

Jim and Charles spoke daily on the phone. They tried to answer one another's questions and pondered scenarios. Jim had conveyed his concern over Gabriel's potential absence from duty. Charles said he would ring Gabriel's office the following day to confirm he was at work. Christmas was fast approaching and the festive period would bring holiday interruptions, so his absence from his office may not be unusual. They both conceded frustrations needed to be restrained and continued to tread cautiously.

Jim had been out walking with Barnstable when Charles sent him a text message. The mobile phone signal was weak on his new daily route – as sparse as an MP's apology – so it wasn't until Jim was within signal range that his phone pinged. The text read, *Goss who IM talking to, Mr Ambrose no less, will call later.* Jim was puzzled: not by the spelling, which he put down to hasty texting, but by the reason behind Gabriel's visit to the Broken Land.

Jim's mind began to race to find answers. Inside, he was trying to suppress the firework of excitement from exploding. The text had certainly lit the fuse and he was trying to dampen his Bonfire Night enthusiasm.

The fact that Gabriel had turned up in the Broken Land meant that some part of their plan had worked and was gaining momentum. Secretly, Jim had become increasingly worried that their adversary might strike again soon. Saviour or not, he did not want to find another file added to 'Operation December'; certainly not one containing Charles' or Lizzie's names.

Charles rang a couple of hours later. 'Well Jim, looks like our plan has worked but it has raised a few more questions, I feel. Mr Ambrose visited. I recognised him, so hung around and forced an introduction. After a few pleasantries he slowly teased his way to the subject matter. He asked if I knew any of the victims. I told him nothing. My portrayal of an innocent soul would have impressed my acting peers but he persisted. His interests lay solely with that of our adversary. He was particularly concerned about Felix, and the physical description of Mr Blue Eyes. Trying to establish when and where his encounter had happened. When I advised Mr Ambrose of Felix's departure, he could not hide his disappointment – he looked tormented. There were a few more teasing questions from him but I explained that the police had all the details. We had told the police everything. I suggested he should pursue his enquiries with them but he explained he was supplementing their investigation. He wanted to cover the case from all angles: make sure we felt safe.

'The rest of our conversation was "rhubarb" as we say in the acting profession. All filler. We talked about the community. He explained how he would improve the area for us. Curiously, as he left, he asked for my discretion if the police asked if he had been there. I naturally assured him he had it, 'Mother' being the appropriate word and all that, and then he wondered off.

'As he left, he bumped into Lizzie. She behaved, for once. It looked like they had the briefest of conversations. They both parted laughing. I managed to take a couple of pictures, I'll send them through.'

Jim's phone pinged again. He opened and studied two photos of a rather tall, well-dressed man talking to Lizzie. One of them showed him with his arm around her shoulders. *What a close shave for Ambrose*, Jim thought. He could have become the next victim entangled in Lizzie's sexual web.

Jim replied, 'I'm not sure what to make of all this. Gabriel seems to be investigating this by himself. Do you think he doesn't trust the police?'

Charles blew into the phone mouthpiece, then answered, 'I wondered the same, or was there another reason? Did he want to expose the killer? Just imagine the headline: 'Crime Commissioner exposes major flaws in local policing methods'. That would inflate his public ratings tenfold and probably give him a position for life.'

Jim thought about what Charles had said. He had a point. In the absence of any other obvious alternative, it seemed the only viable option.

Jim and Charles remained blissfully ignorant of Gabriel Ambrose's' true reason for the visit.

Charles continued, 'Ironically, our saviour, methinks that our foe's deeds may be coming to an end. We now have a three-pronged attack on his malevolence: the police, we two, and now the Crime Commissioner: we're all chasing December.'

Jim sniggered to himself as he considered Charles' last statement. A three-pronged attack maybe, but a 'Dad's Army' approach to catching a serial killer could skew things in favour of the killer. The police were the only qualified investigators and they did not seem to be too fussed about catching him or have any concern for the victims. The fact that they suspected the killer might be one or more of their own was just adding more problems to the case.

As for Gabriel, they had both concluded he might be investigating the deaths alone. They guessed at why. Then there was his and Charles' involvement: hardly Holmes and Watson material. As Jim analysed the merry band that had evolved to track their adversary, he wondered if any success would be achieved more by luck than judgement. Ultimately, he would take that, he thought, before turning once again to the nature of Gabriel's involvement in it all.

'Did Gabriel speak to anyone else?' Jim enquired.

'He just had a brief few minutes with Chrissy at the food station,' Charles answered.

'Did Chrissy say anything?'

'No. I asked, but tried not to probe too much to avoid raising suspicions over our plan. Getting quite skilled at this now. I might add Gumshoe to my CV.'

Jim smiled. Even under pressure Charles had a sense of humour: or was it just a different perception of things?

Jim and Charles ended their call, agreeing to consider the morning's events before deciding what to do next. Charles did not think that Gabriel's visit would be an isolated one, as he hadn't obtained any answers.

Before he signed off, Jim implored Charles to ensure that he and Lizzie kept a close eye on one another, reminding Charles of the gravity of the situation. Charles had laughed off Jim's concern, but despite his blasé front he secretly double-checked every shadow he came across.

They would have to play the waiting game again to catch the killer or, as Charles succinctly put it, *play a game of chess with real people.*

Charles rang Jim every day, as agreed. The rapport between them grew. Their conversations had become more familiar and not just a necessity. They had developed a genuine affection for one another, similar to a father and son. Charles reported, as he had presumed, that Gabriel had revisited the Broken Land. He had spoken to him again and realised that although Gabriel's questions were wearing different clothes, they were going to the same party. It was obvious Gabriel had not got the answer he was looking for. Charles commented that he believed, *his holy grail remained truly hidden.*

Jim suggested that Charles take photos of Gabriel again. Charles did as requested, and then sent them to Jim. Jim said they could keep them just in case Gabriel had other intentions that would impact the Broken Land at a later date.

Nothing seemed to occurring. Patience was starting to wear thin for everyone involved in trying to catch their assailant. The only concrete emotion experienced by all parties was one of confusion, stirred not shaken, with a twist of frustration. Jim secretly worried what would happen next. He could feel the atmosphere getting heavier, like the precursor to a storm. His feelings would soon prove right.

It was three days before Christmas. Shopping tills in the high street rang louder than Christmas carollers. Revellers, wearing party gear, jumped into pubs and spewed out later, giddy with festive spirits. Jim went to the local market. The vendors displayed their goods, decorated by sprigs of holly in a hope of attracting more custom. Jim stood waiting to be served, he stared at the one faulty bulb on the decorations that illuminated a stall and pondered how this mirrored his own imperfect situation.

He peeled off his boots on his return from the market, sending small shards of snow falling from the heavy tread. An excitable Barnstable pounced on them, licking the cold water. Rather than punish his beloved pet Jim just smiled and made a fuss of him.

He gazed to the front door and noticed an envelope partially shoved through, the heavy steel flap trapping its remainder. Jim pulled the envelope free. It felt light, as though its contents were insignificant: how wrong he was.

At that time of year envelopes were normally rigid cards but not this one. Inside was just a single piece of neatly folded paper. Jim unwrapped the message to reveal the contents.

The chase is over, my friend. It is a time of destiny and revelation. Our paths are now determined to cross. No more false smiles for the beggars of the world.

You are cordially invited to a meeting on Christmas Eve. Coordinates to our meeting will be dispatched.

Unfortunately, non-compliance or involving the police will prove tragic for you all.

I know your family and friends.

The Fundamental.

Jim's lips dried, he swallowed hard. Could this be authentic? *No false smile* – the author knew a key trait of the victims' injuries. He looked at the letter again, re-read it then examined the envelope. He was looking for clues; not that he would recognise one anyway. It was a simple, plain white envelope with Jim's name typed out on it.

Jim questioned his involvement in the whole saga again. A simple walk with his dog had led him here. It had been a long time since Jim had had to contend with such huge responsibility and now a gun-wielding adversary had him in his sights. He would just have to find a way of stopping the bullet.

Jim placed the letter on the table and stared at it. He picked it up a few times more and read it again and again. How did the writer know his address? There was a postage stamp and the postmark was a local one. The address had been typed - so there was no handwriting that might have yielded something about the killer's identity. Then he thought about it, handwriting, who was he kidding. If it had been hand written, what difference would it have made? It wouldn't have altered anything. He didn't have a team of experts on side ready to analyse it. There was just him and Charles.

He tried to keep his growing fears in check but failed. *Crane would have access to my address*, he thought. *If Crane is the killer*, Jim determined, *he certainly was not going down without a fight*.

Jim decided to tell Charles in the morning: he would run it past his wingman, in case he had missed something. Jim strolled off to bed, closely followed by Barnstable. The letter remained on the table, its purpose achieved.

Across town, a heavily laden postman was walking his round. The additional burden of Christmas greetings weighed heavy on his shoulder. Even his Santa hat didn't help ease the woe of his burden. As he stooped forward to correct his balance and compensate for the added weight, he went about his task. Little did he know the significance of his duty: he'd just delivered letters to Mr Gabriel Ambrose and to Mr Edward Moffatt. Both had typed addresses with local postmarks: just like Jim's.

Ping! Gabriel heard his phone bleat for an answer. *Not now, I need to get this quote finished.* He had Christmas to arrange. Since his daughter's passing, the season's pressures fell squarely on his shoulders. Not that if took much time or a huge commitment to plan: they no longer bothered with decorations and the Christmas meal would be at Edward's, where at least the pleasant company helped to dilute the bitter memories that the season provoked. At home, his wife, Jessica, only required a bottle and a corkscrew for her to celebrate Christmas.

Ping! His phone demanded his attention again. Unlike other people, Gabriel was not attached or addicted to his phone. It was a device for a purpose. He often frowned at how society had become addicted to such devices. He regularly cursed the hoards that walked through streets like zombies, phones in hand, browsing away, ignorant of their surroundings. The amount of times he had to dodge a phone junkie, high on Facebook or Twitter. *Ping:* a further plea for attention then a rumbling vibration. Gabriel had placed his phone on silent so he could concentrate. The rumbling stopped and there were no further pings. Now only his stubborn resistance prevented him answering, but curiosity got the better of him.

He examined his phone and saw a trail of text messages from Edward. *Call me*, then, *Call me!*, and finally, *Bloody ring me!* Gabriel checked the missed call he had received: it too was from Edward.

In all the years he had known him, he could count the number of times he had heard Edward swear. Swearing did not suit Edward's character. Even adolescent attempts at verbal abuse had not sat right with him. When Edward was younger, he always had an air of gentry about him.

Gabriel returned Edward's call. Edward answered immediately. 'Gabriel, where are you?'

'At work, getting things ready for Christmas and the holidays.'

'Listen to me, Gabriel: go home, check your post and ring me. Do it now,' Edward barked.

'Edward, what's going on? I need to tidy up here before we break up for Christmas.'

'Gabriel, Fuck Christmas! Go home now. Check your post and then call me,' Edward shouted then hung up.

Gabriel was dumbfounded. What was going on? He rushed around the office, switching off the lights before he left.

Gabriel mulled over Edward's outburst and wondered what course of events could have stirred such a reaction in his friend.

He arrived home distracted, with no idea of what he might find there. Entering the house through the normal side door he went in. There was no 'Welcome home darling', nor the aroma of a freshly served meal to greet him: only the dull sound of the TV from the living room and another microwave meal to look forward to. Gabriel passed the living room. He gazed in to see his wife staring at the TV, sat with one of her best friends, Chardonnay. She did not turn to acknowledge him; she just kept on sipping and watching.

Gabriel picked up a small pile of mail still lying on the hallway floor by the front door. He gathered it up and thumbed through it until he came across a plain envelope. It was slightly lighter in weight than the others, and the address was typed out. Gabriel knew immediately that this was the mail Edward had asked him to check for. He opened it then read and re-read it. Taking his phone from his pocket, he hurriedly wrote a text.

Ping! Edward stared at the message: *I'm sorry, Edward.* He knew what that meant. They were both intelligent men and the fact that each had received the same letter drew them to the same conclusion: the past had caught up with them, a past that they had created. Now they had to reconcile their futures.

There were no more texts or phone calls that evening from any of the letters' recipients. In a media-savvy age, it was an old-fashioned letter that had grabbed their attention.

Next morning, Jim woke early, as usual. Even the dark winter's mornings didn't stop Jim from getting up. He ate his breakfast, though his stomach was bloated with anxiety, and then he called Charles. The phone rang but went to voicemail. He decided not to leave a message, but grabbed his keys and set off in his car to find him.

If the letter was to be believed, there was little time left for action. Jim felt like he was trying to smother a bleeding wound on a dying man. His phone rang: it was Charles.

'You rang,' said Charles, mimicking a creepy housekeeper from an old horror movie.

Jim told Charles about the letter, providing as much detail as he could, although there was little to go on.

Jim paused at last, unsure if Charles was still listening. He had often been caught out speaking down the phone to no one. He questioned if those 'lost' conversations were queued up in the atmosphere somewhere, waiting to be heard. He heard Charles breathe heavily into his phone.

'Well my fine fellow, our saviour, I think we are about to take the final hurdle. I believe the message is from our foe. I could argue the contrary, but he obtained your address and refers to false smiles.'

'If the killer is our sergeant, I don't think he's operating in isolation. He is not cunning enough to engineer a plan such as this. We need to tread cautiously – can you come here? We need to devise a plan of attack.'

Jim hung up and drove to Charles in the Broken Land. There was no doubt in Jim's mind that they would soon be face to face with their foe.

Gabriel stood by his car in a park on the outskirts of town. He was waiting for Edward. They'd had a short phone call that morning to discuss the correspondence they had both received and had agreed to meet in person. As Edward approached he could see Gabriel shifting from one foot to the other to keep warm. There had been a fresh covering of snow the previous evening: enough to impact the local roads and alarm the media. Edward parked, got out of the car and approached Gabriel. Gabriel held his head down and whimpered,

'I'm so sorry Edward. This has all been my fault from the beginning. How can he be back? Or if it's not him, who is it? What do they want?'

Edward watched at Gabriel's torment: he looked like an anaconda's prey having the last gasps of life squeezed from him. Edward could have acknowledged Gabriel's comments: yes, it was Gabriel's fault entirely, but he too had chosen to bite the forbidden fruit, and serve as an accomplice by choice. Edward put a gloved hand on Gabriel's shoulder. 'I am your friend and will be until the end. Whatever happens from here, we do it together,' Edward said, looking at Gabriel. 'As for who it is or what they know, we will find that out soon enough. The authorities are not involved, so we have no alternative but to follow instructions. The letter proves he knows where we live. This is our problem Gabriel, we can't afford for any retribution on our families. Our actions cannot haunt them but that does not mean we can't be prepared.'

The two embraced, both holding back tears. Life had led them to that point and fate was about to determine their future.

Unaware of each other's involvement thus far, a common goal was about to bring Jim, Charles, Gabriel, and Edward together.

Meanwhile, in the Broken Land, Jim had shown Charles the letter. They rehearsed possible scenarios. Charles agreed with Jim that the importance of the letter was yet to be revealed. It was a precursor to a more significant event.

Charles read the letter over. He commented how sometimes lack of information carried more sway than more information. There was no doubt in his mind this was categorically the work of the killer.

As they talked, Jim insisted to Charles that, wherever the letter took him, he would attend alone. Charles advocated another course, offering himself and Turnip as companions. Jim argued that that plan could lead to more deaths. The letter was quite explicit about the consequences of enlisting help, he said, adding, 'We don't want to tempt his wrath, do we?' It would be a waiting game, where patience was not a virtue but a requirement.

Across town, similar conversations were being held and options for a plan forward discussed. Gabriel and Edward agreed that it was time to finish the business once and for all; this time with no loose ends. Gabriel did not discuss with Edward he had an alternative plan if things turned sour. Paddy was a phone call away.

The details of their plan of attack emerged. Edward would go armed to the meeting. He still had his grandfather's service revolver from the war and knew he had ammunition. He had never shot a gun before but he'd watched plenty of action movies so reasoned it could not be that hard. You pointed the barrel towards the target and pulled the trigger, didn't you?

Gabriel agreed to Edward's plan. He was happy to follow his friend's lead. He just wanted an end to it all. His life was a mess and he was only hanging on by a thread. That thread, seemingly getting thinner and thinner by the day.

The next day would be Christmas Eve, and all four men spent an evening of unusual anticipation. Charles sat steadfast, smoking cigarettes and listening to the groans of deranged passion emitting from Lizzie's tent. He contemplated the immediate future for them all and the role he had given their saviour, Jim. Would this be their demise? As he inhaled the calming fumes he wrestled emotionally with a sense of guilt and the reality of the situation. It would be a long night.

Jim sat on his sofa, Barnstable curled by his side. The TV was on but Jim was focused on his dog, and gently stroked Barnstable's thick, wavy hair. He remembered the day he had found him roaming abandoned in the street. He had never forgotten the dog's waggy-tailed enthusiasm when he first saw him. It was like two old friends meeting again. There was an instant connection between them. The open fire crackled. Logs glowed red, the picture book Christmas scene. An image plenty might have envied but not the situation. Jim decided to stay up with his mate and watch the morning break. It might be his last.

Gabriel had returned home earlier than normal that day. He had ignored messages from work. He had more pressing things to contend with. He looked into the living room and saw his wife in her usual position; a bottle of wine and a glass at her side. He went to the kitchen, picked up an empty wine glass and grabbed a framed family photograph from the hall. Gabriel entered the living room, reached past Jessica, poured a glass of red from the wine bottle and sat with his arm around his wife. His wife arched her neck onto his shoulder. Gabriel placed the photograph on his lap. It showed the whole family with Tabby. It was a time when they all still smiled. Ignoring the TV they both looked at the photograph and reminisced of better times. As his wife dozed, Gabriel pulled a throw from the sofa over them. There would be no bed tonight.

Edward was at home, sitting at a large table. Food had been prepared and was steaming in large porcelain containers, waiting to be served. It was a family tradition. They always enjoyed a pre-Christmas dinner before the big day. He looked around the table and watched his wife chatting to his daughter and her boyfriend. There was a clatter of crockery as the meal was spooned onto plates. Then there was a hustle of crossed arms, reaching for food while trying to observe table manners. Edward just smiled. He understood that the familiarity of the close family group negated the need for such etiquette. He respected it all the same.

As he scooped portions of food on his plate, he wondered when he would do this again. It was Christmas Eve tomorrow and that would create huge family pressure. Last minute things always had to be done. He would have to make excuses for his absence, which would not be well received but there was no way out of it. Not this Christmas Eve.

Dinner was enjoyed and early Christmas sweets devoured. Edward looked into the night sky from his living room. Time was ebbing away. On any other evening, he would have sat with his family relaxing but this evening he wanted to watch the darkness unfold. He did not want to take the night for granted. He poured a brandy and watched clouds move across the horizon. A bright moon cast grey shadows across space and stars began to appear as it became darker.

Edward sat and rested his head back in his chair. He contemplated his life and tried to gauge how one action could have significantly impacted his life's direction. He calmly concluded that whatever will be, will be. Edward was going to enjoy his own company that evening.

Morning broke: not like the first morning, but similar to most winter mornings. A grey skyline gradually became brighter as the seasonal sunlight clawed at the candy-flossed clouds. Four pairs of tired eyes awaited a message: one that would seal their fates.

Jim left early for the Broken Land, eager to see Charles and make preparations. When he arrived, Charles was swirling his coffee around in a polystyrene cup. 'Good morning fine sir, I do not believe you had the most restful of evenings.'

'Not the best, Charles,' Jim said, placing a nylon bag at Charles' feet.

'Presents for me, Jim? I promise I will not open it until Santa has blessed it. Presents are not real you know, until Santa has blessed them,' Charles laughed.

Jim looked at Charles solemnly. 'In the bag Charles is sixty thousand pounds. It's for you and Lizzie if I don't return. It also contains a note of my address and a door key. I just need you to promise to look after my dog if I don't come back. Inside one of the pockets in the bag is a bank card and details on how to access more funds without arousing suspicion.' The shock of the short speech hit Charles. His temporary joviality calmed, the severity of the task ahead returned, glaring apparent.

'Jim, I'm sorry you had to be our saviour. It's a burden that I should have considered and not arbitrarily assigned. You are a friend, Jim. It's still not too late to alter this path you seem set upon.'

Jim blew a resounding puff of air through his nostrils and said, 'It's not your fault Charles. It's strange, but I feel like this should be my task. I need to tell you something. The evening after I discovered the body, I could have sworn I saw the victim sat on my bed. I told the police: they said it was post-traumatic stress but it seemed so real. When you called me saviour, it was as though I had heard it before.'

'Before you say anything, I know all this does not make sense. It's just . . . I don't want you to feel guilty. There's also the question of what happens if I don't try to stop this – who's next? If the killer turns out to be Crane and whoever else, then I intend to make them pay. I owe Crane from my past and retribution is long overdue.'

'What would you do Jim? How will you enact your retribution?'

'I'm taking a knife. I studied martial arts when I worked in the East. If it's to be my judgement day, I won't go down without a fight. I can assure you of that,' Jim replied.

So much more needed saying, but in this unlikeliest of environments, two men stood in front of one another and were at peace. Charles held out his hand, Jim reached forward and shook it firmly.

'Saviour, I will follow your instructions but I hope that our journey together is far from over,' Charles choked, holding back tears.

'I had better go Charles. I don't know how I am going to receive the instructions and I need to be prepared.'

Charles watched Jim walk away. He remained, clutching the bag that Jim had left him. There was no need to confirm the contents. He trusted Jim implicitly and just hoped to see his saviour again so he could give it back.

Jim slowly made his way home in his car, cautiously dodging the Christmas traffic. Car brake lights sparkled on and off like faulty tree lights. Jim's windscreen wipers started to operate automatically in response to flurries of snowflakes that had started to fall. He heard his phone ping in his pocket. Jim looked for a safe place to pull over and read the new message:

1pm, Coordinates Latitude: 53° 07' 60.00" N, Longitude: -1° 35' 59.99"W.

The Fundamental

How did this guy know his phone number? *It must be Crane*, Jim thought. 'You fat bastard,' he muttered, 'whatever you have in store for me you are not going to get it easy.'

Jim checked his watch. It was five minutes past eleven. He had less than two hours to prepare.

Jim put the coordinates into a web browser on his phone and searched for a result: the location was an hour away. He punched the details into his car's satnav and began the journey.

Ping! Ping! Two more messages were received: two out of the millions sent at that precise moment, without the text abbreviations, the LOLs, OMGs or the emoji's – just a brief message with some coordinates.

Moments later, Edward and Gabriel were on the phone and planning their journey. White lies and spurious excuses were the order of the day. Edward stood at the doorway of his house waiting for Gabriel. He was holding a portable navigation device, freshly loaded with the coordinates. For all of them it was time.

The Fundamental *et al*

'At the next junction take the first exit, then continue for three miles,' the satnav purred. Two cars travelled in the same direction, from town to village, along rough roads that had never seen tarmac. The sound of the steady crunch of compounding stone could be heard under the wheels, slightly muted by slush.

Jim followed the directions: the road had narrowed to a path barely wide enough for one vehicle, save for the occasional passing place. He noticed he was travelling in another vehicle's tyre tracks. Someone had taken the same road recently.

Jim stopped the car. It juddered to a halt, striving for traction on the slippery surface. He could make out a building up ahead with a car parked outside. Looking around, it was the only one around. The building was isolated. The car parked outside didn't look like it had been there long. There was no snow on the body. All its windows were clear, frost free. It had obviously been driven recently.

He guessed he'd reached his destination, and the satnav voice confirmed it. Jim felt nervous, not sure how best to proceed. He decided to approach the building on foot to avoid immediate detection.

The building looked well maintained, similar to a lodge you might hire for a woodland retreat. Getting closer, he saw lights on inside. He crouched as he approached, avoiding the windows to prevent being spotted. Trying to peer in, he couldn't see anyone inside. He felt unusually calm, having concluded that everything was in Fate's hands. As he came closer to the door, his patience started to falter: he wanted it over. Without further hesitation, he opened the door and entered.

There were two men inside, sitting at a table. They both turned to face him. One of the men fumbled for something in his pocket but it fell out and hit the ground: it was a gun. Jim put his hands in the air as the man retrieved the weapon and pointed it at him.

'Whoa! Easy, so is this how it's going end? You're just going to shoot me? No explanation why you have brought me here?' Jim blurted out angrily.

The two men looked at each other: the man without a gun was Gabriel Ambrose. Gabriel reached over and lowered Edward's outstretched arm. He had noticed Edward's arm was getting twitchy with the added weight of the gun. Jim spoke again,

'I recognise you – you're Gabriel Ambrose. What the hell are you doing here? And who is he?'

'I could ask you the same question,' Gabriel replied.

Jim lowered his arms. 'I received a letter then a text message with coordinates to follow, which led me here.'

Carefully, Jim produced the letter from his pocket, opened it to show the two men then tossed it on the floor.

Gabriel and Edward followed Jim's lead, taking out their letters and throwing them down. Jim looked at the three letters scattered in front of them.

'Guess this party was by invitation only,' he said. 'I have an idea why I am here, but what about you two?'

'I think why we're here is the least of our problems,' said Edward.

Jim looked over Edward's shoulder to a clock on the wall. It was a quarter to one. He scanned the room. He could see the place was clean and comfortable. 'Have you looked around yet?' he asked.

'There's just one bedroom, a bathroom and this area. I couldn't see anything extraordinary,' Gabriel replied.

Jim examined the room more closely. There was a large kitchen-diner with a table, and a sofa that faced a log-burning fire and a TV. Lit candles were flickering in several places, emitting a festive cinnamon fragrance. They had been lit for quite a while.

He walked to the table and thumbed through a neat pile of advertising flyers lying there.

'These are for local attractions. I think this is a holiday rental,' he remarked.

Edward had been watching Jim intently; gun still in hand but now by his side. He soon recognised the absurdity of the situation and placed the gun on a small table next to the TV.

Edward rubbed his hands through his thick grey hair, shook his head. 'Why, what, where: it's beyond our control. I am tired; I want this to end. All we all have is questions. I am sick of feeling like a worm dangling on a hook. I just need solace.'

Edward sat down heavily again at the table. Gabriel walked towards the toilet, 'Sorry chaps, I need to go.' The toilet was a good size. Its sides were a timber construction, with a small frosted window allowing a distorted view over some woodland. Gabriel didn't need to use the toilet. He needed something else, something to calm his nerves. He reached into his pocket and pulled out a bag of cocaine. Dipping his damp finger into the white powder, he promptly rubbed it vigorously along his gums. Gabriel let the initial euphoria from the hit of the drug fade before returning to the kitchen. Returning back to the sitting room, he passed Edward, patting his shoulder before he sat opposite.

Jim looked at both men as they stared blankly at the table's surface, subsumed in a mood of dejection and inevitability. He decided he wouldn't join them and made his way to the kitchen area. Looking around, he started to open cupboards. Finding a tin of coffee, he forced the lid open and smelt the brown substance inside. 'Yep, coffee all right,' Jim said, 'I could do with a drink, anyone else?'

Both men nodded. Jim pulled open the fridge but it was empty. 'It'll have to black I'm afraid,' he said, as he filled the kettle from the tap.

Jim did not want to take control: he did not want to be mother. But he didn't want to sit staring at the table either, listening to the second hand ticking down the time on the wall clock.

He placed the cups of coffee on the table. Jim sat at the side, within view of both Gabriel and Edward. He did not really trust either of them and did not want to offer them any advantage if the situation turned sour.

He pondered potential next steps. What would he do? He was remarkably comfortable with the fact that Edward had brought a gun with him. After all, he had not admitted to the others that he had a knife stuck in his sock. It was ridiculous really: it had made him limp slightly, and using it in anger would have been as alien to him as Edward's attempt with the revolver.

Jim watched the two men cup their drinks in their hands, seeking comfort. They sipped, and Jim did likewise. Finally, Gabriel turned to Jim. 'So, we are all full of questions, and wanting an explanation for what is happening here. I know it may not make a difference, but then again it might. Have you any idea why you're here?'

Jim studied Gabriel: he looked frustrated rather than angry. If they had both looked in a philosophical mirror at that point, their physical features would have been the only difference between them.

Jim remembered finding the body and the onerous responsibility he had inherited. 'I think I am here by accident, I just–' Jim stopped. He looked at Gabriel, whose head had started to droop, and then at Edward, whose body was slumped over the table, his dropped coffee cup spilling across its surface.

'Gabriel, Gabriel, what is it?' Jim cried. There was no reply; just silence. Jim looked at the dark stain of spilled coffee pooling across the table.

Tick, tick, tick: time moved on, as it always does, and for a time the sound of the wall clock's hands moving round was the only noise in the room.

Gabriel awoke with his cheek resting on the table. An acrid taste forced his dry mouth to salivate. As he stretched backwards, he realised his arms were bound tightly to the chair. He tried to kick out with his legs but they were also bound tight. Thick bands of tape had been used to fix his limbs. As he wriggled for freedom, the chair creaked and held firm: he was trapped.

At first, Gabriel had not noticed Jim but when he looked up, he saw Jim was trying to wriggle free too, unsuccessfully.

Edward was last to rouse. He promptly started to writhe as the others had. They were like three live fish trapped in a barrel, trying to dance their way to freedom, but with no chance of success. At last, the three men tired and slumped in their seats, at which point they became aware of a small microphone placed in the middle of the table. It was sitting on a piece of white paper that had something written on it. Gabriel tried to read it but he was at the wrong angle and his restraints stopped him from getting a better view. He looked at Edward and asked, 'What does it say?'

Edward did not answer straight away. He just swayed and started to cry out, 'No, no, no!'

Gabriel tried again. 'Edward what does it say? We need to know – we all need to know.'

Edward stopped moving. He looked at Gabriel through moistening eyes. Gabriel focused intently on Edward and spoke calmly, 'Edward, please listen to me. It is important you read the message on the table. Please Edward.'

In a quivering voice, Edward read, 'Confess your sins for a chance of redemption. It's signed underneath – the Fundamental.'

Edward began to tremble as Gabriel spoke again, trying to calm his friend. 'Edward, we need to keep it together. I am as scared as you but we have no alternative but to play this game.'

Gabriel wanted to reach out and place a reassuring hand on his friend but his binds prevented it. If his movement had allowed, Gabriel was not sure his actions would have been convincing. He was trying his best to restrain his own fear.

Jim interrupted Gabriel's thoughts. 'I guess that's what the microphone is for.' He shook his head. 'What sin? The only reason I am here is because I am trying to do the right thing. To stop a killer, deliver justice, is that my sin?'

Jim looked at Edward, then Gabriel, and finally the microphone, and spat out his anger. 'So, you sick bastard – is this what you want? I found one of your victims and I confess I want to kill you. Come out here now, cut my binds and let's end this. But let the others go.'

Gabriel and Edward could see the anger and venom in Jim's eyes. Gabriel imagined a cornered rat and admired Jim's bravery.

Then Edward spoke. 'I need to tell the truth. It's time, and I think I know the reason I am here.'

'Edward no, we don't need to do this,' Gabriel pleaded.

'Gabriel, we should have done this a long time ago,' Edward replied.

Edward then described his part in Josh's murder as Gabriel stared at him. The memory of Josh's death tore at Gabriel's soul. His conscience had always weighed heavy about Edward's involvement in the entire affair.

When Edward had finished his confession, Jim looked at him and laughed, 'Well, that tops mine.' He then turned to Gabriel and said, 'I guess if you can beat that, you get the prize?'

Jim blew out air from his mouth like a bus releasing its air break. 'Is that why we are here? Are we getting to the truth?' Jim asked.

Jim looked at Gabriel, who was doing his best to avoid eye contact. He thought about the email he had sent to Gabriel from Crane, to get him involved and decided not to say anything. There was obviously a bigger picture being painted.

Instead he ventured, 'I have a feeling Gabriel, that yours will be the greatest confession. It's time to pay the piper.'

Gabriel frowned; his heavy eyebrows seemed to weigh down his face. 'Perhaps you're right,' he replied.

He confessed to the part he had played in murdering the street dweller with Josh, to the subsequent plan to remove his teenage accomplice, and how he had involved Edward in the whole sorry mess. He apologised once more to his friend.

He talked of his heavy sense of responsibility to Tabby, even after her death, and to his wife. He tried to argue that it was his desire for justice that had forced him to commit the first murder. He saw Jim shaking his head.

His story complete, the room fell to silence as the three men sat drained, like the discarded remnants of a New Year's Eve party. Empty vessels remained, the effervescence from soda having escaped the three invited guests.

After a few moments Jim said, 'So, you're both murderers? You have killed, or at least attempted it?' Gabriel and Edward stayed silent.

'This guy has asked for confessions, so do it: say you are killers. Then perhaps we might have a chance to get out of here. I don't want to die. I want this guy stopped.'

'I am a killer, I am a killer, I am a killer!' Edward repeated, holding back tears.

'No Edward, I'm sorry but you only acted to help me. I am the killer, it's me, I am the killer,' Gabriel shouted.

By now both Gabriel and Edward, arms bound to their chairs, were choked with tears that rolled down their wrinkled faces unchecked and spattered onto the table top.

Jim rested his forehead on the table, where he rocked his head from side to side. Gabriel and Edward stopped sobbing and stared at Jim; puzzled by his behaviour. As they watched, Jim stopped moving his head and began to sing, 'Smile, though your heart is breaking, smile even though it's aching . . .'

Gabriel's eyes opened wide and his mouth gaped as he listened to the familiar song. As he sang, Jim lifted one arm onto the table and then the next. Finally, he raised his head until he was sitting upright again. Jim's fingers moved up to his eyes, from which he carefully removed his contact lenses, his fingers fluttering in front of his face momentarily before he placed the two filmy discs on the table. By now his eyes were squeezed shut.

As he placed his hands flat on the table again, he opened his eyes: they were a piercing blue. The other two men gasped in recognition.

Jim's stare was like cold steel; his eyes seemed to illuminate the room like the glare of a lighthouse bursting through sea mist.

Gabriel and Edward watched dumbfounded as if thrown into the climax of movie scene without being privy to the story.

Jim spoke again in a monotone voice, devoid of any emotion.

'Gentlemen, let me introduce myself. I am The Fundamental.'

Tick, tick, tick: the second hand of the clock punctured the silence as The Fundamental studied Gabriel and Edward as if they were tropical fish in a tank.

'How are you The Fundamental? What about Jim, and is it you or are you Josh?' Gabriel asked, perplexed.

The Fundamental leant over to Gabriel. He was so close Gabriel could feel the warmth from his nostrils on his cheek. The Fundamental stared intently at Gabriel through one opened eye and then the other.

Pulling back, Gabriel cried, 'What are you doing? Is this part of your sick game, you psychopath?'

The Fundamental didn't retreat, but kept staring at Gabriel's eyes –the left and then the right – repeatedly.

'I wonder? If I pulled out one of your eyes and followed the optic nerve with my fingers, would it travel to the same place as my own? Hmm, just food for thought,' The Fundamental said, without inflexion or empathy.

'And just to correct you on your diagnosis, I am not a psychopath; I am a sociopath with a dissociative identity disorder, if you want to attach a label to me. The good doctor can explain I am sure.'

As he spoke, The Fundamental continued to analyse Gabriel's eyes. 'Hmm, I wonder, perhaps an ad hoc experiment might show if your eyes are connected in the same way as mine? It might prove messy though. Maybe later.'

Gabriel closed his eyes. He could just hear and feel the Fundamental's breath as he leaned forward and licked each of Gabriel's eyelids in turn. Unable to escape, Gabriel wriggled and tried to move his face out of the way. The Fundamental arched his neck and licked his lips to absorb every drop of moisture from Gabriel's tears and, as Gabriel opened his eyes, he returned to his chair with the graceful precision of a ballet dancer.

The Fundamental, still moving his head slowly from side to side in an exaggerated fashion, rose from his chair and made his way to the sink, where he searched for various items in the drawers, placing them on the sink with careful, considered movements.

He began to speak in a languid, monotonous voice, as if reading from a book.

'You both deserve an explanation and therefore, I will offer one. You live in a world of ambiguity, restrained by laws and social consequences.

'I am fortunate: I see the truth of the world and once you have seen its true beauty, every other vision is that of a blind man. The fog of society clouds your eyes, but my abilities allow me to wipe that fog clear. I can gaze into the mirror that shows only the truth but it's not easily done. That's where Jim comes in. You see, Jim and I share the same body but we are poles apart.'

'As I mentioned earlier, my gift is dissociative identity disorder or, split personality. It's quite simple: Jim allows me to exist but what I feel, I see, and my passions are alien to your world. I could not help my flock move on to the other world without my Jim. Jim is my patsy; he is a marionette and I pull the strings. His part in this is innocence. I allow him to live in your society, to build a life, but I am the dominant entity.'

Both men bonded to their chairs, sat listening like school children. They watched intently as the Fundamental continued, 'Jim remains ignorant of our relationship and remembers nothing of my deeds. He only has the memories of our joint existence that I allow him to maintain, and he lives to fuel my ambitions. He does not know I exist, although sometimes there are occasional slips. The best laid plans and all that. You see, I discovered that he had begun to see visions of my flock, and even hear them sometimes. I try to mask my existence but unfortunately, sometimes, our paths cross. It's my eyes: they are a curse. That is why I wear the coloured contact lenses: without them a rage burns, and if it is not tempered then there is only one consequence, chaos. Do not get me wrong, Jim is an intelligent man but only because I allow him to be so.'

Gabriel and Edward looked at one another. Gabriel's eyes were pained with frustration and Edward's were burning red with tears.

‘Can I ask a question?’ Gabriel said hesitantly.

‘Yes, of course,’ The Fundamental carried on his work at the sink, filling a bowl with steaming hot water and inhaling the vapours.

‘What about Josh and how did you become you?’

‘Josh was an alias to get you involved with my first addition to my flock. In your world I only have one true name, my birth name Jim Thomas. If I had used this in our meetings, it might have introduced margins for error. My Jim may have been caught, stopped. That is unacceptable. Josh served a purpose, a function.’

Gabriel sighed, angered he had been so easily duped.

‘How did I become the Fundamental? I didn’t become who I am, I have always been here, trapped by the constraints of your world. What I see as right, you see as wrong, but I would question all of this.’

‘You’re not answering my question. You’re crazy, was the vagrant you killed as Josh your first?’

The Fundamental paused, tapped a pair of scissors on his chin.

‘No. I have evolved over time. I was about ten when I helped my first move on.’

‘Ten, you were a child.’

‘I don’t think I was ever a child. I was just an apprentice to what I am now. I am still not the finished article. There is work to do for me to truly become an artist, a true shepherd to my flock.’

Edward had been quiet, listening to the bizarre conversation. He shook his head and then spoke, ‘you were a child, a juvenile, ten years old, good god, you are a monster.’

‘Your language, perception, so confusing to me. I will offer an explanation. My grandmother was eighty two. She had lung cancer from a lifetime of smoking. Her health deteriorated and my father moved her into our spare room as her conditioned worsened. I sat with her countless hours, watching her struggle to breathe. Her chest was so fragile it barely moved as it tried to expand, craving air. The sound was painful, her gasps only drowned out by the hiss of escaping oxygen from the mask she was forced to wear. We played her favourite songs on the record player, over and over. She loved Nat King Cole, and his song, Smile.'

'One afternoon, I sat with my father, talking to her as best we could. She begged to die, she had had enough. My father just stroked her head and left the room in tears. I remained. I looked into her eyes, they had glazed over. She was so weak. I took a pillow and placed it over her face. She struggle a little as life ebbed away. I held the pillow with one hand and her hand in my other. The feeling as she passed, her soul moved into mine. My eyes they shone brighter than they had ever done, my apprenticeship had begun. I removed the pillow, placed it back at her side and I forced the corners of her mouth into a smile as her body grew cold. I remained and listened to Nat King Cole until my father returned. He cried. I sat and watched him, emotionless.'

Gabriel shouted out, 'you killed your own grandmother!'

'I helped her move on,'

'Didn't your father suspect anything?'

'From that day my father understood I was different. As I physically grew, he was too afraid to help me realise my full potential. He kept me on a tight lead until I was old enough to leave, find my own way in the world. The day I left for college, he said to me, "god help the world" and shut his door in my face. For me and my Jim it never reopened.'

Gabriel and Edward looked at one another. They were both lost, out of ideas, this thing that stood before them seemed devoid of humanity. The Fundamental, he was darkness.

'You mentioned your flock: are they the people you have killed? Are we to join them? We have families!' Gabriel blurted out, spittle projecting from his mouth. His tight bindings, however, prevented any chance of courteous wiping.

The Fundamental did not miss a beat. He placed a mirror in front of him, perched so that he could see his face in it and then placed a pair of scissors and a razor by his side. 'My flock are people I have helped on their way. You two will join them and trying to persuade me otherwise would be futile.'

The Fundamental remained focused on Gabriel; his burning blue eyes knocked at the doors of his soul. Yet Gabriel said, 'What about all the others – your so-called flock? Where do they fit in? If you have murdered many innocent people, who holds you to account for their deaths?'

The question produced no change of character in The Fundamental: if its intention had been something other than to prompt an answer, it had targeted the wrong recipient.

The Fundamental replied in his dull monotone. 'Language is powerful but we choose to use words flippantly, rather than with reverence. Take the word *desperate*: have you two any idea what desperation is? My flock, the street dwellers, came to me willingly with the promise of a meal, a drink, or a place for the night. I spoke to them and, importantly, I listened. Their lives were flaccid and empty. Your world had broken them and tossed them aside. I simply helped them to move on and to fulfil my desire to kill. I even gave them a smile to depart with. Oh, the hypocrisy of it all, when you question my motive in all of this! The truth is like a sour apple in the barrel you call society.'

'My flock stretches far and wide. I even went global with Jim's travels and as I extended my herd, not one country investigated my actions thoroughly. It is a global case of negligence.'

Edward and Gabriel continued to listen, compelled to hear more from their ghoulish narrator.

'Last year, I helped one move on from around here, in this very town. I had passed him every day for three weeks. Winter was biting hard and day to day he struggled to exist, begging for change. He had a small dog huddled at his side. Every day I gave him a hot drink and food until one day, after a particularly heavy fall of snow, I saw just his dog, its lead still attached to the collar, wandering the street. The dog cowered as it tried to shelter from the chill wind and sleet. It looked at the passing crowd. It even followed some of them, but stopped, then gazed back to the vacant space left by his master and returned to his post. It tugged at people's heartstrings: *the poor little thing*, people said – but they asked nothing of the whereabouts of his master. Then a kind soul picked him up and gave him warmth, food and comfort. The dog was found on Barnstable Avenue and I set the seed for Jim to become the new master. And so, the relationship of Jim and his adopted dog Barnstable was created. His owner had become one of my flock.'

'My flock feeds my personal need; a vampire's lust. I choose to act in the winter as it offers release for them from additional hardships and the weather helps mask any evidence of my deeds. They are the forgotten people but I remember them, I remember them all.'

Edward remained still, having resigned himself to his fate some time previously. But Gabriel was angry and he shouted, 'You are just a murderer, a fucking sick murderer. You are not helping those people on their way. You are just killing them! Is this revenge?' Gabriel wasn't sure if it was bravery of the cocaine that spurred him on, but he was up for the fight.

The Fundamental slowly cut at his beard. Clumps of coarse hair dropped to the floor. The only sound that could be heard in the cabin was the snip from the scissors. He then applied shaving foam liberally to his freshly hewn stubble. Taking the razor, he carefully stroked it across his face. 'Sorry gentlemen, I will be with you in a moment. It is always tricky shaving under my nose and I do not want to cut myself.'

Gabriel and Edward could do nothing but observe their captor shave, as if compelled to watch by the most powerful man in the universe.

The Fundamental finished shaving and washed his smooth face before gathering the loose hair and placing it in a bag on the floor.

'That's better, you feel so much fresher after a close shave,' he said, turning towards the two men.

When Gabriel saw the shaved face, one of his questions was immediately answered: it was Josh, undoubtedly, his features only slightly disguised by age. Gabriel knew his destiny was now truly set.

The Fundamental sat back at the table with the two men. He looked at them both, twisting his head from side to side again. Edward refused to make eye contact but Gabriel returned the glare. The Fundamental ceased his action, placed his hands on the table slowly and interlaced his fingers. He began to speak again, without one pulse of emotion. 'Murder is a powerful word; *the unlawful premeditated killing of one human being by another,* sayeth your world. You two tried to kill me; you drugged me and discarded me on a refuse dump. What you did not know was that there were people already there, scouring the dump for items they could sell and reclaim. Fortunately, they found me. They dragged me into a car and dropped me outside the local hospital. I lay outside A&E like a bag of rubbish discarded by you gentlemen.'

'The amount of cocaine you administered made you think I was dead, but I was not ready to pass over that threshold. I was admitted to the hospital as an attempted overdose and slowly recovered my health. Funny, my parents never got over the fact that their son had seemingly become an addict. An addict Gabriel, another powerful word, do you recognise that word Gabriel?'

Gabriel eyes flickered, the unrestrained parts of his body juddered. Edward looked at his friend puzzled. In his head, Gabriel asked, *how could he know*.

'As I said earlier, I created the character of Josh to achieve a purpose, to obtain assistance with my first adventure. To everyone else I was Jim. These people you know as Josh and Jim belong to me. They help me feed my hunger. The pain of your daughter's death was an opportunity I could not help but exploit it to begin my journey. You made it easy for me Gabriel: your anger and need for revenge decided that and I must thank you. Your actions in helping me take the first of my flock were greatly appreciated. Perhaps you are Shelley's Frankenstein and I am the monster?'

The Fundamental paused from his endless monologue. It seemed to go on for an age to Edward and Gabriel but time was what they had now.

'I have a question for you Gabriel, how many more of my flock have you helped me with?'

'Want do you mean you sick bastard?' Gabriel reacted angrily.

‘In your state, your addiction, is it different to mine?’

Gabriel lurched at the Fundamental, his seat creaking in response,
‘What the hell are you talking about, addiction. You’re trying to implicate me in your insanity.’ No deviation in pitch, Gabriel got his response.

‘Tell me Gabriel does Edward, your loyal friend, know of your addiction? Does he know of the sauna club?’ Gabriel froze. He had been caught off guard. Edward interrupted, ‘Gabriel what is he talking about?’

‘Your friend Edward, Gabriel, he meets a select few at the leisure centre, twice a week. I don’t know what they discuss but I do know they help sustain your friends’ habit. My Jim followed you under my direction. I cannot afford slip ups. I have learnt to minimise chances of being exposed by your world.’

‘Shut up, you sick bastard.’ Gabriel shouted.

‘In your drugged induced state, can you recall everything you do Gabriel, can you remember helping me with the others?’

‘What are you talking about, you’re crazy. I didn’t, I couldn’t...could I? What are you doing you sick bastard? Get out of my head.’

Edward spoke calmly, ‘Gabriel what is going on? What is this madman talking about?’

Gabriel looked at Edward, he felt sick, ashamed at his situation.

‘Every so often I take a little pick me up. Just to get me through the day, since Tabby’s death it…’

‘Enough, enough Gabriel, do I know you at all? Is there anything else you are keeping from me? Did you help him kill more people? Is he right?’

The Fundamental sat watching the two friends. His head motioning sided to side rhythmically.

‘No Edward, I haven’t helped him. I only helped Josh, our Josh. It’s a game he is playing. I would never do that.’

Two men, their friendship broken, watched each other closely.

‘Tell me dear friends. Did you two feel anything, any feeling of exhilaration when you believed you had killed me? There is nothing as divine as absorbing a body’s last breath; to feel the muscles relax, to see a life extinguished by one’s own hands.’

Edward spoke, ‘I felt sick to my stomach. I felt inhuman; regretted everything I had done.’

‘I suppose you are disgusted with the morality of it all. Ask yourselves this question, then: when we all look deep into the mirror, are we comfortable with our reflection? Take your situations. You two tried to murder me to avoid blemishes on your careers: you swept me under the carpet. So who is the real monster here: me, the addict; or you two, the businessmen? You placed your personal fortunes before a human life. If you look closely, the scales of morality are not as skewed as you first thought.’

‘You both tried to stop me doing what I was put on the earth to do and I cannot let that go unpunished. From that first day, when I woke up in hospital, I have planned for this moment. It is a moment of pure emotion based on revenge.’

He paused for a moment and the clock continued its rhythmic ticking. Edward was consumed by emotion. It enveloped him; his body shivered and flinched as if affected by palsy. Gabriel’s mind raced; his eyes betrayed his inner turmoil. The Fundamental leaned forward and watched the visual theatre with curiosity.

‘Like birds in a cage craving to be released,’ The Fundamental said.

‘What?’ replied Gabriel, unaware that he was being observed so intently.

‘Your eyes – they move around so quickly. They look like caged birds. I question whether it would be best to release them?’ said The Fundamental.

‘Are you trying to scare me?’ Gabriel shouted.

‘No, just thinking out aloud,’ The Fundamental replied.

Gabriel sensed his sands of time had almost run down. ‘If it was revenge that drove you to do this, then why now?’

The Fundamental began to twist his head steadily again, never once allowing a second to pass that could interfere or divert his view of Gabriel's eyes. 'It was a coincidence. Jim's parents had passed away in an accident and he had little alternative but to return. So fate started the process of my redemption.'

'It was easy to find you. I knew where you were, and that Edward would not be far behind: two for the price of one. Once I was back, I started to add to my flock, to attract your attention. I implicated the police in the deaths: your police. I wanted them to suspect if the killer could be one of their own. That way, you would have to get involved because you are responsible for them. You should have been an escalation as the Crime Commissioner. After all, that was your role, wasn't it? Your police covered the whole thing up; scared of consequence, just as you were.'

'As this plan to gain your attention failed, my revenge was required to explore a new path. I used my Jim's talents to get the information I needed. It's remarkable: your world now sits on the information superhighway and my Jim travels along it freely, picking data as you would strawberries from a field. It was Jim who reopened the door to your closet of skeletons. He sent the message from Sgt Crane to you, when your police authority had failed. I set the seed and convinced my Jim that Sgt Crane was the killer. It was not difficult to convince him as Jim held an historic grudge against him. Crane had tortured my Jim during his childhood. The fuel of retribution just needed a spark.'

'I question the honesty of it all. I would much sooner live in my world: a clear-cut one where actions have definite outcomes. Your world is so immersed in lies and fiction that you cannot even spot the truth any more. Ask yourself: am I the villain, or is it you? How many of my flock would be alive if you and yours had acted, or exhibited a shred of so-called humanity. Refreshingly, I did find a glimmer of light that warmed me through the interactions of my Jim in your world. He introduced me to a place of beauty, where lies are hung like a coat at the doorway. They call it the Broken Land; it's where some of my flock had resided. If you could have witnessed its purity, not for what it has but for what it has not, and the fact that it does not seek anything else. This place and its inhabitants have changed me. My flock will no longer consist of its residents. After all, Jesus would not take his own disciples. I will find another flock to scratch my itch.'

The Fundamental rose: Gabriel and Edward knew it would be for a purpose. Everything he did, each movement, every comment, had a purpose. There was no doubt that he never veered from his road; would never seek refuge from it until he had reached his destination.

The two captives saw cupboard doors opening and closing. The Fundamental walked towards them. He was holding a bottle of liquid in his hands and reading the label. He mouthed the instructions as he stood behind Edward then held the bottle over his head and began to squirt its contents over him. The fluid poured down Edward's hair. As it reached his cheeks, Edward caught the pungent smell of solvent. Gabriel watched The Fundamental's macabre actions; saw Edward shaking his head violently, hoping to disperse some of the liquid but managing only to spread it further across his body.

'No please, no, not this, please I beg you not to end my life like this!' Edward stammered. He'd had a mortal fear of fire since he was burned as a child.

The Fundamental moved to Gabriel and repeated the process. Gabriel held his head down and watched the liquid drip to the table.

Edward continued to beg. 'Gabriel, please talk to him. He will listen to you. Don't let me die like this Gabriel. Not like this.'

Gabriel called out to The Fundamental as he walked back to the kitchen area with the bottle of solvent in his hand. 'So that's it? You are going to burn us to death?'

The Fundamental did not turn as he squeezed the last remnants of the fluid onto the cooker top and along the kitchen work surface. 'Yes. Fire is an excellent medium for removing evidence and this particular liquid burns at a higher temperature, so there is less chance of error. Apparently, it does what it says on the tin.'

Gabriel looked at Edward, who was crying inconsolably and pleaded for his friend. 'I can see how I deserve this but not Edward. He just tried to help me.'

'There is no ambiguity in my actions. I only hear the continued hypocrisy of your language. Edward was party to my attempted murder, a contract he engaged in freely. Therefore, he is as guilty as you.'

The Fundamental then put his finger to his chin as if pondering something briefly. 'I will give you a chance, but it is your last predicament. The service revolver you brought with you – I will place one bullet in the chamber and release one of your hands to fire it. It is then up to you: take your own life, or Edward's.'

Gabriel's face told a story. Across his features the last episode to the saga of his life was being played out.

'Tell me Gabriel, are you right or left-handed?' The Fundamental asked in his prescribed manner.

'Right,' Gabriel replied.

Edward watched as The Fundamental emptied the revolver's chamber, leaving a solitary bullet inside. He then looked at Gabriel intently and spoke with a jittery voice, 'Gabriel, please choose me! Get it over quickly. Don't let me burn.'

Gabriel saw Edward's red eyes, puffy with fatigue and anguish. Edward smiled at Gabriel. 'It is OK my friend. You would be saving me from so much pain. You have always looked after me.'

The Fundamental moved forward and cut the bindings from Gabriel's left arm. Gabriel watched. 'I said I was right-handed,' Gabriel said.

'I know,' replied The Fundamental, 'but with one hand free, you might try something stupid, so, I now place you at a disadvantage. Anyway, I will be behind you to offer assurance.'

The Fundamental produced a small blowtorch and ignited the gas. He placed the revolver on the table. It was a stretch away from Gabriel, so he could just reach. He then took his position behind Gabriel.

'It is your time now Gabriel,' he whispered.

Gabriel pulled the gun towards him and manipulated it into his palm. It felt uncomfortable: not that he had ever held a gun before, but it sat awkwardly in his hand.

Edward watched Gabriel as he struggled with the weapon. 'Gabriel, do this for me, your friend. Please save me the pain. You know my fear of fire. I will always be your friend.'

Gabriel stared at Edward. He looked past his gaze and into the history they had shared together. Gabriel's eyes welled with tears. He could hear the sway of the flame from the blowtorch as The Fundamental waved it behind his back. Without hesitation Gabriel aimed the gun at Edward and pulled the trigger: *click.*

'What the fuck?' cried Gabriel. Edward looked at his face with despair.

'I must have loaded the wrong chamber,' replied The Fundamental.

Gabriel aimed the gun again, pulling the trigger repeatedly until a loud bang delivered a crescendo of reverb followed by silence.

Edward's head rocked backed, then forward, his chin resting on his chest. Blood poured from a bullet hole in his head. The hiss of the blowtorch stopped. He forced the gun under his chin and frantically started to pull the trigger again. *Click, click, click* but there was no action from the weapon.

'Only one bullet,' The Fundamental said.

Gabriel fuelled with hatred replied, 'murdering bastard: you will not get away with this!'

The Fundamental's pulse kept its steady beat, like a metronome. 'Emotions cloud the issue. They get in the way of purpose. I will get away with this; your death will see to that.'

'The story is due to unfold; each morsel of information ripped from it like a children's game of pass the parcel – a parcel wrapped by me, and the prize is my freedom. You see, you fit the police's suspect perfectly: a man tormented by the grief of his daughter's suicide. You sought vengeance for a daughter who had been supposedly raped by a street dweller. My Jim even has photographs of you in the Broken Land seeking out potential victims. High on drugs, a cocaine addict, you were a man out of control. This and the commentary from the inhabitants there, will add to implicating you. The final piece in the jigsaw came from your very mouth. I have on tape your confession, with you admitting to being a killer. Oh and Edward, poor Edward. He tried to confront you and you shot him: yet another death down to you. Unable to live with yourself, you decided to end it all in a blaze of glory.'

'If the police examine the lodge's reservation schedule, they will see it was booked under your name, with your account details. My Jim's expertise has no bounds.'

Gabriel slapped the table with his free hand. 'That's all the applause I can give you. So what happens now to you and Jim? Will you add to your flock?'

The Fundamental let out a small, audible breath through his nostrils. 'I will feed a story to Jim about this evening. He will be none the wiser of our adventure. I will task him with editing the tape recording then fabricating and submitting the necessary evidence. He will act without remorse; remember, I control his actions: one body, two minds.'

The Fundamental got to his feet, stretched his neck and arms and then picked up the contact lenses from the table. Placing them in a cup taken from his pocket, he walked steadily to the kitchen and reached deep into one of the drawers. He pulled out a bag and placed the contents on the table. A pair of gloves, a knife and a staple gun.

'Hook, line and sinker,' He said calmly to Gabriel.

'What?' Gabriel asked.

'These are the tools I used to move my flock on. I will pop them in your car boot as I leave. I only need the finishing touch, the icing on the cake.' The fundamental moved behind Gabriel, reached into his pocket and pulled out the bag of cocaine. 'I knew your little trip to the toilet earlier was not a call from nature. I'll leave this in your car, for the police to find.' He moved to the kitchen, turning on all the gas rings in turn. The hiss from the escaping gas filled the room. Holding the evidence in one hand, the blowtorch in the other, he made his way to the door. Standing in the doorway, he lit the torch and placed it on the floor, facing towards the table.

The roar from the blowtorch flame tore into the atmosphere. The Fundamental gazed back towards Gabriel once last time. Gabriel's free arm was stretched out, pawing at his fallen friend.

The Fundamental closed the door and started walking hurriedly away as the torch's open flame flared into the fuel-filled air. Outside, he placed the cocaine in Gabriel's glove box and the evidence bag in the boot. He stopped to insert his contact lenses. They made his eyes itched and he blinked repeatedly to moisten them. He was now Jim again.

A raucous boom shattered the silence as fiery shards peppered the winter sky with premature Christmas festivity.

Jim shook his head.

'Shit! Shit! That could have been me! Gabriel, you bastard! That could have been me!' he shouted towards the burning building.

Jim ran to his car, climbed in and started the journey home. As he drove he tried to calm his heartbeat. He was unaware of the web that had been spun and implanted into his brain by The Fundamental.

Jim felt the urge to tell someone of the evening's events, but somehow he knew he had tasks to finish. He needed to fulfil the epitaph of guilt that surrounded Gabriel Ambrose.

Crane

It was not to long before Jim was home. The winter weather had long since dispersed the Christmas Eve traffic. Taxis were ferrying home tipsy revellers and shoppers laden with last-minute bargains and gifts. As he opened the door, Jim was met by an eagerly awaiting Barnstable. The dog ran towards him, back down and tail wagging between his back legs. For a brief moment, all was forgotten and all was good in the world. Jim bent down to fuss his pet. Barnstable smelt and licked his freshly shaven face. As he did, Jim was pulled back into the evening's events and the implanted memory of Gabriel insisting he remove his beard before his attempted execution.

Thoughts and visions tormented him as he stroked and cuddled Barnstable. He subconsciously knew he had things to tidy up, tasks to finish. He was not going to let Gabriel get away with this. In his mind, Gabriel's position had led him to the ultimate corruption of his role: murder. Jim was determined to see justice done.

He made his way to his desk and started to mentally assemble a list of actions he needed to complete. Little did Jim know his hands and thoughts where being manipulated by a sinister author.

Firstly, he created an email from a Good Samaritan, the real detective, who wanted to remain anonymous. The same man who had saved the "Cheese Plant" he wanted to include but recognised that could expose his identity. He had to remain hidden. The mail went to DI Rand and the local press. This time the press' involvement was vital for the cases conclusion. The whole fabrication surrounding the case needed to be made public. There would be no more cover ups by the Police.

He wrote of Gabriel's drug addiction and his deranged hatred of street dwellers since his daughter's death. He also included images of Gabriel at the Broken Land that he had obtained from Charles. The information and anonymous messages left to appropriate people started the links of evidence being gathered that would firmly chain Gabriel to the murders.

Jim soon finished his preliminary task. Further evidence leaks may have to follow, but Jim realised he must employ a measured approach, not to over-indulge. If Gabriel's guilt was to be successfully revealed, Jim recognised the need for caution. He had to let the wheels of the system do its bit, without drawing attention to himself in anyway.

The Fundamental's plan was being enacted. He was a mental sculptor; Jim his muse. As Jim made his way to bed, he felt a virtual pat on the shoulder for a job well done.

Before he could rest, he needed to let Charles know what had happened. He needed the Broken Land to sleep peacefully again. Jim wanted its inhabitants to have the confidence to peer into shadows once more.

Jim grabbed his mobile and started thumbing through for Charles' number. Barnstable jumped to his side and lay with his back pressed to his leg. Jim felt comfortable: he actually felt happy.

He dialled and heard the trill of the dial tone. Charles answered immediately, 'Saviour, is that you?'

'Yes Charles,' Jim answered, as his stomach turned over. He felt like an expectant father, nervous and consumed by anticipation.

Jim spoke again, 'It is over Charles; you're safe.'

There was an awkward moment between the two: words were difficult to find, let alone speak. For one second, Jim thought he heard Charles whimper.

'Jim are you OK? Can you tell me what happened?'

'I'm fine, well I think I am.'

Jim then told the story that he thought to be the truth. In his mind it was, but his puppeteer The Fundamental had fabricated it all.

He'd followed to the coordinates as instructed. When he'd arrived, he'd discovered Gabriel Ambrose and Edward Moffatt already there. They all confirmed they had received letters and subsequent coordinates to that location. It was a waiting game, they all waited for the allotted time to arrive. Gabriel had made everyone a drink to try and calm us down. The drink had been drugged, and he'd passed out. He woke to find himself tethered to the table, along with Edward, but Gabriel was free. Gabriel had then covered them with some sort of liquid: Jim explained that he'd recognised the aroma of fuel and had believed he was about to die.

Gabriel had then started to tell them of his deeds: the murders he had committed. He'd told them of his hatred of the street dwellers. He'd blamed them for the death of his daughter and how they needed to pay the ultimate price, as she had done. He'd dispatched them like animals. It was not murder in Gabriel's eyes: he was doing the world a favour by removing the scum from the earth; preventing them repeating the vile act that had been performed on his daughter.

Gabriel had also become privy to Jim's investigations into the murders. That was why Jim had been invited to the lodge: to be removed from the picture. Gabriel had needed to tidy up loose ends before his impending re-election.

Jim described Gabriel's deranged nature and how it had tested sanity itself. He wondered if even Charles' reluctance to judge anyone would be compromised by Gabriel's behaviour.

Steered by The Fundamental, Jim continued the fabrication of the evening's events. Every aspect was covered.

Jim explained how Gabriel wanted Jim to meet his maker free from hair, to be pristine and pure: this was the deranged and uncompromising nature of the man he had faced. So he forced him to shave off his beard, so he could form the perfect smile upon Jim. He shaved with one hand, that's all he would release.

He recalled Gabriel's arrogance and his need for society to remember what he had done. Jim told how he had recorded his admission to the murders on tape. In Gabriel's eyes he was not guilty because the murders were not a crime. But the taped conversation revealed more. It also described Edward's role in the macabre affair.

Edward was not innocent. He had been Gabriel's accomplice but had repented his actions. That was why he had been tied up like Jim. Edward argued for Jim's life but it was in vain. Gabriel shot him. He afforded his friend no mercy.

Then there was the final struggle. Gabriel had cut one of Jim's hands free to allow him to clear his eyes of the toxic substance which had been poured over him. That was enough for Jim to work loose his shackles as Gabriel moved around the kitchen. At the opportune moment, Jim had made his move and pounced at Gabriel. They had wrestled to the floor, kicking and punching. Jim had managed to get free and, with Gabriel on the floor, he'd run to the door to escape. In the doorway he'd spotted a lit candle. Avoiding his own clothes with the naked flame, he'd tossed it towards Gabriel. He'd watched as flames ignited along Gabriel's arm and body: some of the flammable liquid he had poured over Jim and Edward must have spilled over him.

Jim narrated his version of events passionately and Charles absorbed them like a sponge. After all, he had no reason to doubt the word of his saviour. They both had questions about what had happened, but each understood that to try to answer them would lead them along a darkened path neither wanted to follow.

The conversation came to an end.

'Thank you,' Charles said quietly.

'I'm just glad it's all over, Jim replied, though something told him that would not be the case. His eyes itched and he longed for a release from the lenses but somehow Jim realised that his eyes had seen enough for that evening.

Jim slept solid until morning. He had no dreams, only a formulated recognition of the previous day hung in his head. Walking around the bedroom he felt lighter as if a huge weight had been removed from his shoulder. It wasn't until he looked in his mirror and saw his shaven face that he realised the gravity of the previous day. Gazing at his reflection, his attention was interrupted by a barking Barnstable. The dog was on his bed, excitedly wagging his tail. Jim sniggered and recognised what he wanted. Barnstable was staring at a roughly wrapped dog toy Jim had bought him for Christmas. 'Get it then boy,' Jim said. The dog instantly responded and a shredding of paper was heard, followed by the raucous shrill of the new toy being squeezed. Jim realised it was Christmas morning, Christmas Day had arrived.

The seasonal events were soon in full swing. Festive lunches were enjoyed, children played with their new gifts and fathers stretched out in armchairs fighting seasonally-induced sleep. Jim had nothing planned for the day in particular. He took Barnstable for his morning walk, wished everyone who he passed a *Merry Christmas* and smiled at children sledging in the park. Everything seemed right in the world. There was one place he missed, he had to go to. He had to visit the Broken Land.

A short drive and he was there. The roads were quiet, people cabined up, enjoying the big day. Approaching the food station, he saw Chrissy serving meals.

As Jim got closer, Lizzie called out. 'Well, you cannot keep away, Mr Thursday Night.'

She walked quickly to him, flinging her arms around him and kissing him firmly on the lips. As she pressed her lips on Jim's, she tried to squeeze Jim's mouth open with her tongue. Jim pulled away and laughed. Lizzie gave a coy giggle and whispered in his ear, 'You can't fault a girl for trying. You know it's not over between us. You make me feel so happy Jim, a happiness I haven't felt in a long while. Come on, your sitting next to me,'

She grabbed Jim's hand and walked him towards the food station. Jim saw Turnip staring at him. He thought, 'Oh shit! He knew Turnip was one of Lizzie's regulars. He did not fancy spending Christmas Day in his local Accident and Emergency unit. As he got closer, he looked at Turnip and said, 'Turnip.'

Turnip looked at Jim. His features softened and he replied, 'Turnip.'

Lizzie looked at them both and laughed, 'Now, now boys, don't fall out over little old me. There's plenty of me to go around. My appetite is only getting stronger.'

There was a solitary clap of muffled hands. They all turned and saw Charles patting his gloved hands together. He approached Jim, placed one hand on his shoulder and through his aged mouth said, 'Merry Christmas Jim, our saviour.'

Both men smiled. Tears bulged in the corners of their eyes. What a journey they had been on together they both appreciated.

'Come Jim, I'm sure Chrissy has a spare meal, join us,' Charles said.

Jim followed Charles to the food station. He wished Chrissy Merry Christmas and gratefully took a meal.

Jim asked himself, which land was actually broken: his or Charles'? They all sat happily around makeshift tables eating their Christmas lunch in absolute harmony. No pretence, no reverence: it was motive-free and pure. Chrissy joined in and produced a box of Christmas crackers whose gifts and hats soon adorned the diners.

Charles provided the entertainment. He recited excerpts from Dickens' *A Christmas Carol*. Lizzie continued her game of enticement, repeatedly winking in Jim's direction. Jim blushed like a chastened schoolboy but welcomed the attention all the same.

Soon, Christmas carols started. All sat dumbstruck as Chrissy sang in a quiet, beautiful voice. The others, encouraged by the season, tried to join in: Jim mouthed the chorus and politely mumbled the rest and they all rocked from side to side to the festive tune, arm in arm. Jim wondered when he last felt as happy, with people he truly wanted to be with. Both Jim and his blue-eyed maestro were content.

It was a day of contentment; a day of joy and a time for enjoying the moment. The fog of responsibility and concerns of tomorrow were conspicuous by their absence. Jim and Charles laughed and paid their individual homage to the season.

As the temperature cooled, the small party slowly dispersed. Charles thanked Jim again. 'No one will ever know what you have done for us. You are the sort of hero that the Greeks would worship.'

Jim blushed then hugged Charles gratefully. As Jim turned away, Lizzie was waiting. She came towards him and grabbed his hands in hers then spoke, 'Jim, there is no more Thursday night thing for us. There are no weekday things; it's you Jim. I'm all about you now if you want me? Come back with me?'

Jim did not speak. He just looked into her eyes and followed. Polite society may frown on their relationship: a vivacious older woman, a street dweller, she had nothing to tangibly offer in terms of wealth or goods but everything to offer in terms of life. Happiness was hard to find and Jim had spent a lifetime searching the world for it, only to discover it had been on his doorstep all along.

There would be no seasonal of cheer for the local police: just parcels of questions holding gifts of retribution. DI Rand got his man. He had suspected someone within the force but the Crime Commissioner, never. At the scene of the lodge fire, his car had been found with the evidence inside. DNA tests on the knife and staple gun linked them to the victims. The bag of cocaine was also discovered. A few influential calls from the sauna group confirmed Gabriel was guilty. Well rehearse speeches from the proprietors of Aubrey's shadier clubs nailed his fate. *He was a troubled man a drug addict*. As for the sauna group, they said they only communicated infrequently. It was important that they distance themselves from Gabriel, to keep their business operational.

The lodge fire and explosion didn't leave many remains. Skeletons where shattered, only dental records confirmed who the two skulls belonged to. One of the skulls was pierced by a single shot confirming Jim's story. The messages in the victim's mouths were also explained. Gabriel in his role had full access to the police central data system. He was their data guardian, a thankless task that was a tag on to his duties. This meant, he had unlimited access to all the officers personal information held on the system.

Alibis in support of Gabriel's innocence were barren. The murder dates had been carefully chosen by the Fundamental using Jim's skill. Gabriel had been at home for each of the murders, he had the opportunity to kill them. His time at home would not have been easily confirmed. His wife lived in the land of the ripened grape.

For the police it was cut and dry. Gabriel had the motive, the opportunity and tools to complete the job. He was identified as the killer. *Who would have thought it?* became the common phrase for a while from the people who knew him, but his guilt was readily understood and accepted. Everyone who had known Gabriel since before his daughter's passing had recognised the change in his character.

The press had a field day, heads rolled, positions became vacant and public shook their heads in disbelief. The recriminations did not go on for too long. The fact that the victims were vagrants saw to that.

A new Crime Commissioner was elected, *promising to rid the area of corruption* and *restore the public's faith* in the force. Messages carefully scripted by the sauna group.

The Fundamental's game of chess had yielded a well-structured checkmate for Gabriel Ambrose. The local authorities promised change but Charles and Jim had little confidence anything would alter significantly. Ultimately, the great unwashed still needed washing and importantly, the Broken Land remained broken.

Christmas and the New Year soon passed. It was colder than ever. The festive season was a memory and people with little to look forward to, psychologically started to feel the chill more. The papers struggling for stories since the murder expose, emphasised the conditions. Historic pictures of people wrapped in winter clothes, blanketed with snow, under a headline of "New Ice Age" became the norm. They did it every year.

Jim was spending more time at the Broken Land, in particular with Charles and of course, Lizzie. Their relationships grew stronger. One morning, Charles grabbed Jim's attention. 'Have you heard the news? Hot off the press this one Jim,' he said.

'No Charles. I had a bit of a heavy night last night. I found a bottle of Scotch I had in the cupboard and decided to give it a go. If I'm honest I can't remember a thing. I woke up in bed naked. I ached when I got up I must have slept funny. I must have been in a mess; I'd put my clothes in the washer before I went to bed, so I guess I must have puked. There was a smell of bleach everywhere and the mop was on the floor. I had to put my clothes in the dryer this morning.'

Jim shook his head. Charles looked directly at Jim and spoke again, 'They found Sgt Crane this morning: he'd been beaten to death.'

Jim looked to the floor, his mouth dried, he felt ill and dizzy. He mumbled, 'Crane dead.'

Charles watched his friend's reaction. 'Jim, you OK?' he asked sympathetically.

'Crane . . . I can't believe it.'

'It is what it is Jim. From what I know of the man, his history will not go down in any annals. I do not glibly speak ill of the dead but I am more concerned with the living and you. Perhaps this was a fitting end for this man.'

Jim knew Charles was right and respected his counsel. Another episode in his life was over: Crane the Pain was dead, Lizzie's attacker was dead, a husband to a missing wife was dead.

Jim sat with his thoughts, unaware that The Fundamental had been at work again. At home, his washing machine had held clothes stained from the previous evenings events. They were now infused with artificial aromas from the washing detergent.

Jim's hangover masked something more sinister than a whisky-induced coma. When the police investigate Crane's attack more closely they'd uncover a lot more but not everything. A subtle clue had been left: a smudged letter written in the dust on the Crane's cupboard: 'F'. It was a late Christmas present to Jim from his patron.

***

The Previous Evening

The more time Jim spent with Lizzie, the greater his need to understand what had happened to Abby Crane. Lizzie didn't speak of her anymore. It was just Jim didn't want her turning up and ruining their blossoming relationship. If Abby turned up now, he would reluctantly leave it for Lizzie to decide. If Lizzie chose Abby, he'd accept it and although heartbroken, move on.

Lizzies other partners ceased. She spent the odd night at Jim's and since he became Lizzies' solo partner, she certainly kept him fit. His house was detached. He had neighbours but they were not too close as to eve's drop or listen in. Good job as the couples groans from love making were often and loud.

Lizzie had visited during the day. She had taken Barnstable a walk with Jim. It was a lovely image, a Christmas card picture, a loving couple walking hand in hand on a winter's landscape. Their little dog running slightly ahead, leading the way.

It was true, they did love one another. When they returned back to the house, the inevitable happened. Lizzie ripped Jim's clothes from him before he had even chance to knock the snow from his boots. Barnstable snuggled in his bed, ignoring the sex show in front him. He only barked when their love making got a tad too noisy for him.

Lizzie left to return to the Broken Land. Jim wanted her to move in but she explained her responsibility to Charles and he understood. The place, The Broken Land had a pull about it, almost magnetic to its inhabitants.

Jim now sat in the house on his own. He had deliberated about the situation with Crane. He made up his mind. He was going to visit him, find out once and for all what happened to Abby.

His address was easy to find, a little peruse on the police network and he had it. It was evening, Jim had checked Cranes shift pattern. He had worked the morning shift and with his customary visit to the Broken Shoe over, he guessed he would be home. Cranes address was not too far, so Jim decided to go on foot. He was determined to get the information from Crane, so took a sharp knife with him for intimidation.

The weather was freezing, dank. Perhaps the papers were right and the "New Ice Age" was coming, he thought.

Approaching Cranes house, Jim saw lights on inside. He walked up to the door, shielding from the snow which had started to fall again. Jim knocked. A few moments later, Crane appeared. He looked through a side window to the door, spotted Jim and opened it. 'Jim, what are you doing here?'

'Hello David. Sorry just wanted to catch up, hope you don't mind. I got your address from a neighbour.' Crane didn't look shocked. He smiled and welcomed him in glad of the company. Other than work and the Broken Shoe, his was a solitary life. Jim looked around as he entered. The house did not seem lived in, not homely at all.

'Do you want a drink Jim?'

'Love one David,' Jim was amazed that Crane had welcomed him so freely. He reasoned correctly and understood he probably didn't get many guests.

Jim watched Crane, stumbling around the kitchen for a glass. He had obviously had a good drink already. He returned with a glass tumbler, half filled with some kind of liquor. They sat around a small table. Jim took a swig of his drink, drawing his teeth back as he tasted it.

'Crickey, that's a bit keen David.'

Crane laughed, replied, 'Haven't got a clue what it is? Jim why are you here?'

Jim toyed with the best way to proceed. Should he dance his way to the ultimate question or dive straight in. He put his trunks on and went for it.

'Where is Abby David? Where is your wife?'

Cranes demeanour altered, 'There I was thinking you had come to pay me a visit as a friend and you have to bring her up. What is she to you anyway?'

'David, where is she?'

'What is my wife to you?' Crane shouted.

'She is a friend of a woman I know.'

The last answer fuelled Crane's rage more. 'A woman you know. Tell me, this woman, is she one of the tramps, the scum that live in the old car park?'

It was now Jim's turn to get angry, 'Don't you dare Crane?'

'It is. It is the whore from the old car park. What a fuck Jim, I had good times with her.' Crane coughed with laughter.

Jim's eyes burned, they begged for release, he had to comply. Crane watched Jim slowly remove his contact lenses.

As his eyes cleared, he focused back on Crane, steadily and in control. Crane observed Jim,

'I knew there was something different about you last time we met, I can remember now from school. Little Jimmy, Jimmy blue eyes.'

'Sorry Mr Crane, let me introduce myself, I am not Jim. I am the Fundamental.'

Crane sat back, perplexed by this last statement. With one rapid movement the Fundamental took the knife from his pocket and drove it threw Crane's hand, pinning it to the table. Crane squealed in pain. The Fundamental got up, clasped Cranes head between his hands,

'Shush, there's a good boy. I am going to ask you a question Mr Crane. Where is your wife please?'

'What the hell is going on? Jim what is going on?'

The Fundamental, motioned his head side to side, never losing his focus on Crane, 'Jim isn't here anymore. Where is your wife Mr Crane?'

'What do you mean Jim isn't here. What's this Fundamental thing?'

The Fundamental released Cranes head and wandered into the kitchen. As he did, he produced a pair of rubber gloves and steadily put them on. He started opening draws, investigating their contents. Crane recognised the sound of cutlery rattling in the last one he opened. He looked over and watched the Fundamental pick kitchen implements from the draw. As each item was chosen, the Fundamental swung it or stabbed it in mid-air performing a test of its impending use. Crane tried to move but realised his hand was firmly attached to the table. The Fundamental approached him, armed with a carving knife and a wooden rolling pin.

'Not a lot of choice, these will have to do.'

'Not a lot of choice for what?' The Fundamental stood directly in front of Crane again. 'Where is your wife Mr Crane?' The question repeated in his lifeless voice.

'I'm a police officer. You won't get away with this?'

The Fundamental swung the carving knife to the table. Two of Cranes' fingers from his clamped hand were instantly removed, rolling loose on the table top. Crane screamed out aloud. The Fundamental grabbed his head in his hands again, 'Shush, Mr Crane where is your wife?'

'Screw you, Crane shouted.'

Spittle from his mouth landing on the Fundamentals face. The Fundamental backed away, wiped the spit with his finger and then put it in his mouth and swallowed,

'The taste of death Mr Crane.'

Crane watched in horror. The Fundamental grabbed Crane's other arm, pulled it forward on the table top and began hammering it with the rolling pin. The beating was precise, purposeful. Crane watched as his hand disfigured before him. The Fundamental stopped, caught his breath and spoke again, monotone and deliberate, 'Where is your wife Mr Crane?' Crane was shaking with fear, he understood his assailant could not be reasoned with, he eventually broke, 'The basement.'

The Fundamental had his answer. He pinned Crane's beaten hand to the table with the other knife. This was easier as the bones had been smashed offering little resistance to the blade.

'Where's the basement?' Crane moved his head to show the way.

The Fundamental followed his eyes and spotted a small door leading off the hall way. Leaving Crane in the living room he made his way to the doorway. He opened the door, there was a stair case leading down, its sides grey unpainted, showing the bare concrete walls. The Fundamental turned on a switch at the top of the corridor. The stairway lit up, showing the route. He eased his way down. At the bottom was another door, bolted from the outside. Carefully releasing it, he swung it open. The smell of faeces hit him straight away. Rather than shy away, he accepted the smell and moved forward. There was a dull light ahead and he could just make out what looked like a metal cage. He then heard a week pitiful voice, 'Hello, please, hello.' The Fundamental moved beside the cage bars, inside he could see a shape. He asked, 'Mrs Crane, is that you?'

'Yes, please help me. God help me.'

A quiet reply from the darkness was barely audible. The Fundamental, feeling around, discovered the entrance to the cage, pulled open the door and entered. A woman sat in one corner of the cage. She was emaciated, not capable of standing. The stench was terrible, her clothing stained with urine and excrement. Empty cartons of food stacked around her. She barely possessed the energy to talk.

'Thank God, you have saved me.'

The Fundamental gently moved into her field of view. She saw see his bright blue eyes. He was now close enough that she heard his breathing.

'Thank God, thank you for saving me,' Abby cried. She barely had the energy to weep.

'Hmm, I think we are at cross purposes. I am not God, I am the Fundamental. I am here to remove a problem.'

He stretched out his hands and clasped them around her neck. Squeezing tightly she didn't have the strength to resist. Her body soon became limp, exhausted of life. His eyes burned brighter blue, energised by her departing soul. Gently lowering her dead body to the floor, Abby Crane was no more.

Crane sat at the table, pinned by the blades, every movement agony. He heard steps getting louder from the basement and assumed his wife would shortly be with him again. The Fundamental walked in to the room alone.

'Where is she?' Crane asked. 'Did you find the bitch?'

The Fundamental ignored Crane. He reached into his coat pocket and pulled out a small bag. It had been placed there earlier under the guise of Jim. He unwrapped it, revealing a pair of paper overalls. Stood before Crane he removed his coat and started to put them on.

Crane watched, 'What's the plan now, you going to kill me? What about the bitch?' The Fundamental continued to dress. He pulled the hood of the suit over his head, picked up the heavy rolling pin and without pitch or fluctuation in his voice he spoke, 'Your wife is my flock, you will shortly join her Mr Crane.'

Crane didn't speak anymore. He bowed his head ready for his punishment. The blows rain down on him, one after the other. Retribution for his Jim, the Fundamental exacted a long overdue revenge. The playground had gone once and for all.

***

The Present

In the Broken Land the world moved on and the days turned to months. Jim and Charles' friendship flourished. In a curious way, Jim looked upon Charles as a father figure. He offered Charles the opportunity to move in with him but Charles declined. He explained he was a custodian of the Broken Land and there he would remain.

Lizzie lived between both places. She kept her word to Jim and enjoyed her new found chastity. Jim just had to keep up the pace of love making.

People came, people left, until one day a flustered Charles came to Jim's attention. It was autumn and Jim had been helping serve coffees from the food station. Charles was with Turnip. Jim noticed Charles examining Turnip's face and head, wiping his cheek with a handkerchief taken from his pocket. Turnip turned towards Jim. Jim could see heavy bruises and blood about his face. Turnip, keen to avoid eye contact, just nodded in his direction. Charles slowly walked over, returning the handkerchief to his pocket.

'Is everything OK Charles?' Jim asked.

'I'm afraid not, dear boy. We have a new occupant in our land: a violent man. He has attacked Turnip and tried to force himself on Lizzie. Lizzie has handled herself admirably but I am afraid Turnip has come off second-best. There will be no comfort in our little Eden until he decides to leave,' said Charles.

Jim pondered the situation briefly. 'Let me speak to him. He will not scare me Charles.'

'Thank you Jim, but that may lead to other problems. We all value your friendship and you are too important an asset to the Broken Land to lose,' Charles answered reluctantly.

Both toyed with their dilemma, sitting at a vacant table, staring at half-drunk coffee cups. Charles rubbed his weathered fingers across his top lip. He blew through his mouth as he calculated what do to next. Jim turned away, putting his hands to his face to delicately remove his contact lenses. Charles hadn't noticed and as Jim stared into the distance, he spoke in a sombre, flaccid voice, devoid of emotion. 'I am sure it will get sorted. All good things come to those who wait. December will soon be with us.'

Printed in Great Britain
by Amazon

33002676R00130